Katrina~

May you always know
God's deep love for you.
God bless~
Natalie Replogle

A
RESCUED
LOVE

can it really be happily ever after

Natalie
Replogle

Published by White Feather Press.
(www.whitefeatherpress.com)

ISBN 978-1-61808-117-9

Printed in the United States of America

Cover design created by Ron Bell of AdVision Design Group
(www.advisiondesigngroup.com)

White Feather Press

Reaffirming Faith in God, Family, and Country!

Acknowledgements

Thank you to God Almighty for the amazing gift of your unconditional love. May Your love always be the foundation of everything I do and say. I pray this novel serves to glorify you and impact your Kingdom.

Gregory, I believe we are a great testimony that things only get better with age. Twelve years, baby! Oh how I love being married to you! You are my best friend, my protector, my haven, and most definitely my better half. Thank you for being my biggest fan and cheering me on as I pursue my dream – and for showing me an incredible love that makes writing romance easy.

Jarrett – I can't believe you are almost a decade old … how did that happen so fast? I remember you walking around with your blanket and monkey with a squeaky voice that could capture my heart in an instant. Now you're up to my shoulders, full of ideas and growing up without my permission. I love watching you begin your relationship with Christ and how you have come to realize how much He loves you as you lean on Him through all your ups and downs.

Brayden – It feels like just yesterday I was watching you sit in the hospital bed fighting for your life at age two and now you are seven, full of life and a walking miracle that proves God has His thumbprint on you. I always pray, without fail, that you will follow Christ all the days of your life and that you will do great things for Him. I love your tender heart, your compassion for others and how you are always so sincere and quick to apologize.

Kyla – Oh, my sweet girl. I can't imagine my life without you. Each day you bring our family so much joy with your crazy sense of style, silly faces and fun-loving with a side of sassy attitude that puts you way beyond your years. Sigh, if only you could stay 4 forever – but I'm looking forward to watching you grow as God molds you into the woman He has created you to be. You, my darling blue-eyed beauty, are going to be a world changer!

Mom & Dad (and also my father, Gregory Snider, who has already gone to his Heavenly home), thank you for telling and showing me at a young age who Jesus is and how much He loves me – there isn't a time in my life that I haven't known God or His love for me. Thank you for being incredible role models and examples of Christ followers. I have a lot to live up to.

Susan Begay, when I look back over the last five years and this exciting and surreal journey I have been on, you are always the first person that comes to mind. Without you I would have endless grammar mistakes, but most importantly, I would never have had the guts to pursue a writing career. Thank you from the bottom of my heart for the continuous hours you take to work on my manuscripts, give ideas and shower me with encouragement. You are truly one of the most generous people I have ever met.

Kathi Shaffer, we might live hundreds of miles apart and only be related through marriage, but you are truly family to me … and you had me at hello. I still remember the first time meeting you and how we jumped into a friendship as if we'd known each other all our lives. Thank you for taking the time to read over my book. You are such a blessing!

Thank you to Darcy Holsopple of Darcy Holsopple Photography for taking my author's picture. Not only are you crazy talented, but you are also a beautiful person inside and out.

To my White Feather Press family, Skip and Sara Coryell, thank you for your continued support and believing in my story and the message I want to share with others. I appreciate all you have done to help me chase after my dream.

CHAPTER ONE

JULES ANDERSON CLOSED THE HEAVY DOOR OF ROOM 302 BEhind her as she slipped out into the empty hallway. She looked down into the screen that displayed the patient's chart, trying to blink the tears away. This patient hit too close to home. Swallowing the lump down in her throat that continued to push itself up, she stepped away from the room that stirred up memories she had tried for years to repress.

Being a pediatric nurse brought many rewarding and heartbreaking days. She rejoiced on the days when she brought a smile to a child's face and gave comfort in a very scary time, but then there were the days that crippled her in an instant when her cruel past came back, reminding her of what she'd lost and the continual pain that surrounded her heart.

On the other side of the door, which grew in distance with each purposeful step, lay a little five-year-old girl fighting for her life against pneumonia. With each ragged breath sweet Lexi took, Jules breathed deeper in an attempt to keep her emotions in check. In no way did she want to break down in front of the parents that sat clutched together, desperation straining their features.

Sure, she'd had patients before with pneumonia, but none that had reminded her so much of her little sister, Jenna. Being the same age and gender proved to be hard enough, but the soft strawberry-blonde curls that framed her face had put her over the edge.

When Jenna had turned two, she had been diagnosed with Children's Interstitial Lung Disease. Right before her fourth birthday, she came down with a bad cold that turned into pneumonia and ultimately took her life. Jules had only been eight-years-old at the time but could still remember coming up to the hospital room and sitting with her sister, reading to her and watching cartoons when she was coherent.

Jules made her way to the bathroom, taking a few necessary minutes to compose herself. She leaned over the sink, splashed a handful of cool water onto her face, hoping to shock the tears into ceasing. Grabbing a paper towel, she patted her face dry.

She looked up in the mirror, only to grimace. Streaks of mascara pooled around the bottom of her eyes. She used the towel to clean up the black residue. Taking a deep breath, she discarded the towel into the trash and headed back to her station to finish updating Lexi's chart.

Becky, the other nurse on shift with her today, eyed her coming as she finished up her phone call. "Okay, thanks for the heads up." She clicked the phone back in its slot and finished writing the notes she had been taking. Giving her attention back to Jules, she drew her eyebrows together, "Hey, are you okay?"

A soft smile leaked onto her face, "I will be." Jules pointed down to the notes Becky had just written. "New patient?"

Becky hesitated a moment but let her concern pass. "Yes. That was the ER. A boy has been brought in. They aren't sure what is going on, but the parents refuse to leave until they get answers. They have already done blood work and are sending him up here for admitting."

"Have they sent the doctor's report yet?"

"They are sending it as soon as possible. They have also marked the blood work STAT, so we should be getting results soon."

"What is the boy's name?" Jules asked. One aspect in helping patients feel comfortable started with knowing their name. A simple gesture but so very important.

Becky looked down at her paper. "Brandon Spencer. Two-years-old."

Their slow morning looked to be picking up quickly. A new patient diversion might be just what Jules needed. "Would you mind doing a little swap with me? I will take care of the new patient if you oversee Lexi." Confusion filled Becky's eyes. "Lexi reminds me a lot of my sister, Jenna." The two of them had worked together long enough for Becky to know plenty about Jules's past and understand that simple statement.

Becky stood up and wrapped her in a hug. "Of course."

"Thanks. I just need to update her latest stats, and then you should be set. She's scheduled to have another x-ray this morning. We are just waiting for a call from imaging to let us know when they have a break in their schedule."

"All right. I'll take care of it."

By the time Jules finished up Lexi's chart, the elevator pinged, announcing they had company. An orderly emerged pushing a wheelchair that swallowed up the little bleached blond boy accompanied by whom she assumed were his parents tight on his heels.

Jules approached the group with a gentle smile, welcoming them. She checked the orderly tag. "Thanks for bringing them up, Bill. I can take them from here."

"No problem." The older man turned, leaving the way he came.

Jules squatted down on the balls of her feet, putting her at eye level with the boy. "Hi there, you must be Brandon." Brandon nodded, a small smirk flitting across his lips from the attention. "Well, Brandon, my name is Miss Julia. I'm really sorry to hear that you aren't feeling well, but we are going to do all we can to help you feel better, okay?" He sat still, just staring at her. She looked down at his Thomas the Train shirt, realizing how to break the ice with him. "I like your shirt. Thomas is my favorite train." She had seen her fair share of Thomas movies over the last couple years working on the pediatrics floor. It had become knowledge that helped immensely when trying to get a child to feel comfortable around her.

Brandon's eyes lit up. "Choo-Choo. Thomas is blue."

"Wow, you are good with your colors." She stood up. "I think we have a few trains in the playroom that I could find for you once we get you all settled in your room. Would you like that?"

"Yes!"

"Okay then, let's go find your room." Jules made her way behind the wheelchair. She caught the attention of the parents. "Hi. My name is Julia. I will be Brandon's nurse today."

The man stepped forward. "I'm Ryan, and this is my wife, Janet."

Jules pointed to the room straight across from the nurse's station. "Brandon will be in room 305." The parents followed her into the room. Once settled, she went to the closet and pulled out a hospital gown and socks, placing them on the bed. "If you could get Brandon into these, I will be right back to start up his chart."

Jules returned ten minutes later with her computer and a couple trains she hoped would raise Brandon's comfort level with her. Having the child relax usually helped the parents to relax as well.

Brandon sat in the bed, his tiny legs sticking out from the peach gown that displayed fluffy bears wearing party hats. She had noticed how weak he seemed before, but the gown amplified his pale complexion.

Leaning over the bed, she handed Brandon the Thomas

and James trains. A smile broke on his face as he reached up and took them from her. He cradled them in his arms. Lying back against the bed, he rolled over on his side and began playing with the trains on his pillow. Jules had hoped this would be the outcome. It would be easier to talk to the parents if Brandon stayed occupied.

She pushed the cart that the computer sat on closer to the parents as they took a seat in the chairs pushed up against the window. "Mr. and Mrs. Spencer, I know that you gave details down in the ER, and I do have that report, but if you don't mind, I would like you to go over his symptoms with me. That way we can make sure we haven't missed anything."

"We've been talking about his symptoms for weeks – a lot of good that has done us so far!" Ryan Spencer's words spewed toward her. She rocked backwards slightly from the surprise of his anger.

Janet Spencer placed her hand on her husband's arm. "Ryan, she is just trying to help us."

He moved his arm from her touch. "I'll believe it when I see it."

Oh boy! Maybe switching patients with Becky hadn't been the best of ideas. Becky had an extra layer of skin when it came to dealing with challenging parents. "Mr. Spencer, I know you are concerned about your son and want answers. I hope you realize that I will do my very best to make that happen."

Janet nodded, looking over at her child and then back at Jules. "I'm sorry if we come across difficult. It's just..." – she cleared her throat and swiped her eyes with her fingertips – "it's just that it has been a very long road, and it is breaking our hearts watching him suffer."

Jules could remember that road very well with Jenna, re-calling the strain it had put on her parents knowing that their child was sick but not having any answers. "It's all right. Just know we *all* want Brandon to get better. If you could just talk me through what has been happening, it would be a great start."

"Of course." Janet reached down into her purse and pulled out a pad of paper. "I wrote down everything so I wouldn't forget. Do you just want this?"

"No, I'd prefer to hear it from you."

"Okay, it started three weeks ago. Brandon has never been the healthiest of kids, but he came down with a 103 degree fever that lasted several days. We took him into the doctor's office, and after checking him out, they determined it was probably just a virus and sent us home."

"What do you mean that he hasn't been the healthiest of kids?"

"Since birth he just seemed to get sick, often with many ear infections, colds and fevers."

"Okay, thanks for clearing that up. Please continue."

"A few days later he woke up from his nap with a swollen gland the size of a golf ball."

Jules typed along on the keyboard, making sure she got all the information. "Did he still have the fever?"

"Yes. It had gone down some, but it was still high enough that I was concerned. They checked him out once again and sent us home with the explanation of it still being from the virus."

So far nothing seemed out of the ordinary. "Okay, then what happened?"

"A few days later, along with the continued fever, his eyes became bloodshot. I took him into the doctor, and we returned home with the same diagnosis – a virus."

Jules stopped typing. "Was his fever still as high?"

"It usually stayed between 101 and 103 degrees. At some point during the day, it would lessen to a low-grade temperature. It would fluctuate often."

Ryan sat forward in this chair, his earlier-tensed features easing slightly. "I don't know if this means anything, but I noticed a few times when I came home from work that his hands and feet seemed a bit swollen."

Jules put the notation in Brandon's chart. "Any information is helpful, Mr. Spencer. Have you noticed any respiratory or bowel problems?"

Janet shook her head. "No. I don't think so."

"How has Brandon's demeanor been?" Jules asked.

"He has been very tired, not much interest in playing with toys. Mostly lays around and cuddles with us, but then things got really weird and started to worry us. A week ago my great-uncle died and on Wednesday we attended his funeral. At the funeral lunch, I put Brandon in a high chair to eat. When I got him out and put him down to stand, he collapsed onto the floor crying in pain, unable to stand. At first we weren't sure what to make of it, so we just kept an eye on him. But yesterday, when he still refused to walk, I called the doctor's office again. This time they didn't see us and just said that sometimes viruses can work their way into joints and that we were to call back after the weekend if he still wasn't walking."

Jules kept her appearance calm while her insides screamed. She now understood their hard conclusion of believing that no one would help them.

Janet continued, "Last night as Brandon came crawling to me, I realized that this had gone on long enough. I knew right then that if we didn't do something our child was going to die. Instead of calling the doctor's office today, we just brought him into the ER." Swiping the bangs out of her eyes gave Jules a glimpse into her determined stance. "So here we are. I'm sorry if I come across with the Mama Bear complex, but I'm not leaving this hospital until someone tells me what is wrong with my child."

Keeping a tight rein on professionalism by refusing to

high-five the woman and say to Janet "You go, girl", Jules instead finished her notes. "I'm sorry for your last few weeks." She checked the time. "Brandon's blood work should be back soon. Dr. Henson should also be here soon making rounds."

Jules grabbed the thermometer and stepped over to Brandon. "Hey Brandon, your trains told me earlier they weren't feeling well either. Can I check and see?" He handed her Thomas, and she pretended to take the train's temperature. "Thanks. Can I check yours, too?" He nodded. She slid it across his forehead. 102.3 degrees flashed back at her. What was wrong with this child? She had never heard of all these random symptoms together with the time frame so spread apart.

Jules excused herself and made her way to the nurse's station. While sending a page to Dr. Scott Henson, her stomach did a flip, and she wasn't sure if the nerves came from the puzzling patient or the realization that she had to spend the shift with her ex-boyfriend.

CHAPTER TWO

A HALF-HOUR LATER JULES SENT OUT ANOTHER PAGE FOR Scott. Where could he be? He was already an hour late for rounds. Blood work for Brandon had come back and decisions needed to be made. If he wasn't here soon, she would need to page another doctor.

Letting her thoughts drift to how things would go spending her shift with him made her shoulders even more rigid. In the last few months, Jules's love life could have been made into a soap opera. It wouldn't take long to prepare her acceptance speech for the Daytime Emmy.

Scott played a huge role in that drama when they broke up over the summer after she found out he had been cheating on her with another nurse from the hospital. They had finally sat down a few weeks ago and hashed out their failed relationship. Jules thought they had left it on good terms. They wouldn't be getting back together, but both agreed to stay friends. So why wasn't he returning her pages?

Time had expired. Grabbing the phone to call another doctor, she paused when she spotted Scott walking down the hallway from the back elevator. She headed toward him, slowing as they approached. He looked horrible. A red line highlighted his eyes as if he hadn't slept in days. His hair wasn't combed, and a couple days of no shaving showed on his face. The white coat tried to hide his outfit, but his untucked, crumpled shirt underneath could still be seen.

"Where have you been? I've been trying to get a hold of you for almost an hour." She tried to keep a calm tone. Despite them having a personal relationship, he was her superior.

Scott ran a hand through his unmanaged hair. "I'm sorry. I was in the middle of something and couldn't get here until now. What do you need?"

"We have a new patient, Brandon Spencer, two-years-old. His blood work has returned and it doesn't look good."

Scott followed her into the nurse's station. Bringing up Brandon's blood work, she turned the computer for him to see. She watched his face as he read, wondering what caused this man who always seemed put together to look the way he did. He grimaced, clicking around the screen to bring up the chart. "Huh? Those are some strange symptoms."

"That's what I thought."

Removing his glasses, he ran a hand down his worn face. "His blood work shows his inflammation level at an eighty-nine. Over a hundred and we are talking death. That high of a level tells me something is wrong with his heart. Let's get him an echo ordered immediately, and I want the results sent STAT to the Cardiologist, Dr. Hahn. Give his office a call and give them a heads up."

She picked up the phone, her fingers flying over the numbers. "On it."

§ § § § §

JULES PULLED A CHAIR UP NEXT TO SCOTT AS HE SAT AT THE DESK, a medical book spread out before him. "Anything I can help with?"

He jumped from the sound of her voice. "Oh, hi. Sure, I'm just trying to figure out a diagnosis from Brandon's symptoms."

She placed her hand on his arm. "Hey, are you okay? You just don't seem … yourself."

Scott rubbed the scruff on his chin, not making any eye contact with her. "I'm fine. It's just been a long couple of days." He finally looked over at her, his smile never reaching his eyes.

Holding his gaze, she wondered if she should push harder and how he would respond if she did. She resolved with letting it slide. They needed to focus on Brandon. Tapping the book Scott had been researching, she changed the subject. "Want me to be your sounding board?"

"I'd like that."

She grabbed a pad of paper. "What do you have so far?"

"His main symptoms include – fever, swollen glands, bloodshot eyes and inability to walk. Although, seeing how his inflammation level is so high does explain the reasons behind him not walking, but mixed with the other symptoms, it just seems odd."

"Could it be just an extreme case of the flu?" Jules suggested.

"Maybe, but it would be a far stretch and doesn't make sense with some of his symptoms. It wouldn't hurt to test him. Put it on the list."

Jules made a column for maybe's, no's, and tests they wanted to run. "What about an infection? Could it be a type of Adenovirus? He has a fever and the bloodshot eyes."

He flipped back to Brandon's chart. "Did the parents say if he has had any problems with respiratory, diarrhea or urinary problems?"

Jules shook her head. "I remember asking them. They said no."

Scott's lips thinned as he thought. "Then I don't think that could be it. Those symptoms usually go hand-in-hand."

Writing Adenovirus down in the 'no' column, she questioned him. "Is there something you are leaning towards?" Scott had a knack of working through the possibilities with ease and confidence. She had no doubt he would come to a diagnosis soon.

"I don't know. I keep going back to him maybe having some type of autoimmunity disorder. A lot of his symptoms correlate – fatigue, muscle and joint pain, swollen glands and fever."

"His parents did say that he has been a sickly child since birth with multiple ear infections, colds and fevers."

"Interesting." He tapped his pen against the book. "But …"

"But you don't think that's what it is?" she gathered.

"I can't place my finger on it exactly, but it just doesn't seem right. Heck, this whole case doesn't seem right." Scott released an exasperated breath. "I just keep going back to how high his inflammation level is and the continued high fevers. My guess is something to do with his heart, but none of these diagnoses fit in with heart problems."

"Maybe we should work that angle first." Jules suggested. "Focus on heart problems in children and see if any of the symptoms match up." Brandon had already left for his echo, and they would be getting the results back soon enough, but that wouldn't lessen Scott's pursuit. He'd rather be a step ahead of the game than wait.

"Good idea." A soft smile separated his lips and he reached out, squeezing her hand. "See, this is why we are so good together, Julia."

Sure, she enjoyed working alongside Scott and the excitement that pushed her heartbeat faster. She had never denied it, but she could tell his comment went so much deeper than work related. A long time ago maybe things could have worked out between them. She probably could have gotten past him cheating on her and worked towards repairing their relationship, but that was all before Derek came into the picture.

Oh, how Derek Brown had burrowed a hole into her heart over the last couple of months. By her request, they had started out as friends, but it had finally come to a point where she realized that despite pushing him away, she wanted him to be more than a friend. The last few weeks she had been crossing off her list the things she needed to deal with before she could truly give over to her yearning to try a relationship with Derek.

High on that list, besides finding closure and forgiveness with Scott, was the trip she had made to reconcile with her parents. Jules had hoped that making amends with her parents would free her from what had been holding her back from a relationship with Derek – allowing herself to trust and let him in.

Since returning, her disappointment deepened with each day. She had been back from her trip for over a week, and she still hadn't had any contact with Derek. He knew when she would be getting home, and it hurt that he made no effort to get in touch with her.

Maybe it was just his way to let her down gently that he was tired of waiting around. Even if Derek didn't want her now, she couldn't consider being with Scott again. He wasn't Derek. Not by a long shot. Either way, now wasn't the time to allow the depressing thoughts to trickle in and take her captive.

Jules squeezed Scott's hand in return, but quickly pulled her hand to her side, not wanting to give him the wrong idea. "We do make a good team at work." For the next twenty minutes they researched heart problems in kids, placing ideas on the list as they went along.

"Hmm," Scott said, leaning back against his chair. "I can't believe I didn't think of this sooner."

Jules looked up from the screen, "What is it?"

"Listen to this – Kawasaki Disease is a disorder that produces inflammation of many tissues of the body, high fever, red eyes, rash, peeling of skin on hands, swelling of the lymph nodes in the neck and can affect the heart and blood vessels."

Jules had seen Kawasaki Disease a couple times before, but the other patients had sores in their mouths and peeling of skin on their hands, and none of them stopped walking from it. But Brandon's condition had been weird from the very beginning with how spread-out the symptoms were and how his fever fluctuated. In fact, when he left for his echo, he didn't even have a fever anymore.

"You know, he is only missing a few of those symptoms. Plus, Mr. Spencer did mention how Brandon's hands and feet seemed swollen at times. It's a good possibility." She agreed.

"There isn't much we can do until we get the results back from Brandon's echo, but I have a hunch it is going to confirm Kawasaki Disease. I'll call a friend from college and get his opinion." He pulled out his cell phone, his eyes locking on hers. "Why don't you call Dr. Hahn's office and reiterate our need for results as soon as possible."

Jules nodded, placing the call. Her heart tightened, knowing that if Brandon had been suffering from Kawasaki Disease this entire time, the outcome could be much worse than any of them imagined.

Chapter Three

Taking a deep breath, Jules followed Scott into Brandon's room. Dr. Hahn's office had called five minutes earlier confirming Kawasaki Disease. Now the time came to break the news to his parents. There were times in this profession that sharing a diagnosis brought good news and answers that proposed hope. This would not be that moment. Scott cleared his throat as they entered, grabbing the attention of Ryan and Janet.

Ryan looked up from his phone. "Finally."

Janet lay in the bed alongside Brandon, stroking his head while he slept. "Hi, Dr. Henson." She looked over at Jules. "Julia." Janet sat up, swinging her legs over the side of the bed. "Do you have the results back from the echo?" she asked, keeping her voice low.

Nodding, Scott pulled the extra chair over and took a seat. Jules noted that he might not be a great boyfriend, but he excelled at being a doctor. His bedside manner and sincere care brought him hugely positive reviews from the patients and their families.

"Mr. and Mrs. Spencer, we have received the results from Brandon's echo. Dr. Hahn, our pediatric cardiologist, has taken a look at the test, and we agree that Brandon has something called Kawasaki Disease."

"Kawa-what?" Ryan asked, leaning forward in his chair.

"Kawasaki Disease. It is a rare childhood disease. This condition involves inflammation of the blood vessels and also includes the arteries, veins, and capillaries. Occasionally, it can also affect the coronary arteries. Unfortunately, the echo has shown this has occurred in Brandon. Because of the inflammation, the arteries narrowed which prevented blood flow. Not only has this happened, but also a part of his coronary artery has stretched and weakened, causing a bulging." Scott used his hands to explain as he showed what a normal artery looked like, and what size Brandon's was now. "His bulging is minimal, but if not dealt with immediately, he will likely have an aneurysm."

Janet gasped, covering her mouth with her hands. "What?" she cried through her fingers, her wide eyes revealing her fear. "An aneurysm. I don't understand. How did he get this Kawasaki Disease?"

"Regrettably, Kawasaki Disease is a poorly-understood illness, and the cause isn't known. What little research that has been produced shows it could be the body's response to a virus or maybe an infection that correlates with an auto-immune disorder; however, no specific virus or infection has been found. At this point, it's mostly speculative."

Ryan stood up, thrusting a hand through his dark hair. "For weeks we have begged doctors to help us, and you're telling me my child has to be on his deathbed to figure it out?"

Standing, Scott raised his hand, hoping to settle Ryan as swear words filled the room. "Mr. Spencer, I totally understand your frustration, but please understand that we are working with a very rare disease we really know nothing about. It only affects about four thousand children in the U.S each year, and many of those cases are different. I have yet to see a case like Brandon's. The diagnosis of Kawasaki Disease cannot be made by a single test but only by carefully examining the child, hearing the history of onset symptoms, and eliminating other possibilities. Because Brandon's symptoms were so spread out, a conclusion for a diagnosis couldn't be made until everything was put together."

"If we hadn't brought Brandon in, he would have died!" Scott flinched as Ryan pointed his finger at him.

"You're right. Chances are he wouldn't have made it through the weekend, but you did bring him in, and we now know what is wrong. We may not know what causes Kawasaki Disease, but we do know how to cure it."

"How?" Janet reached for a Kleenex and blotted her eyes. "How do you cure it?"

"Brandon will be admitted into the hospital for a few days. We will start him on a high dose of gamma globulin. This will be given through an IV and will typically be run over ten to twelve hours. If his fever reaches above 101.5 degrees during treatment, it will have to be run again. He will also be on a large aspirin regimen, probably about twenty children's aspirin a day for the next few weeks to help thin his blood since his arteries have narrowed."

Janet leaned down, placing a kiss on Brandon's pale cheek. "So that's it? After the treatment he will be cured?"

Jules glanced over at Scott. Her breath caught, wondering how he would word Brandon's long term care. He paused, his Adam's apple bobbing slightly. "I'm not sure. Brandon's case is a little different. Most patients usually have the fever for a few days, and when caught within ten days, they make a complete recovery. As you know, Brandon's fever has lasted almost twenty-one days. The percentages for him having a full recovery have dropped immensely. I'm not saying that he will for sure, but there is a good chance he may have some cardiovascular complications from this. Only time will tell."

Ryan spun around, punching the back of his chair. "This is insane!"

Covering Brandon's ear with her palm, Janet shot a look at

him. "Ryan, please keep your voice down."

He shoved his arms out to his sides, "I have a right to be upset!"

"I'm upset, too, but it won't help if we get Brandon upset also. And don't take this out on Dr. Henson. He's the first person to actually help us."

Ryan took a few steps toward Scott. Adrenaline pumped through Jules's veins, worried about what he would say or do to Scott. "You doctors are all the same. You only care about one thing … yourself."

Scott blinked slowly, not allowing any emotions to show. How could he just stand there while his character was unjustly disdained? Jules didn't want to judge Ryan Spencer. She didn't have a child that had just been given the diagnosis of a rare disease – and she prayed she never would – but that still didn't give him the right to treat Scott so poorly.

Stepping back from Ryan, Scott turned toward Janet. "Julia will start Brandon's IV, and I will get an order started immediately for the gamma globulin. If you have any further questions, please don't hesitate to ask. I should be around for the rest of the day, and if I'm not on this floor, I can be easily paged." With that he left the room, leaving Jules alone with Brandon, Janet, and Ryan – the hothead whose glare could burn a hole in the back of Scott's head.

CHAPTER FOUR

JULES STARED DOWN AT HER SALAD, WILLING HERSELF TO TAKE A bite. Her upset stomach twisted in knots. For the first time in months, she couldn't bring herself to eat for reasons other than the mental battle that raged in her head daily. Trying to get Brandon's IV in had proven to be more difficult than she thought it would be. He might only be two-years-old, but he was strong. It took his parents and Becky to hold him down while she administered the needle, leaving the tube inserted. In order to keep the IV in place, she used a board to keep his forearm straight and cloth adhesive tape to keep it secure. His large drops of tears that raced down his cheeks broke her heart.

It didn't help to have Ryan breathing down her neck while she worked either, acting as if she was trying to hurt his child. When she left the room, Brandon was resting comfortably while watching a Thomas the Train video. The gamma globin had been started and at this point he had no fever.

The waiting game had begun. In the next twelve hours they should be seeing a positive change in Brandon. By tomorrow he might even be up for walking down to the playroom for a few hours.

Becky joined her, setting a diet coke down in front of her. "I thought you could use one."

"Thanks." She smiled, twisting the cap open. "Not going

to lie, I'm glad it's Friday, and I'm off this weekend." She already had plans to stay home all day tomorrow, but the stress of today sealed it for her.

"Lucky you. I'm back here on Sunday."

Jules scrunched up her nose. "Sorry." After taking a long sip of her drink, she continued. "How is Lexi doing? Did she get an x-ray then?"

"Yes. Scott is in talking with her parents now. The x-ray showed improvement in her lungs."

Relief melted the tightness in her stomach. "That's great!"

"So … how are things between you and Scott?" Becky asked, placing her elbow on the desk, her chin in her palm, her bob-cut hair swinging from the movement.

Becky didn't know much about Jules's relationship with Scott. Of course most of the staff had overheard through the grapevine of Scott's unfaithfulness, but no one really had the entire story. Jules was cautious when it came to sharing details with those she worked alongside. She liked Becky. They had become good friends at work, and she seemed to really care about Jules as a person, not just someone trying to get the inside scoop.

"Okay, I guess. We had a good talk a few weeks ago. We aren't going to get back together, but we want to stay friends."

Becky leaned in, keeping her voice low. "So him acting weird today doesn't have anything to do with you?"

Interesting. So Becky noticed it, too. "I don't think so, but —"

"Julia!" Her breath caught as her name screeched out from Brandon's room. Janet came skidding to a stop just inside the door, eyes wide, white knuckles gripping the doorframe. "Julia, help! I think something is wrong with Brandon!"

Jules sprang from her chair, following after Janet. Approaching the bed, she could see what sparked her fear. Brandon lay on his side in the bed, shaking. She checked him over, quickly ruling out a seizure. Placing the back of her hand on his forehead, her skin warmed instantly by the slight touch. He was burning up.

"He has a fever that is rapidly rising." She grabbed a cloth from the closet, wetting it with cold water from the sink and placed it behind his neck.

Janet sat next to Brandon on the bed, wrapping him in her arms, rocking him back and forth as tears rolled down her cheeks. "He's dying, isn't he? We didn't get him here fast enough." A cry escaped from Janet, smothering Jules with the mother's heartache.

"His body is just reacting to the accelerated high fever."

Ryan paced behind his wife and child and then came to a halt. "What! You are just going to let him convulse like this?" He pointed down at his child. "This can't be right. Why aren't you helping us?"

"Mr. Spencer, I know this is a very scary time, but we just need to give his body a little bit of time to respond to the medication. I can give Brandon a dose of pain and fever reducer medicine to help take the edge off. Dr. Henson is on the floor right now. I will go and consult with him. I'll be right back."

Jules couldn't get out of the room fast enough. Ryan Spencer made chills roll down her spine – and not the good kind; however, she did feel badly for him and Janet. It was sad to see families come in that didn't know Christ and the hope and reassurance only He could give. It didn't make the hurt any less to watch their child suffer, but there was a divine peace that easily identified those who loved God. Jules needed to stay sensitive to the Holy Spirit and keep looking for opportunities to share with the Spencer's about her faith.

Well, maybe she'd start with Janet.

Scott stood at the counter when she came out into the hallway. "Scott, can you take a look at Brandon? His fever is rapidly rising and I want to make sure I'm not missing something."

He blinked slowly, not hiding his hesitation. After his last interaction with Ryan, she didn't blame him for not wanting a round two. "Yeah, I'll go check in on him." He looked down at his watch and back up at her. "Is your shift over at five?"

"Yes." She cocked her head to the side, confused by his casual question. "Did you need something?"

Clearing his throat, he stepped closer to her, keeping his voice low. "Not really. I just wanted to talk to you about something. Could we grab a coffee or dinner later?"

If Scott hadn't been acting so differently today, she probably would have asked for a rain check so she could just go home, but his look of desperation made her initial response change. "Um, sure, I could do coffee." A cold January night called for a hot coffee.

"Great. I'll check on Brandon, and then I have a conference call I need to take. I'll be back before your shift ends, and I'll walk you out to your car." He walked away, leaving her to wonder about what he needed to talk to her.

Jules stepped into Brandon's room ten minutes before her shift ended. The rest of the afternoon expired without any commotion, but she wasn't sure what mood Ryan would be in when she entered. Finding Brandon and Janet both asleep and Ryan absent, she quietly made her way to the dry erase board, erasing her name and putting the next nurse's name on shift in its place.

"I'm sorry for my husband's rudeness."

Startled, Jules spun around to find Janet awake in the chair. "Don't worry about it. I know this is a very stressful time for you all. I'm sorry if I woke you."

"You didn't, I was just resting my eyes." Janet sat up further in her chair, rubbing her eyes. "You'd think after weeks of not sleeping well I'd just fall asleep from exhaustion." She looked over at Brandon, "But until I know he will be okay,

I'm not sure I'll be able to fully rest."

Janet seemed like a good mom, and her love for her son was evident.

Stepping over to the cart, Jules picked up the thermometer and ran it across Brandon's forehead. She breathed a sigh of relief. "His fever is down, only low-grade now, and his color looks good. By tomorrow I bet you'll have a hard time keeping him in one place for too long."

Leaning over, Janet ran a hand over her child's head, tears filling her eyes. "That would be wonderful."

"Janet, can I get you anything before I leave for the day?"

She shook her head. "No, thank you. Ryan left shortly after Brandon's high fever scare. Said he needed to grab some things from home and more clothes for our stay. I'm sure he'll be back soon." Tightening her arms across her mid-section, Janet waited a moment before continuing. "I've never seen Ryan this intense before."

"His son is very sick. He has the right to be upset."

"He may have the right to be upset, but not to treat you and Dr. Henson so poorly. I'm very sorry. He won't apologize, but please accept my apology."

Jules couldn't help herself. She walked around the bed and bent down, giving Janet a hug. "Please don't worry about it anymore. It's fine. Really."

§ § § § §

THE QUIET WALK TO THEIR CARS AMPLIFIED THE AWKWARDNESS between Jules and Scott. This trip to the coffeehouse would be the first social time they had had since the evening a few weeks back when she informed him that she didn't want to try a relationship again with him. Riding down the elevator to the parking garage had Jules wondering if this evening would get any better. Maybe she should go with her original thought of asking for a rain check for another night. If it wasn't for the fact that Scott wanted to talk to her about something imperative, she'd swing the conversation that way without another thought. But despite her desire to go home, put in a movie and curl up on her couch, she wanted more to be a friend.

The doors opened, exposing the shadowy cement parking garage with only a few lights above to guide their way. They turned left, arriving at the row that held their vehicles. Scott had his own personal parking space up front, but it wasn't his BMW parked in the spot.

"Did you get another car?"

"Yeah, I decided to get something new."

Jules would hardly call his current car "new." Compared to his fancy BMW, this was an old rust bucket. The look she gave him out of the corner of her eye brought a tired smile to his face. "Different. Is that a better adjective?

"Sorry. I'm just surprised. I thought you loved your car?"

"I did. I just love no car payment more."

Although Jules had parked further away, Scott insisted on walking her to her vehicle. As their footsteps pounded along the cement, his stride quickened, and Jules had to work to keep up. A car door slammed shut.

Scott jumped, pushing her to the side. "I'm sorry, Julia." He grabbed her arm, bringing her close to him again.

"Are you sure you're all right?"

Putting his hands on his hips, he looked down at his shoes, scuffing his toes against the floor. "No, I'm not." He let out a defeated breath, bringing his eyes up to reach hers. "I've got some things going on. That's why I wanted to have coffee with you. I could use a friend right now."

Jules wasn't really sure what she could offer Scott, but if he needed a listening ear, she would be willing. She reached a hand up, squeezing his bicep. "Of course, and I'm happy to be that friend. I'm worried about you, Scott."

He placed his hand on his arm, covering over her hand. "Thanks. I knew I could trust you." Looking around the garage, he pulled her toward her car that sat parked four spaces down. "We should get going. It's not safe."

"Safe? What are you talking about?" She tried to slow down their pace, but even with her resistance he didn't slow a bit. "Scott, what is going on?" She finally worked out of his grasp and stopped short of her car.

Scott turned, "Julia, please just trust me and get in the car," he pleaded.

"No. Not until you tell me what is going on." she demanded, while straightening her stance. Determination laced her words.

"I promise I will tell you everything over coffee, just get in the car."

They began their stare down, neither budging.

"Doctor Henson!"

They turned to find Ryan Spencer stepping out from around a van, pointing a gun at them. A scream escaped from Jules as Scott pushed her behind him. Scott lifted his hands, palms up, in a motion of surrender. "Mr. Spencer, please don't do this!"

Jules's legs began to shake from the fear pumping through her veins. She grabbed hold of Scott's coat to keep her from falling. She scanned the parking garage in hopes of seeing someone to call out for help.

Empty.

They were alone.

Ryan stopped advancing but kept the gun pointed at them. "Scared? Afraid you're going to die?" He shuffled his feet back and forth, clearly agitated. "Now maybe you have an idea of the fear we have dealt with these last few weeks. It's a horrible feeling, isn't it?"

"You are right," Scott agreed, "it is a horrible feeling, and I'm sorry you had to experience it, but this isn't going to help your son. Now put the gun away, and we can forget this ever happened."

"I see, so you can walk away fine, but my son has to suffer for maybe the rest of his life?"

"Okay, listen. Let's get Julia in her car, and we can talk about this." Scott put his arm behind him, gently pulling her away from him and toward her car. "This only needs to be between the two of us."

Ryan looked between her and Scott. His nostrils flared. "What, so she can call for help? I don't think so." He jabbed the gun toward them, the motion causing him to stumble forward.

The blast from the shot immediately caused Jules's ears to ring. She screamed, falling back against her car. Through the haze she thought she heard Scott yell at her to get in the car and then heard another shot.

Her eyes darted over to Ryan, whose hand covered his mouth, eyes wide. Bringing his hand down he swore and then yelled, "No! No! No! How did that happen? I didn't mean …" He looked all around and then darted away, climbing into a beige van and speeding through the garage.

Jules covered her ears, hoping to stop the ringing. She looked behind her to find Scott on the ground, a pool of blood growing on his chest. "Scott!"

CHAPTER FIVE

R USHING TO SCOTT'S SIDE, JULES DROPPED TO HER KNEES TOO fast onto the cement. Pain radiated through her knee-caps from the hard impact. She took deep breaths, trying to slow down her heart rate. She had been trained for situations like this. She just never thought she'd ever have to use the skill, and nothing ever prepares you to see someone you care for, someone you once loved, suffer like this.

"Scott! I'm here." Panic clouded her thinking. What should she do? He was breathing, but his breaths were ragged. Sucking in a deep breath of air, she pushed the shock off. Scott needed her. She threw her purse down. Ripping open his shirt, she could see the entry the bullet had made just right of the center of his chest. Realization gripped her that chances were slim he would survive. She pushed her right palm against his chest, applying pressure to the wound. He moaned, gurgling from fluids, never opening his eyes. With her left hand she fumbled around in her purse to find her phone. As she dialed 911, she leaned down and implored, "Hang in there, Scott. I'm getting help. You are going to be fine."

The call connected. Jules gave dispatch the information they needed. Thankfully, being in the hospital parking garage would bring help very soon. Putting the phone down, she rose up higher on her knees, placing her left palm on top of her right. Blood began leaking out from under him. Her scrubs turned a dark red. Realizing she couldn't get the bleeding to stop, her adrenaline flickered like the overhead lights above her. His pulse began to decrease rapidly.

"Come on, Scott! Stay with me!" Tears began to blur her vision.

A car drove past. She tried to flag the driver down, but their angle had them hidden too far behind her car. She turned back to Scott. "Hold on!"

The moment his heart stopped beating, she felt its void against her fingertips that she pressed to his neck. "No!" The word ripped from her throat. She began compressions, calling out the number of thrusts as an act of sanity. Sirens bellowed in the distance, closing in on them quickly. Between compressions, she noticed hospital staff stepping out of the elevator and rushing toward them. New hands replaced hers. She crawled around and sat by his head. Sobs erupted as she put her mouth down to his ear, begging his heart to beat once again. Begging God to let him live. Two police cars arrived. A couple EMT's pushed a gurney up to them. She looked around at the others working on Scott, their grim faces slicing her heart in two. Eventually they stopped compressions.

"What are you doing? Help him!" She knew there was nothing more they could do, but the pain cut deep just watching him lie there, bare chested, gray pallor, lifeless.

The man next to her turned, compassion filling his eyes. "I'm sorry. He's gone."

§ § § §

JULES SAT IN THE BACK OF THE CRUISER, NUMB. SCOTT WAS DEAD. A life taken away at its prime, senselessly. Red and blue lights caught her attention from the rearview mirror. She turned in her seat, leaning slightly out of the open door, to see an unmarked car slow down and stop behind the squad car she occupied. Her breath caught when a familiar face emerged. Detective Trevor Hudson. She had met Trevor last month when her best friend, Ava, had been kidnapped, and he had helped with the investigation in finding her. She didn't know him well or really anything about him personally for that matter, but just seeing him now put her at ease.

Trevor approached the officers at the scene. They talked for a few minutes, and then one of the officers pointed in her direction. Trevor nodded, heading her way. When they made eye contact, his steps slowed as he recognized her, and then he rushed forward. Reaching her, he got down on a knee.

"Jules." He hesitated, "You're my witness?" She nodded her head in answer, not trusting her voice. "Are you okay? Were you hurt?"

She swallowed the lump in her throat. "I'm fine." Fine. She was far from fine. "No, I wasn't hurt."

"Has someone been called to come and be with you?"

"I ... I don't have anyone to call." The depression over that fact could have strangled her if she'd let it.

"What about Ava?"

"No." She had already told herself that wasn't an option. "She and Matt just got home from their honeymoon. I'm not going to burden her with this."

"I'm sure she wouldn't look at it that way."

"I'm not calling her."

"Okay, how about someone here at the hospital? What about Derek?"

Derek. What she would give to have his arms around her right now, but she wasn't about to throw her needy self at him, especially if he didn't want anything to do with her or even worse, comfort her out of pity. "It's okay, Trevor, really. I'd like to just give my statement and go home, if that's all right?"

He stood up, loosening his navy tie a small fraction. "Of course, let me take care of a couple things, and then I will get your statement. Stay here. I'll be right back." Once he left, she leaned her head back against the head rest. She closed her eyes, wishing when she reopened them that she could be anywhere but here.

CHAPTER SIX

D EREK BROWN'S SQUAD CAR CAME TO A SCREECHING HALT IN-
side the hospital's parking garage. Trevor's phone
call informing him that Jules was a witness in a murder had
him rushing from his house, an uneaten supper sitting on the
table. He hadn't even taken time to get back into uniform. His
jeans and sweatshirt would just have to do. He wanted to kick
himself for not getting in touch with her sooner. She had been
back from her trip for almost a week, and he had been too
scared to make the first contact, as if not talking to her would
eventually make everything work out the way he wanted it to.

He had dealt with rejection in the past, but to hear it from
the woman he could see himself spending the rest of his life
with – that rejection he wasn't sure he could recover from.
But none of that mattered now. Trevor hadn't given him any
details other than Jules had been a witness to a murder, was
alone, and he thought she could use some support.

Did Jules even want him here? She'd made no effort to
contact him. Maybe he needed to get a clue. Spotting Trevor
deep in discussion with the head of the CSU, Derek waited to
approach so as not to interrupt. While scanning the garage,
auburn hair sticking out from the back of a squad car caught
his attention.

He rushed forward in her direction, calling her name out as
his throat tightened, "Jules!"

She heard him the second time he called. Her eyes widened with shock and then filled with relief. Stepping out from the car, she waited for him to approach. Derek hadn't expected her to throw her arms around his neck, but he welcomed it when she did. Pulling her tight against him with his left arm, he used his right hand to gather her hair and hold her head against his neck.

Pulling back, she used her palms to push the tears aside. "What are you doing here?"

"Trevor called me."

Her cheeks flushed pink. "I'm sorry. I told him not to bother you."

Derek pushed down the disappointment that flooded his heart from the realization that maybe he was right earlier and she didn't want him here. Using his curled pointer finger, he pushed her chin up, making her look at him. "Jules, you are never a bother."

Her shoulders slackened. Taking a step into him, she slid her arms around his chest. "I'm glad you're here."

Hope sprung from her words. "Me, too." A black body bag laying on the ground near her car caught his attention. He cleared his throat, "Have you given a statement yet?"

Stepping away from him, she turned her back to the scene and shook her head. "No, I'm waiting for Trevor." She pulled out a tissue from her coat pocket, wiping her eyes and then nose. "He's dead, Derek." Looking up at him, sadness strangled her words into a whisper. "I just can't believe Scott is dead."

"Wait. What?" Having not received many details entailing what had happened, he had no clue that it had been someone she knew. Not that he gave Trevor a lot of time to explain. The first sentence had him grabbing his keys and heading out the door. "I didn't know, Jules. I'm so sorry."

"Jules, if you are ready, I would like to take your statement now." Trevor stood behind them, hands on his hips, compassion lacing his words. His five-o'clock shadow amplified his exhaustion. He had mentioned earlier to Derek in passing conversations that he was on a big case this week. The lack of sleep showed.

She nodded. "I am." Looking up at Derek she asked, "Can you stay with me?"

Glancing over at Trevor for confirmation, he answered with a gentle touch against her back. "I'm here for as long as you need me."

Trevor started the grueling process of taking her statement. "Just start at the beginning, Jules, and I'll interrupt if I have any questions."

Jules began by sharing about the new patient, Brandon, and the harshness of the father. Derek stood beside her, noticing the tremors that sparked from the memories she shared. When she reached the part about agreeing to go to coffee with Scott, Derek couldn't deny the jealousy that flushed through him. Maybe it was his imagination, but he grabbed onto the fact that when she mentioned they were going out for coffee as friends, she kept her focus on him, wanting him to know that's all it was.

"Did you and Scott usually go out after work together?" Trevor asked, looking up from his notepad.

"No. Scott and I used to be in a relationship and since that ended we hadn't really spent any time together outside work."

"Why was today different?"

"He said that he needed to talk to me about something."

"Do you know what?"

"No, but he just didn't seem like himself today. That is mostly why I agreed to the coffee."

"How did he seem different?"

"More stressed, tired. He also mentioned that it had been a long couple of days."

"Okay, so tell me what happened when you got down here to the parking garage?"

Jules paused before answering, taking a moment to soak in the scene and her thoughts. Derek rubbed her shoulder in silent encouragement. Her strength impressed him. Despite her grief and processing through the last few hours, she spoke with clarity and confidence. Her voice did tremble at times and a few stray tears appeared, but she would pause, collect herself and move on with the information.

She started at the elevator as she walked them through her conversation and movements with Scott until they reached her vehicle. Trevor stroked his chin as he digested her words. "So you have no idea why he thought it wasn't safe? Do you think he had an idea that Mr. Spencer was after the two of you?"

Wrapping her arms tightly against her mid-section, Jules frowned. "I don't know, maybe? We never had a chance to talk about it before Ryan came out from around the van with his gun pointed at us."

Derek tightened his fists into a ball just thinking about her in harm's way. The idea that she could have easily been in a bodybag alongside Scott, made him nauseous. By how many feet had she been spared a bullet? Respect for Scott grew as Jules continued to explain how he had protected her, putting her safety above his own.

"Can you show me exactly where Mr. Spencer stood?"

Jules's green eyes searched over Derek's face. He clasped her shaking hand. "You can do this. I'm right here."

With a tight smile, she squeezed his hand in return. Making her way across to the other parking spaces, she stopped at an empty one. "Ryan came out from behind a van that was parked here. He moved forward until he stopped," she looked around, "right here."

She covered her palms over her face. Derek took a step forward, ready to comfort her, but Trevor put an arm out to stop him. "She needs to remember. Give her a second." Agreeing, but not liking it one bit, he stayed still, keeping his eyes glued on her.

Taking a deep breath, Jules straightened her frame, determination returning with vengeance. "Ryan started yelling at us, asking us how it felt to be scared of dying and that we would finally understand how he and his wife felt. Scott tried to talk him down, but Ryan stayed persistent with anger about us being fine while his son might have to suffer for the rest of his life." She ran a hand through her hair. "It just happened so fast. I don't remember if he said anything else."

"You are doing great, Jules," Trevor confirmed, "just a few more questions."

"Okay."

"Tell me about when Scott was shot. How did that happen?"

"Ryan was jabbing the gun at us, Scott pushed me toward my car and the next thing I knew, Ryan shot. My ears were ringing, but I think I heard Scott yell at me to get in the car, and then another shot. Ryan started freaking out. I looked back and found..." she cleared her throat, "I found Scott on the ground. Ryan took off in the van. I called 911 and started working on Scott." She looked down into her hands, still stained from Scott's blood. "I tried to stop the blood, but I couldn't."

Derek didn't give Trevor a chance to hold him back this time. He hurried to her side, pulling her willingly into his arms. Resting his chin on the top of her head, he whispered, "Jules, you did all you could."

"There was just so much blood. Maybe if I had done something differently ..."

"This isn't your fault."

Trying to hold back a glare as Trevor approached, interrupting their moment, Derek moved to the side. "Jules, I think

I have what I need for now. I'll be in touch if I have any further questions. I'm going to need to keep your vehicle here for a while since it is a part of the crime scene," Trevor stated.

"Jules, I can take you home and bring you back to get your car when it's cleared from the scene," Derek suggested.

"Okay, thanks." She turned her attention to Trevor. "Am I safe now? Is there a chance that Ryan could find me?" Derek rubbed a hand along her arm, hoping it offered an ounce of comfort. He had been thinking that very question but had been waiting to ask Trevor when she wasn't around.

Trevor nodded, "Let me check on that." He returned a few minutes later. "You're safe. When you told the dispatcher Ryan's information, we were able to get a BOLO out on his van immediately. He is now in custody."

Jules's weight shifted. Derek placed his arm under hers to keep her steady. He needed to get her home. Shock would be wearing off soon, and she no doubt would be hitting her max with the emotional drain of the situation. "I'll take you home now."

"Thanks." She looked down at her scrubs saturated with blood. "Can I change my clothes before we go?"

"Sure thing." Trevor stepped forward. "I'm sorry I didn't think of it sooner. Let me get you a new pair of scrubs."

"I have an extra pair in my vehicle. Can I just use those?"

"Yes. Feel free to change wherever you feel comfortable." Trevor slapped Derek on the shoulder. "Make sure she gets home safe."

"Will do."

Changed, Jules stepped out of the bathroom. Derek held a plastic bag in his hand, ready for her to put the soiled scrubs in. "I'll get these washed for you."

"No need. You can just burn them. I don't think I'd ever wear those again."

"Understood." He led her to his squad car. Guiding Jules

into her seat, he fussed with the seat controls to make her more comfortable.

Her cold hand slipping over his stopped his motion. "Derek, you don't have to go to all this trouble."

Smiling, he pushed a strand of hair behind her ear. "I want to." He stood up, "Now put your seatbelt on," he said and shut the door.

§ § § § §

JULES UNLOCKED HER FRONT DOOR AND PUSHED IT OPEN ENOUGH for her and Derek to get through. He closed it behind them and then helped slide her coat off, hanging it on the hook near the door. She hoped she hadn't offended him with her quiet demeanor on the way home. The last four hours had been a blur, and she had a lot to process. Not wanting him to leave yet, she asked, "Can I get you a cup of coffee? I have decaf."

He laid his hands on both sides of her arms, "Tell you what, why don't you go wash up while I make us a pot of coffee."

Examining her hands, her stomach churned. Good point. "Okay, thanks. I'll hurry."

"No hurry, I'm not going anywhere." Jules couldn't deny how those words warmed her heart.

She thought she'd be quick, but once the hot water from the shower poured over her, eliminating all trace evidence from the day, she stood motionless, not wanting it to end. If only the water could remove the memories.

Thirty minutes later, clothed and hair dripping wet, she walked into her kitchen to find Derek at the table with two mugs of coffee and a bowl of chicken noodle soup waiting for her.

"I figured you missed dinner and might be hungry." He stood up from the table and walked around to pull her chair out. "I hope that's okay? I found a can of soup and used my extended knowledge of cooking to heat it up for you."

Food was the furthest thing from her mind, but she wouldn't dare turn away his thoughtfulness. "Thank you." She sat down at the table, taking a sip of the coffee. "I hope you made enough to include yourself. I'm sure you missed dinner, too."

"Well, I left it sitting on my kitchen table, but by this time, I'm sure it's in Max's belly," implying his Golden Retriever. A smile escaped. It felt nice after the day she had. Derek made his way over to the cupboard and got himself a bowl, filling it with soup. She liked how at ease he seemed at her house and hoped it continued. After a few bites, he placed his spoon down and leaned forward on his elbows. "You aren't eating very much."

She looked down at her half-eaten bowl. "Sorry, I guess my stomach is a little upset."

"It's understandable. You've been through a lot today." He reached across the table and took hold of her hand. "How are you holding up?"

"It doesn't seem real. I think reality will set in once I get back to work and have to face the fact that Scott isn't there anymore." A lump formed in her throat, just thinking of the void in her life from his absence.

"Well, just know that you have people that care about you and want to help you through this, myself included." He pulled back his hand, checking his watch. "I have to tell you something, and I hope you don't get mad at me."

She gave him a curious look. "How could I when you put it that way?"

"I'm worried about you and didn't want you to be alone tonight. So, while you were in the shower, I called Ava. She will be over soon and plans to stay the night with you. And selfishly, I didn't want to endure Ava's wrath when she found out I knew about what happened and didn't tell her."

"I don't blame you. I'm sure I'll get the third degree my-self." Relief smoothed out her knotted stomach. She didn't want to mention to Derek her unease about being alone to-night. It wasn't his problem to worry about. Having Ava here tonight would make the night at least a little more bearable. "I'm glad you called her. I wanted to, but I just felt guilty about her spending time away from Matt since they just got home a few days ago."

"I don't think I could have stopped her from coming over."

"Probably not."

Their eyes met, and they shared a knowing smile. Jules's heart squeezed as his baby blues sparkled back at her. Having Derek here with her felt good. Really good. As if something had been missing from her life, and she finally found it.

"Are you finished with your soup? I can put it in a con-tainer for you. Maybe you'll want it tomorrow."

She nodded, keeping her eyes on him as he picked up her bowl and moved to the other side of the kitchen. "Containers are in the cupboard left of the microwave."

"Got it." He followed her instructions, finding a Tupperware dish to put the soup in.

Once he placed the leftovers in the refrigerator, she stood, meeting him in the middle of the kitchen. Pushing up on her tip-toes, she wrapped her arms around his neck, in need of his strength. "I'm so glad that Trevor called you. I don't think I could have handled tonight without you."

He pulled her closer, whispering in her ear, his breath slid-ing along her skin. "I'm glad he did, too. But next time, you call, okay?"

A throat clearing interrupted them. "Sorry. I had a key and let myself in."

She turned to find Ava standing in the doorway of the kitchen. "Ava!" She left Derek's embrace, missing his tantalizing touch already. She gave Ava a hug, thankful to have her here. "Thanks for coming."

"How many times have you camped out at my place for me? Derek should have called me sooner. In fact, you should have been the one to call me."

"I know. I just didn't want to ruin your first few nights at home."

"I appreciate you wanting to put my needs above yours, but being with you right now trumps a night at home with my husband. Matt agrees."

"I'll let myself out while you girls do your thing." Derek announced, already heading out of the kitchen.

"Let me walk you out," Jules submitted, not wanting to see him go yet.

"While you do that, I'll go get settled in the spare bedroom." Ava reached down and picked up her bag. "Thanks again for calling me, Derek."

"Yep, see you later."

Jules followed Derek to the door. He slipped on his coat, pulling his keys from the pocket. He ran his fingers through his hair, his nervous trait showing. "So I was thinking. I have the day off tomorrow. Would you like some company? I could come over and bring lunch and a few movies."

She stepped forward, surprised and yet happy about his suggestion. "I'd like that, but there is one condition."

"What's that?"

"Tomorrow has to be a diet coke, sweat pants, no make-up kind of day."

"I guess, but I really wanted to try out my new mascara."

Jabbing his arm, she grinned. "And you can bring that sense of humor, too. I'll need it."

Pushing a stand of hair behind her ear, his gaze softened. "You're a strong woman, Jules. You'll get through this. Go talk to Ava. Get some sleep. I'll be back around noon for a day

40

of us being couch potatoes."

She waited to shut the door until he drove away, waving until she could no longer see his brake lights. Earlier she hadn't wanted to go to sleep, for fear of the nightmares she knew would appear – but at least the sleep would speed up the time until she saw Derek again.

Her stomach lurched, thinking about tonight and how she wouldn't be able to control the memories that would press her down. With Ava here, she wouldn't be alone, and she took comfort in that, but it didn't take away the fact that Scott was gone. Needing a sense of control over her life, she did what she always did, what she fought against every single day. Walking into the bathroom, she closed the door and stuck her finger down her throat.

CHAPTER SEVEN

CURLED UP ON THE COUCH, JULES DID HER BEST TO CONCENtrate on the comedy movie playing and not on Derek sitting a mere few inches away from her. He had arrived at noon, as promised, and she opened the door to find him with Subway sandwiches and a case of diet coke in hand. Already on their third movie for the day, they hadn't left their seats except for more drink and bathroom breaks. So far it had been the best day she'd had in months, and one she needed after yesterday and her long night.

After three in the morning, she had finally fallen asleep, only to be awakened multiple times from reliving Scott's death. She tried not to disturb Ava, but her sobs easily made it through the thin walls, bringing her friend in quickly to her side. By sunrise, she had finally fallen into a restful sleep, except for the few minutes she aroused, hearing Ava leave. The aroma of coffee woke her up shortly before Derek arrived, not giving her much time to get ready. Needing coffee more, she decided against a shower and instead pulled her hair back in a ponytail, changed into more appropriate sweatpants and a long-sleeved shirt.

Derek picked up the remote and shut off the television as the credits rolled. "Want to order some pizza for dinner?"

Pushing down the apprehension of the amount of calories that were in one slice of pizza, she smiled, "Sure. I can go order and have it delivered. What kind do you like?"

"Chicken supreme is my favorite, but I'll eat about anything."

"That sounds good to me." Jules went to the kitchen to get the number on the to-go menu, placed the order, and then returned to her spot on the couch she'd claimed all day.

Derek leaned forward, tucking the blanket tightly around her. "How are you holding up?" he asked.

She shrugged, "Better than I thought. Today has really helped."

"I could get used to these lazy days with you." He admitted. Their eyes caught, neither turning away. She wasn't sure whether she was ready for where this conversation could head, and yet she anticipated it all the same. Jules decided to let Derek take the lead and broach the subject when he deemed fit.

After a few beats he cleared his throat. "So, did you hear we are supposed to get a bad winter storm next week?"

Weather. He wanted to talk about the weather? Jules paused, disappointed by his diversion, but not really surprised since they had been skirting the subject. "No, I haven't, but it's January in Northern Illinois, so we're due for some bad weather."

Leaning his elbows into his knees, Derek looked down and then back at her, a frown tilting his soft lips downward.

"What's wrong?" she asked.

"I'm sorry Jules, but I don't want to talk about the weather," he admitted.

"Neither do I."

"Would it be extremely insensitive of me to ask if we could talk about us?"

Always a true gentleman. "No, I think we need to talk." Her words squeaked out, barely above a whisper. After months of playing tug of war with their feelings, could it be that finally they were on the same page at the same time?

"I'm sorry I didn't contact you when you returned from your trip. If I could do it all over again, I would have offered to pick you up at the airport, despite my fear of your rejection."

"I don't blame you. I haven't made it very easy on you since we met."

A soft laugh filtered through a smirk, "No, you haven't." Jules playfully pushed his shoulder in response. "So, how did your trip go visiting with your parents?"

She reflected on her week of soul searching and the eye-opening experience it had been for her. "The time with my mom after Matt and Ava's wedding went well. We spent an entire day walking along the beach. I was able to share my hurt and frustration over her leaving me, moving down to Florida, and wanting to start a new life without me. We were able to handle the conversation well, each sharing our emotions over the matter without getting defensive." She smiled, remembering the sun-filled day. Jules had even told her mom about Derek. She couldn't remember the last time she and her mom had talked about a boy she liked. It felt like a small victory between them. "I think our relationship had its first breakthrough."

"That's great, Jules. How did you leave things with her?"

"We are going to make more of an effort to talk and visit. I guess spending a couple weekends a year in Florida isn't all that bad." The thought of maybe one day Derek taking that trip with her warmed her heart.

"No, I'd say not. How did it go with your dad?"

Her shoulders sank slightly. "Not as well, but it's my own fault. I thought after years of not seeing me he'd want to spend all this time together. I assumed our talk would go like it had with my mom." She shook her head. "Boy, was I wrong. He picked me up from the airport and took me out to dinner. It was so awkward. The following two days he had to work, so I only saw him for a few hours in the evening. My last night there I brought up my feelings about him leaving us. He pretty much blamed everyone else for his actions and at one point said, 'I don't remember inviting you to come here'." Tears stung her eyes even now from his hurtful words. "I think I went into the visit with high expectations. For years I've been dreaming of connecting with him, having a moment where as his daughter I'd feel loved and wanted."

Derek leaned back against the couch, crossing his arms at his chest. "Jules, there is a difference between unrealistic and realistic expectations. Yours were very valid. I'm sorry it didn't go as you hoped."

"Despite the trip not going well, it really gave me the closure I needed. He's not walking with the Lord or hearing God's truth, and I'm not responsible for his actions or response – only mine. So when I left, I hugged him, told him I forgave him and then walked away. I don't know if we'll ever have a relationship, but I'm done letting my hurts from rejection affect the plans and people God has put in my path." Her heartbeat escalated at reaching this point in their conversation that sparked the unknown of what Derek would be thinking. The doorbell rang, giving her a few minutes to prepare what she wanted to say next.

§ § § § §

DEREK ANSWERED THE DOOR, PAYING THE PIZZA DELIVERY KID and tipping him an insane amount, not wanting to wait for him to make change. He stuck the pizza in the oven, turning it on low to keep it warm before heading back out into the living room. There was no way he would let their conversation stop there. Hearing Jules's review of her trip gave him a better understanding of where she stood the last few months. He understood the expectations she placed on her parents. He had often done the same with his. He needed to take her example and work at making amends with his family. But right now, the beautiful redhead nestled up in the couch commanded all his attention. She seemed to be more ready, giving him the cue to bring up the discussion of them.

Entering the living room, he stopped short when he found Jules crying while reading something on her phone. He came to her side, kneeling down in front of her, "What happened?"

"I just got a message from work letting the staff know about Scott's funeral arrangements." She grabbed a tissue from the side table, drying her eyes.

His heart squeezed, wishing he knew the best way to comfort her. He used his thumb to swipe away a lone tear slipping down her cheek. "What are the arrangements?"

"Wednesday morning there will be a memorial service for him."

"Do you want to talk about it?"

She sat motionless for a few seconds, staring off, deep in thought. Bringing her feet down to the floor, she leaned forward toward him. "No, I don't. To be honest, I don't want to talk about my parents, or Scott's death, or what happened yesterday. I want to talk about us."

His breath caught from her admission. Hope pulsed throughout his veins. "Jules, my feelings for you haven't changed. If anything, they have grown. I want to be with you. I want to be the last call you make every day. I want to know everything about you. But I think the question we face now is how do you feel?"

She stood, wrapped a blanket around her, and walked over to the bay window. The sunlight streaming in highlighted the gold strands in her hair. He followed, staying behind, giving her space. Wind whipped through the bare trees, swaying the branches with its gusts. His nerves squalled through his gut just like the wind while he waited for her response. Turning to face him, she let out a breath as a small smile emerged. "I want to be with you, Derek. Everything you just said sounds wonderful. To be the source of your attention makes my heart skip with happiness ..." her smile faded quickly, "but ..."

Stepping forward, Derek ran his hand down her arm. "Jules, I don't want your grief over the death of Scott to push you into a relationship with me. There is no need to rush anything. We can let the dust settle for awhile."

She shook her head. "No, that's not it. If anything, Scott's death has made me realize that I shouldn't take life for granted. That I shouldn't allow my fear to rule my life anymore. My hesitation is because I feel like I should tell you something before this conversation goes any further."

"Okay." He drew the word out, bracing himself mentally for what she would say next.

Taking a deep breath, she closed her eyes. Determination appeared when she opened them. "I've been dealing with something the last few months, a secret I've kept to myself, and if we are going to be together, it will affect you also." She pulled the blanket tighter against her. "I have an eating disorder. It started over the summer when Scott and I broke up. As you know, I've been dealing with my life feeling out of control, and I found a sense of empowerment when I could control my weight. It started off by not eating much, and sometimes not anything, on some days. Then when I needed to eat around others so they wouldn't find out, I would eat, but then I'd just go and throw up afterwards. I've been gaining freedom from it day by day with the Lord's help. It is still a daily battle at this point, but I am seeing victory in many areas. I had a bit of a relapse last night, but I know that is going to happen. I'm not going to be healed of it immediately, but I am seeing progress. I hope you meant it when you said that you wanted to know everything about me, because here you go, as raw as I can get."

Derek stood silent, not sure how to respond to her exposed secret. Looking back he had noticed that she was losing weight, and it was weight that she didn't really have to lose. Jules kept her eyes down on the floor, yet to make any eye contact with him. He stepped closer to her. *God, give me the wisdom to speak the right words.*

"Julia." He waited until her eyes found his. "I can only imagine how hard this was for you to share with me. We all have things in our life that we struggle with, and your struggle doesn't change the way I feel about you at all. In fact, you telling me this gives me hope because you are letting me in and trusting me." He placed a loose piece of hair behind her ear. "Do you want to talk about it more?" He would leave it up to her whether she wanted to go into more depth or wait for another time.

"Not right now. I just wanted to tell you so you weren't blind-sided later on."

"So, Ava doesn't even know?"

"No. You are the first. I will tell her, but I'm just not ready yet."

"I'll respect your decision to wait, but can I just say one thing?"

"Do I have a choice?" A soft smirk flirted across her lips.

He laughed. "No." Placing his hands gently on her shoulders, he continued, "We all care for you, Jules. We want to help and encourage you. Satan wants us to keep our struggles hidden so he can work them to his advantage, but when we bring them to light, God can use them to His advantage."

"Since when have you been so smart?"

"You just stick with me, pretty lady."

She shorted the distance between them. "Hmmm, I think I will."

"Best decision you've ever made."

"Time will tell."

He wanted to kiss her, but instead, kept his lips to himself. "Well, I'm up for a challenge. And just for the record, next time we are in public, I'm introducing you as my girlfriend."

"I've been called worse."

He pulled her into a hug, smiling from their banter. "Are you sure you're ready to start a relationship with me?" He asked, giving her one last chance to back out, because after this moment he was giving everything he had.

"I'm ready. It shouldn't have taken me this long, but I'm glad we are here now. Are you sure you want to deal with all my baggage?"

Derek couldn't believe after months of pursuing her, the time had finally come to see if there could be a future for them. He wanted to dig deeper into her eating disorder, ask questions, find ways that he could help, but he would wait. "What makes you think I don't have any baggage to bring to the table? How about we start with yours and work mine in slowly?" His family flashed through his mind. Desperation to make a conscious effort to make amends with them changed from a want to a necessity.

"Smart and full of good ideas, I'm a lucky lady."

"I'm catching on to a hint of sarcasm."

"See, I told you, smart." She slipped her hand into his, fitting perfectly. "So what's next? Where do we go from here?"

"Well, we are going to get you through the next few days, with me by your side, if that is okay with you." He had plans to be her shadow until after the memorial service. She wouldn't walk through this alone.

"I'm more than okay with that."

The smell of pizza teased him, causing his stomach rumbled. "Good. Now that we have that settled, how about some dinner?" He cringed, realizing what food waited for them. "I'm sorry. Pizza probably isn't what you want to eat. I can order you something else or take you out."

"No. Pizza is okay. I might just eat one piece and have a salad. Do you think you can handle an entire pizza to yourself?"

He squeezed her hand, pulling her into the kitchen. "You just wait, you're about to witness something real special."

CHAPTER EIGHT

DEREK DROVE HOME, UNABLE TO QUIT SMILING. HE TURNED right and headed north to his house. He only lived about fifteen minutes away, but he'd drive hours every day if he had to, to see her. The moon peeked out behind the clouds, leading the way. It was so bright he could probably shut off his head lights and still see the road.

Jules's auburn hair flashed across his thoughts, her porclein skin soft to the touch, her full lips he dreamed about touching against his. He had wanted to kiss her but didn't want to push too quickly. After dinner Jules lit some candles, mentioning how her favorite way to relax was by filling the room with their lavender scent. He didn't mind the smell or the fact that they sat for hours laughing and talking by just the light from the candles as the soft glow illuminated her emerald eyes.

Since she had a rough night before, he didn't stay too late. He could sense her tiredness and need for sleep, by continually covering her yawns with a hand. She promised to lock up and head to bed as soon as he left. Instead of kissing her like every fiber in his being yearned to do, he opted instead to pull her into his arms at the front door before he left. The cold wind licked his face as he jogged to his truck. Jules had waited at the bay window, waving at him, blowing out the candles as he drove away.

He decided to stop and fill up the gas tank so he wouldn't

have to get up so early in the morning to do it before church. Twenty minutes later Derek turned into his neighborhood, slowing down as he reached the section of houses that were heavily populated with kids. His phone started ringing as he pulled into his driveway, its screen displaying Trevor's name.

"Hey Trevor, what's up?"

"Are you by chance with Julia?"

"I was, but I just left her place about a half hour ago."

"Okay. I just tried to call her a couple of times, but she isn't answering."

She had mentioned wanting to take a shower before bed, so she probably just couldn't hear it. Or maybe she was so exhausted she had already fallen asleep. He hoped for the latter. "Is there a problem?" he asked as he looked down at the dash clock. Why would Trevor need to talk to Jules at 8:30 on a Saturday night?

"I'm not sure. I just have a few questions. If it was any other case, I would wait until the morning, but since I know her personally, I thought I'd just give her a call."

Derek shut off his truck, letting the silence clear his mind. Something must be really bothering Trevor for him to be calling. "What's going on, Trevor? I thought this was an open and shut case?" Jules had witnessed the whole thing. What other questions would need to be answered?

Trevor's hesitation spoke volumes. Finally he said, "I thought it was, too, but the case has taken a weird turn and to be honest, it's not making sense with Jules's statement."

A desire to defend her burned in Derek's chest. "Are you saying you think Jules gave a false statement?"

"No," he answered quickly, "I didn't say that." He cleared his throat, "It's just that her statement isn't lining up with the evidence."

Derek gripped the steering wheel with his free hand. "Like what?"

"Jules said that she heard two shots, but the gun we found on Ryan Spencer had only been shot once."

"Did you check to see if he owned another gun?" It was a foolish question. Of course Trevor had covered all the bases, but he still had to ask.

"Yes, he only has one gun registered in his name. We searched his place and came up empty. Ryan is also adamant that this was the only gun he had and that he did not shoot Scott."

"And you believe him?" The words roared out, his blood pressure spiking.

"I'm just following the evidence, Derek."

He took a deep breath, needing to get a handle on his emotions that caused his outbursts. He wouldn't be able to help Jules or with this case if he lost his temper or appeared not to be open-minded. "Okay, I'm sure it was very traumatic for Jules, and she got confused. She said her ears were ringing after it happened. In a cemented parking garage, without ear protection, I'm sure it threw her off. But why does it matter whether it was one shot or two? He did it."

Trevor's pause almost brought Derek out of his seat. "We found a second bullet."

"What?"

"We found a bullet embedded into the cement wall by Jules's vehicle. We won't get ballistics back until early next week. The M.E. pulled the bullet out of Scott today. We should get results for that next week also."

Drumming his hand along the wheel, Derek began to understand the confusion Trevor had about the case. It wasn't making sense. "Is there a chance the bullet embedded into the cement wall is an old bullet?"

"There is always a chance, but it just seems to be too much of a coincidence to me."

For the years he had been on the force, it had become clear

how few and far between coincidences happened. His gut tightened, uneasiness gripping him over what this new information might mean and how Jules would take it. One thing he knew, she wouldn't be asked the questions without him present. "I can run over to her house, ask her a few questions, and see if I can get her statement a little clearer."

"I'll join you. Make it a little more professional."

"That's fine." He started up his truck, the purr of the engine slicing through the night. "I can get there in fifteen minutes."

"I'm working on another case now. I shouldn't be too far behind you."

"Sounds good. That should give me a little time to prepare her for the questions." The last thing he wanted was to upset Jules and drudge up the memory again. Especially after their amazing day together, he didn't want it to end this way. But they needed answers, and she was the only one who could give them.

"How is she doing?" Trevor asked, his concern for her apparent and genuine.

"She's hanging in there. Jules is a strong woman. Last night was rough, but she seemed better today."

"I'm sure it helped spending time with you today," he teased.

He would have usually answered with a joke, but he was in no joking mood at the moment. "I hope so. I'll see you in a bit."

Derek ended the call and placed one to Jules. Her voicemail clicked on after five rings. He left a message, letting her know he was on his way back to her house. Retracing the roads he had just traveled, he ran through his mind the questions that needed to be asked, while others emerged from wondering how she would handle them. Would the stress of the case push her into a setback with her eating disorder? Now that they were in a relationship, would she allow him to be her rock or would she push him away? The questions consumed him until the smell of smoke distracted him. He turned onto Jules's road, looking for the source of the smell. His adrenaline surged as he pulled up to her house. Black smoke melted into the dark sky as flames dashed out from her front bay window.

CHAPTER NINE

DEREK JUMPED OUT OF HIS TRUCK AND SPRINTED TOWARD Jules's house, screaming her name. "Jules!" He canvased her yard, hoping to see her safe. A knot grew in his stomach when he came up empty.

An elderly couple stood across the street, watching the house burn. He ran up to them, his breath ragged. "Do you know if the woman living here got out?" he asked, not sure how friendly this neighborhood was and if they would know Jules by name.

The woman shook her head as the man gave the address over the phone. "I don't know. I haven't seen her. We were watching television and just noticed the fire a couple minutes ago. We aren't physically able to go in and help, but we called the fire department."

Derek zipped up his leather coat and put on his gloves. "I'm going inside to find her. If I'm not back when they show up, make sure to tell them that there are two people inside."

The woman nodded as he took off running. He assessed his options, knowing he couldn't go through the front door, being too close to where the source of the fire appeared to start. He ran around to the back of the house. Her back door opened up into the kitchen. He wiggled the knob. Locked. He yelled her name again. Not waiting for a response, he picked up his leg and kicked his foot through the glass window in the door. Unlocking the door through the broken window, he moved into the house, glass crunching beneath his boots. Oxygen sucked out of his lungs as he stepped into the kitchen. He grabbed a towel lying on the counter and tied it around his mouth and nose.

He had only been to her house a couple times and had no idea which room was her bedroom. Making his way down the hall, he opened each door. The first seemed to be the spare bedroom. The door on the right was a bathroom. The last door on the left, he opened, knowing this had to be her room. A dim lamp sat in the corner by a chair. Light leaked out from under a pocket door that he assumed led into her master bathroom.

"Jules!" he shouted, hoping to get her attention before she came out, sure that she wasn't expecting company to be standing outside her bathroom door. He banged on the door. "Julia!" She had about three more seconds before he barged in.

"Derek?" Her confused tone came muffled through the door. She slid the pocket door open slightly, eyes wide, her wet hair dripping down onto her cotton tank top and pants that probably revealed more than what she would be comfortable with under normal circumstances. "What's wrong?" Worry clouded her eyes.

He grabbed her hand, pulling her from the bathroom. "The house is on fire. We have to go!" He saw a robe lying on her bed. He picked it up, draping it around her. She slipped her hands into the arms and tightened the rope around her waist as he took off the towel covering his face and wrapped it around hers. "Stay with me."

She nodded, but said nothing. Eyes filling, she gripped his hand. Her bedroom fire alarm started blaring, causing her to jump. Why had it taken so long?

Leading her back through the house as he came, closing doors along the way, he noticed how much thicker the smoke had gotten in the living room. He coughed, and with his free hand, tried to pull his coat up over his mouth. Remembering the glass that was broken in the kitchen, he turned and picked her up, carrying her out the back door. An eruption of coughs exploded in his chest as he tried to breathe in the fresh, cold air. He placed her down in the grass, bending over to catch his breath.

Jules rubbed his back while clutching his arm with her other hand. Sirens bellowed from a distance, closing in. Her pink manicured toes reminded him that it had easily dropped below freezing by now and he needed to get her someplace warm. He straightened his frame, slipped off his coat and laid it across her shoulders. "Come on. We need to get out front."

The fire trucks pulled up as he and Jules made their way down the drive. The firemen jumped off the trucks, pulling out gear and hoses, making their way to the front of her house. After telling the firemen that the house was empty, Derek took Jules over to his truck that was still running. Heat slithered out as he opened the door, hoisting her up onto the seat. Shutting the door he ran around to the driver's side and jumped in. His chest tightened when he caught her staring at her house with tears pooling in her eyes, her chin trembling.

"My home … I don't know what happened." She blinked, sending tears trailing down her cheeks. He reached out, placing his hand over hers. Scooting closer, he wrapped his arm around her shoulder and brought her against his chest as her sobs filled the truck.

§ § § § §

JULES SAT IN MATT AND AVA'S EARTH-TONED LIVING ROOM, SUR-rounded by moving boxes stacked against the walls, trying to decompress what had happened in the last hour. She couldn't take her eyes off the canvas that hung over the fireplace. Ava's wedding gift to Matt. The picture of the beach with the sunset lowering to the trees put her in a trance, soothing her.

After Derek had consoled her in the truck, he called Matt and Ava. Ava picked her up and brought her back to their house while Derek and Matt stayed. Derek assured her he would stay and find out what he could and then meet back with her at Matt and Ava's house. She wanted to stay nestled in his arms but agreed to his suggestion. She really couldn't stand watching anymore, and he probably sensed that before she did. She longed to have him sitting here with her, holding her hand, being the rock he had consistently been over the last few months, whether she deserved it or not.

Running her fingers through her damp hair, she looked up to find Ava stepping into the living room with a mug of hot tea. She reached out, taking the cup, "Thank you."

"No problem. Do you feel any better since your shower?"

Jules had taken another shower when she arrived at Ava's to get the whiff of smoke out of her hair. Ava had graciously loaned her sweat pants and her Chicago Bears pull-over sweatshirt to replace the skimpy outfit she had on earlier. Hopefully Derek had been too focused on the fire to notice how little clothes she had on. If it wasn't for the fact that her house was burning, she might have been more embarrassed by her forced lack of modesty.

"I do. Thanks for the clothes." She took a sip of the tea. Gesturing toward the wall of boxes, she asked, "How is unpacking going?" Matt and Ava had moved into their house the day after they returned from their honeymoon, almost a week ago.

"Oh, you noticed our lovely décor?" Ava took a sip of her tea. "Slow, but it's finally starting to feel like home. We finished our bedroom first," she looked up, a slight blush coloring her cheeks. She moved on quickly, "and we finished the kitchen and bathrooms today. Next week we plan to go through all those boxes." She looked up at the canvass above the fireplace; the one Jules couldn't take her eyes off of. "That was the first thing we did. Do you like it?"

"It's beautiful. Lucy did a great job painting it, and it looks perfect there." She remembered the day she moved into her house. The joy of finally owning something that was just hers and the accomplishment of working hard to make it happen. Her throat tightened by the thought of it being gone. "How much longer do you think the guys will be?"

Ava wrapped her slender fingers around her mug, "Matt called while I was getting the tea ready. They are wrapping up now and should be here in the next half hour. I'm so sorry about your house, Jules. Hopefully they got to it soon enough that the damage just stayed in the living room."

"Me, too. As we ran though, it looked to have stayed contained, but we won't have those answers until later, I'm sure." She swallowed the lump forming in her throat. *It's just a house, it's just stuff* – at least that is what she had been preaching to herself. She was so thankful that she was alive, but watching her home burn surged an emotion of pity through her, despite the thankfulness.

"I'm just so glad that you are okay. It could have been so much worse, Jules."

"I don't know what brought Derek back, but I'd hate to think what would have happened if he didn't." When he got here, that was one of the many questions she had for him.

"What do you mean, back?"

Jules realized she hadn't told Ava about she and Derek spending the entire day together. She filled her in on the details. "And forty-five minutes after he left, he's pounding on my bathroom door telling me my house is on fire." She closed her eyes at how surreal the last two days had been. The rollercoaster of emotions from witnessing Scott die, to starting

60

a relationship with Derek, to watching her house burn. She needed a vacation from life.

"So you and Derek spent the entire day together? Interesting ..."

"He knew I needed a distraction and wanted to keep me company."

"He does make a very good distraction, doesn't he?" A teasing smirk hitched up the corner of Ava's mouth.

She should have known Ava would read between the lines and push until she got the information she wanted. "Yes, he does." She couldn't hide the smile that grew as she thought of him and their day together. "We had a really good talk and I guess we are going to try this relationship thing out."

Ava's eyes widened. "Finally!"

The doorbell rang. "Who is that?" Jules asked, being too soon for the guys to return. Moving the curtains to the side, she tried to see the porch and who could be there.

"Your support system," Ava stood up, heading to the front door, "but this conversation is far from over."

Opening the door, Ava's siblings Josh, Lucy and Jake filed into the living room. She hadn't cried since standing in the shower, but seeing their concern and the fact that they had come here for her brought a fresh batch of tears to the surface. She grew up with not much of a family, but the Williams family had made her their own throughout the years.

After the hugs, they sat around the living room and she gave them a review of what had happened over the last two days, intentionally leaving out the fact that she and Derek were now together. She watched Ava as she passed over those slight details. It wasn't that she didn't want people to know, but she hadn't had a chance to really wrap her mind around it yet.

And the fact that she had shared her deep, dark secret with him. The reason for telling him about her eating disorder came two-fold. He needed to know the truth before they took this next step, it was only fair. But if she was really being honest, she told him because if he was going to leave her because of it, he needed to do it now, rather than later. His caring and sweet reaction shouldn't have surprised her, but it did. He had even wanted to talk more about it but didn't push when she wanted to change the subject. She couldn't believe the freedom she experienced when the words finally came out, knowing she didn't have to deal with this struggle alone. Looking over at Ava, guilt crept through her thoughts. She needed to tell her. But not tonight.

Lucy and Ava disappeared into the kitchen to make popcorn while Jake and Josh stayed to keep her company. Josh sat in the recliner, while Jake took a seat beside her.

"Have you heard how your patient, Brandon, is doing?" Josh asked.

"I haven't. My co-worker Becky is back on shift tomorrow. I think I'll call her and get an update."

"I'll be praying for him. For healing and the fear and confusion he is probably having about why his dad isn't with him in the hospital."

"Thanks. I've been thinking about that, too."

Jake scratched his five o'clock shadow, lost in thought. "You know, Jules, I can't stop thinking about what you said about Scott acting weird and the things he said in the parking garage. Call it a professional hunch, but it doesn't seem to settle with me."

Around the city, Jake was well known as a gifted investigative reporter. So good that The Chicago Tribune wanted him, but he turned down their offer so he could stay close to his now fiancée, Erica Miles.

"It was very out of character for him," she agreed, "but he's gone now. I guess it doesn't matter." That wasn't true. To her, it did matter. She wished he could have had the chance to confide in her. Now she would never know.

"Well, if you ever want me to do some digging, don't hesitate to ask."

She leaned her head over, laying it on his shoulder. Never having brothers, she hadn't understood the protection they gave, until now. She could get used to this brotherly love. "Thanks."

Jake ruffled her hair, "Anytime, Jules."

Yawning, she slipped her hand over her mouth for the hundredth time over the stretch of the evening, trying to hide it.

Josh caught her. "Why don't you try and get some sleep? We can wake you when Derek and Matt get here."

Maybe a few minutes wouldn't hurt. Being sleep deprived wouldn't help balance her emotions. Jake stood up, fluffed the pillow, and directed her to lie down, whether she wanted to or not. He grabbed a blanket from the side of the couch and covered her up. The smell of buttered popcorn filled the room as Jules's eyelids grew heavy. She didn't fight it. Sinking deeper into the couch, she let sleep consume her.

Muffled voices filtered into the room, bringing Jules back to consciousness. A warm hand pressed against her shoulder. "Jules."

Derek. His tenor voice drew her eyelids open. Focusing, she caught his tender smile. "Hi," she whispered, not expecting her voice to sound so groggy.

"Hi. Sorry to wake you," he helped her sit up, "but we need to talk."

Rubbing her eyes, she contemplated a cup of coffee but decided against it. She would never fall asleep tonight if she had caffeine now. "That's okay." She wanted to add, 'I'm glad you're here. I missed you,' but she wasn't ready to admit those feelings yet.

Derek sat down beside her and draped his arm across the back of the couch, pulling her close. She scanned the room, finding everyone's eyes on them. Either she had slept hard those few minutes or everyone came in with ninja like skills. Jake sat in the oversized recliner with a large bowl of popcorn and a knowing grin. Matt and Ava shared the love seat without an inch between them, while Josh and Lucy sat in front of the stone fireplace. Putting her attention back on Derek, she asked, "So what's the damage?"

His gaze looked across the room to Matt and then back on her. "It's not a total loss, it could have been much worse. The damage stayed mostly contained in the living room, but you will have to replace everything in there. The kitchen has some smoke and water damage, but a deep cleaning should make it good as new. Luckily, the bedrooms and bathrooms are fine. They are far enough down the hall and with the doors closed, that area was spared."

She absorbed the news. It wasn't as bad as she had feared. "Can I still live there?"

He shook his head. "Not right away. Insurance will need to look at it first. Your front window and back door are boarded up for now, but you'll have to get someone in there to repair the damage before you can move back in."

She fought against the tears that made her feel weak. "I guess I can move into a hotel for a while." Not ideal, but her options seemed limited.

"No." Ava piped in, "you're not staying in a hotel. You can stay with us."

Staying a few weeks with the newlyweds sounded like an awkward option. How could she break the news to Ava without hurting her feelings?

"You know what," Lucy said, "my roommate moved out, and I've been looking for a new one. Why don't you just stay with me, Jules, until you can return home?"

Lucy's offer made the most sense. She gave an appreciative smile. "Thanks, Lucy. That would be great." Ava's face fell slightly. Jules scrambled to find a compromise, "But since it's so late, maybe I could just stay here tonight, and then starting tomorrow, I'll stay with Lucy."

"Yes!" Ava responded with gusto.

Jules caught Matt's eye to judge how he felt about a third wheel for the night. "You are always welcome to stay here," he reassured.

Nodding, she wrapped the blanket tighter around her. Not sure she was ready for the answer to her next question, she proceeded anyway. "When can I get my stuff?"

"We came up with a game plan while you were sleeping. Tomorrow afternoon we all want to go with you and help salvage what you can save and help you pack your things," Ava informed her on the group's behalf.

Looking around the room, Jules became humbled by their support. Ending with Derek, she held his gaze a few seconds longer than the others. "I'm fine, really. I'm sure you all have better things to do than go through my house."

"Jules, you're family. That's what we do for each other," Josh encouraged.

Family. It felt so good to be a part of something. So often she considered herself as a loner. Her against the world. But tonight, she was reminded of the support system she always had, but failed to let them in. Swallowing hard, she tried to push down the "ugly cry" burning to release. "So speaking of my house, did they find out what started the fire?" She had been wondering all night what had happened. Maybe a short circuit?

Derek grimaced before answering. "The Fire Investigator took a look and believes it came from your candles."

It took a few seconds for the shock to clear. "What? How? I blew them out before I headed to bed. I remember."

Derek grasped hold of her hand and squeezed. "Maybe you thought it was totally out, but it didn't fully go out? One candle was lying on its side, very close to your curtains in the bay window."

Closing her eyes, Jules tried to replay what she did. Dread engulfed her. "After I blew out the candles, I did bump the table with my foot. I didn't look back to check, but I also didn't hear anything fall." Frustration toward herself grew. "You mean this could have all been avoided if I'd just turned around and checked?" Her stomach tightened and her demon emerged, taunting her that if she would just throw up she'd feel better.

"Jules, it was an accident," Derek reassured, but his attempts fell flat. This was her fault.

"So why didn't the fire alarms go off? If they had, I could have called for help quicker." That question had confused her from the beginning.

Matt leaned forward, grabbing his hands over his knees. "Your fire alarms in the kitchen and living room didn't have batteries."

"What?" She darted a look at Derek, who nodded the confirmation. "No. That can't be true. I always switch out my batteries twice a year at each time change. I put new ones in two months ago." It made no sense.

"Is there a chance you took the old ones out but forgot to replace them with new?" Jake asked, airing the question everyone, including herself, wanted to ask.

She couldn't deny how tired she'd been last fall. Without eating well and getting the right nutrition, she'd struggled with fatigue and stress that had mounted into her finally admitting she had a problem.

"I ... I guess it's possible." Embarrassment grew as she confessed how careless she might have been.

"You're safe, Jules, that's what matters," Lucy interjected.

Looking over at Derek, she smiled. "Thanks to Derek. You never told me what brought you back to my house."

He couldn't hide the tightness in his features. His jaw constricted. "It's late. We don't need to get into that tonight."

Clearly, Derek was trying to protect her for some reason. It should feel sweet to her, but instead it only irritated her. "I want to know now." She softened her resolve. "Please."

Releasing his hold on her, he ran a hand through his sandy blond hair. "All right. Trevor called me when I got home, needing to speak with you. I offered to meet him at your place to go over more questions. I called him and told him about the fire. He said that he will get in touch with you sometime next week."

"What did he want to talk about?"

"It seems that they are having conflicting information with your statement and the evidence."

Jules rubbed her temples with her fingertips, trying to massage away the growing headache. Maybe Derek had been right, not wanting to push the subject tonight.

Continuing, he brought up a hand to her shoulder. "You said that Ryan took two shots. Are you still sure about that?"

Over the last twenty-four hours she had been replaying what happened over and over – and it transpired the same every time. "Yes, there were two shots. I'm sure of it." His frown surprised her, confused her even. "What aren't you telling me, Derek?" Her heartbeat began to race in an erratic pattern, waiting for his reply.

"Ryan Spencer's gun was only fired once."

Dropping her head, she reached her emotional limit for the night. She had been wrong about all the events of tonight. Had she also not remembered correctly what really happened in the parking garage? Could her mind be playing tricks on her?

"So what does that mean?"

Derek sighed, "I don't know."

CHAPTER TEN

JULES WIPED OFF THE ASHES THAT COVERED HER HANDS ONTO HER jeans and then placed them on her hips, surveying the progress. Derek, Matt, Ava, Jake, Erica, Lucy and Josh had been helping her sift through her belongings for the past two hours to see what could be salvaged.

When she heard of the damage, she had assumed the fire had destroyed most of her living room. Shockingly, that wasn't the case. The front window and outside wall bore most of the charred fire damage; the rest of the living room damage had been from smoke and water. All her furniture, bookshelf, tables, lamps and electronics had been ruined. Picture frames on the walls had the glass blown out and the edges curled up. Black soot with its own art creation ran down her painted yellow walls, turning them a dirty brown color. Water stood a half inch in places along the floor, the carpet unable to fully soak up the excess. Earlier this afternoon, her insurance agent had been out to the house, assessing the damage and adding up an estimate for her. The agent was confident everything would be covered, and then some. She had wanted a new couch, just not this way.

Derek had backed his truck up to the front door so the guys could haul out the useless furniture and items. He volunteered to take it all to the dump tomorrow. Erica and Lucy worked in the kitchen, cleaning up the glass from the door and washing down the cupboards and counters. Jules and Ava had spent their time going through her bookcase, sorting out what knickknacks and pictures could be saved.

Ava held up a picture of the two of them from middle school. "I remember this day. We had just won our basketball tournament."

Grabbing the photo, Jules examined it closer. "And I remember that hair style. What was I thinking? I mean, look at my bangs. Could I have gotten them any higher?"

"And yet, back then we thought we were hot stuff. Look at my braces and the neon rubber bands around them. They could have glowed in the dark," Ava pointed out.

They laughed, reminiscing more of the past. They had always been each other's rock in life. Together they had encouraged and supported each other in all their ups and downs through years of dealing with teenage drama, broken hearts, life's disappointments and talking out their dreams. Things would change now that Ava was married. It had to. They would always remain close, but now Matt needed to be Ava's rock, her go-to person. And some day, maybe, hopefully, Jules would have someone as well.

As if on cue, Derek came in from outside, bringing in a rush of cold air. He unzipped his Carhart coat, exposing his flannel shirt that transformed his eyes to a brighter blue. Pulling off his hat, his hair shot out in all directions. Jules held back the urge to run her fingers through his untamed hair. "What picture is this?" he asked, taking it from her hand before she could object. Looking between her and Ava, he laughed. "This is the two of you? Let's just say you've aged well. Jules, look at your hair. Your bangs barely made it into the photo."

Grabbing the picture back, her lips thinned to keep from smiling. "Speaking of hair, yours could use a mirror and a little TLC."

He leaned in, "I saw the way you looked at me when I came in. It can't be all bad."

Eyes wide, she glanced at him as he winked back. Despite being together, she wasn't ready for him to see how much she really cared. Holding back gave her some control, because once she told him how she really felt, he would hold her vulnerable heart in his hands.

"Is the truck loaded?" she asked, needing to change the subject that caused heat to run up her neck.

"Yep, not an inch to spare. I'll take it to the landfill tomorrow and come back later this week and do it again."

"Thank you."

"You're welcome." Stepping close, he placed a hand on the small of her back, a move so natural, it was as if he had been doing it for years. "How's it going in here?"

"Okay, I think. Lucy and Erica are about done in the kitchen, and we finished up the bookshelf. We were able to save a few things." She pointed to the box sitting on the chair.

While going through the bookshelf, she cried only once – when she discovered the collage of her and Jenna had burned up, along with the picture Jenna had colored of the two of them together. The irreplaceable items hurt the worst.

"Any more pictures I can look at? I could use a good laugh," he teased.

"If I have to, I will burn them myself before you get a chance." He curled his arm, twisting her into his chest. Close enough that his minty breath ran across her cheeks. In her peripheral vision she watched Ava step away from them.

"They can't be that bad."

"Trust me. I had a few awkward years. This red hair might be cute now, but when big and crimped, not so much. Oh, and in seventh grade my glasses were larger than my head and thick as Coke bottles. I'm blind as a bat without my contacts."

"I'm sure I could find a stash of pictures that would make

yours look adorable. In eighth grade I was a little chubby, had a buzz haircut, and wore sweat pants every single day. I probably don't have many pictures as proof of that time period, though. I'm pretty sure I embarrassed my mom with the way I looked. Usually my appearance didn't line up with her social events."

He looked off into the distance, lost in thought, a storm brewing behind his baby blues. Laying her hands against his chest and curling her fingers into his shirt, she brought his focus back to her. The left side of his mouth twitched up as his eyes locked on hers. The intimacy became an electric current between them. His eyes dropped to her mouth. Stepping further into his embrace, her body tingled with anticipation.

Matt, Jake and Josh came in from outside before their lips touched. A few feet into the room, the guys stopped, noticing for the first time the situation they intruded upon. Involuntarily, Jules pushed off quickly, stepping away from Derek, crossing her arms at her waist.

"Did we interrupt something?" Matt asked with a discerning grin and questioning eyes that darted between her and Derek.

"No," Jules responded too quickly, with a perfect mixture of guilt and embarrassment. Disappointment tightened Derek's features, but he made no comment nor pulled her back against him.

Jake blew into his cupped hands. "Did we miss the memo it was break time? I'll go find Erica and have a little break myself." He slapped Derek on the back as he passed by, disappearing into the kitchen.

"I think we've done all we can do today, Jules. If you have your bags packed, Josh and I can load them into Lucy's car," Matt suggested.

"Yes. They are back in my bedroom." Before they started on the bookshelf, Ava had helped her go through her room, packing up her suitcases and a few boxes of things she'd need for her extended stay at Lucy's place.

"I can help," Derek said, walking out of the room without looking back.

§ § § §

DEREK TRIED NOT TO BE OFFENDED WHEN JULES JUMPED OUT OF his arms like she'd found a spider crawling on him. It shouldn't bother him, but her reaction upon being caught in his arms gave his confidence a hard blow. Maybe she wasn't ready for the public display of affection, and he had pushed her before she was ready? But she was the one that invaded his space first. He rubbed his forehead from the confusion.

Two suitcases sat in the middle of the room with three boxes stacked next to them. Standing in her room, for the second time, he had time to glance around, taking in her personal touches that reflected the woman he had grown to care for deeply. From the soft blue comforter covered with a stack of pillows in bold colors, each a different design, to the Bible verses etched up on the wall above her headboard, this room was all Jules. He breathed in the scent of her flowery perfume, letting it intoxicate him. Matt grabbed the suitcases while and he and Josh split up the boxes. He turned to find Jules standing in the doorway, not realizing she had followed them.

"Derek, can I talk to you?"

"Sure." He turned to the guys. "I'll be right out to finish helping."

"No problem. Take your time," Josh said over his shoulder as he and Matt exited the room.

The box wasn't light by any means, but in an effort to keep his hands to himself, Derek stood holding it, waiting for her to begin.

"I just wanted to make sure everything was okay between

us?"

Eyebrows smashing together, he tried to figure out what she meant. Then it hit him. Jules was the most observant person he knew, and being a cop, that said a lot. She had noticed his frustration even though he had tried to hide it.

He nodded, "Of course," and paused. "I haven't asked yet how you are handling today. It can't be easy." His words sounded stale – the conversation forced. Guilt crept through him. He had been so selfish with his emotions. Worrying more about his pride than the toll this day had taken on her.

"No, it's not easy, but I'm doing better than I thought I would." She stepped closer, never taking her eyes off him. "But quit changing the subject. I know I hurt you by my reaction when the guys came in, and for that I'm sorry. I guess I'm not used to "us" yet, and I panicked a little."

His arm muscles burned as he adjusted the box. Had she packed bricks? "Jules, you have nothing to apologize for. I understand you have a lot going on, and the last thing you need to worry about right now is me. I'm sorry if I've pushed too soon."

Stepping forward, her ponytail swayed from the movement. She stopped at the box, his barrier. "You didn't. I've just been single for a while, and it's hard to change my train of thought. Plus, to be honest, Matt, Jake and Josh are like brothers to me, and I just got caught red-handed with my boyfriend. It was purely a subconscious move."

Derek laughed at her metaphor and smiled from the fact she called him her boyfriend. Progress was being made. "I promise to watch myself around the three amigos from now on." He would have put up his fingers in the scout's honor, but he was holding fifty pounds. "What did you have in this box anyway? Cement?"

She bit her lip to hold back a smirk. "Books. My Bible, a journal, a few novels and self-help's, and a couple text books

I've kept from college to keep me refreshed."

Naturally he had grabbed the box of books while Josh probably made off with the box of socks. "I'll go run this out to Lucy's car."

"Not yet. You know what I've wanted to do all day?"

Intrigued, he asked, "What's that?"

Jules took the box out of his hands and set it on the bed. "This." She stood up on her tip-toes while running her hands up his arms and locked them behind his neck, bringing him against her into the tightest hug.

Without hesitation, his arms enveloped around her thin waist, beginning his self-pep talk to not push, especially after he just told her he wouldn't. He held her close, wishing he could erase for her the grief from the last couple of days. Against his desires, she leaned back. He loosened his hold but caught the mirror image of his longings in her eyes. The hair on the back of his neck stood at attention as her eyes dipped down to his lips. A long time ago he had told her he wouldn't kiss her until she had no regrets. His hormones pumped throughout his veins, unable to focus on the answer to that. A deep ache traveled through him, wanting to respect her wishes and yet wanting to show her the passion he'd been holding back all these months.

"Derek." The way Jules said his name changed to a tenderness he had not heard from her yet. "Are you finally going to kiss me, or are you going to think about it some more?"

A relieved breath thrust out. He wrapped his hand behind her neck, pulling her slowly to him. Enjoying the anticipation, he smiled, hovering over her mouth. A rush of pleasure exploded through him as his lips covered hers. Deepening the kiss, his pulse quickened as she responded, her soft lips exploring his. Putting his other hand on the small of her back, he drew her in tighter.

With strength he didn't call his own, he lessened his hold,

finishing the kiss by grazing her cheek, slowly making his way to her forehead.

"Derek, Jules, are you ready … for …" Matt stood at the doorway like a deer caught in headlights. "Sorry." He cleared his throat. "We're talking about heading out to get some dinner. Do you want to join us?"

Matt really needed to work on his timing. They would have a talk later. Derek began to release Jules, knowing earlier how uncomfortable it made her to be this close to him in front of people, but she kept her grip tight on his arms.

"Sure," Jules answered for them. "We'll be right out," never taking her eyes off Derek.

Derek heard Matt walk away as Jules got up on her tip-toes, brushing her lips with his, initiating round two without any objection from him.

CHAPTER ELEVEN

DEREK CLOSED HIS LOCKER DOOR WITH A HEAVY BANG THAT echoed throughout the empty room. Turning, he stuffed his gear into his bag and zipped it shut. He ran his hands down his khaki pants, hoping to smooth out the wrinkles from his lack of iron expertise. One at a time, he rolled up the sleeves on his electric blue shirt. The outfit was probably a little overkill for his plans, but he wanted to make an impression. Since he'd officially started dating Jules, he had either been in work clothes or sweats. It wouldn't hurt to remind her of what he looked like all cleaned up.

A whistle from the doorway made him turn. His eyes rolled from Matt's smug grin. "What are you so dressed up for? It wouldn't be because of a certain redhead?"

Derek's glare could have sliced metal. Of course he probably deserved it from all the times he gave Matt a hard time when he was dating Ava. "As a matter of fact, it does." Slipping on his coat, he tried to ignore Matt's intense focus on him.

"You know I think of you as a brother, Derek. But Jules is also like family."

"And your point is?"

"Don't break her heart."

Had they just entered the virtual reality of the Godfather? All Matt needed to do was rub his chin and talk in a hoarse voice.

"Trust me," he lifted up his bag and flung it over his shoulder, "we both know if any heart will be broken out of this, it will be mine."

He didn't mean to sound so glum, but when it came to his relationship with Jules, he was all in – and he wasn't a hundred percent sure she could say the same. Patience was not his virtue. If he wanted things to work out, he needed to reach deep inside and pace himself. Their kiss last night boosted his hope. Every so often Jules would let him witness her heart, the emotions she felt. In his arms, she gave him a peek of the desire she kept bottled up.

"Well, what I walked in on last night didn't look like her getting ready to break your heart."

No, yet the kiss brought up a new fear. They had jumped another big hurtle, but in the process he had fallen for her even harder. Her words said she was ready, but a part of him didn't fully believe it.

"Speaking of, you need to work on your timing. You're a mood killer."

"Excuse me for breathing or walking into a room. I apologize for being so insensitive."

Matt's dry humor brought out a laugh. He was a good friend. The best, actually. One that didn't put up with his sour behaviors, gave it to him straight, and could keep up with his quick wit.

The two of them had met when they both entered the academy at the same time. Their friendship had grown the strongest when they both trained and applied for the SWAT team. Matt had a way of pushing him past his breaking point and making him a better cop.

Matt crossed his arms and perched his shoulder against the wall, as if he was holding it up himself. "So what are your plans tonight that have you looking all GQ?"

Sitting his bag down on the floor, he straddled the bench and took a seat. "Jules has decided that she wants to go see Brandon at the hospital before he is discharged. I'm going to take her, and then we'll grab some dinner afterwards." Now that he knew of her struggles with eating, he had to put more effort into a restaurant – one that had a decent and healthy menu for her to choose from.

"Did you try and talk her out of it?" Matt asked, acting just as surprised as he had been when Jules brought it up.

"Yes, but when the woman puts her mind to something …"

"Touché. I live with one. I get it."

Derek shook his head. "I tried to tell her that her intentions were pure, but Mrs. Spencer might not see it that way. That's when I volunteered to be her sidekick for the visit." It had taken awhile to convince her, but finally she complied after he promised to stay in the shadows unless needed.

Matt straightened, pushing off the wall and sauntering over to his locker to retrieve his things. "What is Jules hoping to get from the visit? To be honest, I don't see it ending well."

Turning to keep him in view, Derek shrugged. "I know, and I have to agree, but try telling her that." He could be wrong, maybe it would go well and give her the closure she needed. But in case it didn't, he wanted to be there.

The door to the locker room swung open. Their boss, Lieutenant Rogers, stepped inside. "Good, you're both still here." He rubbed his fingers along his mustache that looked like a bloated caterpillar. "We just got a call that there is a high security warrant going down in the next hour. We don't need the whole team, just a chosen few. I'd like the two of you to be on that team."

"Yes, sir," he and Matt said in unison.

Derek took off his coat and began unbuttoning his shirt, all the while dreading the call to Jules he had to make.

§ § § § §

JULES WALKED BRISKLY ALONG THE SIDEWALK TOWARD THE HOSPItal, wrapping her coat tighter around her mid-section. A winter snowstorm threatened, and a few flakes fell from the sky as a bitter alert of what wasn't far behind. The cold wind licked her face and sent her hair up into a whirlwind. Despite the tangles forming in her hair, she didn't care. Parking in the parking garage wasn't an option. She had a half mile walk from her vehicle, but it was worth the frostbite forming on her nose as long as she didn't have to go near the space where Scott died.

The call she'd taken yesterday from her co-worker, Becky, about Brandon likely being released today had urged the visit. Just being with the little boy one day had been enough for him to play on her heartstrings. She wanted to see him one last time, to see for herself the improvement he had made over the last few days.

Stepping into the hospital, she made her way to the elevators. With a deep breath, she pushed the button for the third floor. Rifling through her purse, she found her ChapStick and applied it to her dry lips. She smiled, remembering her kiss with Derek last night. He was good. Really good. The kind of good that meant he'd probably had a lot of practice. They hadn't broached the subject of past relationships yet, but just the thought of him kissing other girls caused a snake of jealousy to wrap around her spine. Thankfully, his lips were now hers alone.

She wished he could be here now. When he called to inform her of the SWAT call that dissolved their plans, her heart sank with disappointment. She finally grasped what Ava had to deal with. Derek's sincere apology was evident, but it didn't fix the pain of his absence. At first she'd protested him coming along to the hospital, but once he convinced her, she realized how much she really just wanted him with her. For a second time, he tried to talk her out of going to see Brandon, especially since he couldn't join her, but she had to go. Scott had lost his life over this child and she had to see him one last time. To see for herself that his health was restored – to know it wasn't a total loss.

Willing one foot to move in front of the other, she left the elevator and walked out onto the pediatrics floor. The nurses' station stood empty. Not wanting to cause attention, she slipped down the hallway and into Brandon's room. He sat on the bed, eyes glued to the Thomas the Train video. Rosie cheeks spread across his healthy complexion. Before he had had a gray undertone, but today a splash of peach highlighted his skin. Blue eyes gleamed as he smiled when he spotted her standing in the doorway.

Stepping through the doorway, memories of the room filled her thoughts: The hours she spent taking care of Brandon, talking to Janet, watching Scott break the news about Kawasaki Disease, the anger that had burned from Ryan's eyes. Scott … it hurt to walk back into the hospital, knowing he wouldn't ever be here again. That they would never have the chance to research together, discuss cases, and see that what they did mattered. She'd never see him smile, chew on his pen cap when in deep thought, or hear his laughter that made the rough days bearable.

Brushing off the thoughts, she gave a warm smile. "Hi Brandon, I hear you're feeling better."

Pulling his blanket against his chest, he returned a smile. "I all better."

As she stepped forward, she noticed a packed bag sitting on the chair. He no longer had the IV in his arm. He was going home today.

"Julia?"

Turning, she found Janet standing in the doorway with

a cup of coffee in hand. "Hi Janet." She tightened her arms around her waist, suddenly uncomfortable by the woman's presence. It wasn't her fault that Scott had died. Jules needed to keep that in mind.

Janet stepped into the room, stopping short of Jules. "I didn't know you were on shift today."

Jules shook her head. "I'm not. I heard Brandon was being discharged and I wanted to see him before he left." They both shifted their gaze to him. "He looks great."

"He does, doesn't he? I wish Ryan could be here to see him." Jules froze, trying to hide her shocked reaction over hearing Ryan's name. After a sip of her drink, Janet continued. "I just have to sign papers and then we are out of here." She sighed. "I can't get out of this place fast enough."

The same feelings threaded through Jules. It was good to see Brandon, but she needed to leave. "I'm glad Brandon is better. I'll be praying he has a full recovery."

She moved to leave, but Janet placed a hand on her arm. "I'm very sorry about what happened to Doctor Henson."

How did she answer that? Her mouth grew dry. The elephant in the room just stepped on her chest and deflated all the oxygen from her lungs. "Yes, it is a terrible loss," barely squeaked out. "How are you doing?" The words came without her thinking through it first. Truth was, she didn't want to know anything about Ryan except that he was miserable in jail. But his family was innocent and despite her sadness, they needed compassion.

"It's been a long few weeks, that's for sure. With Brandon's illness, being admitted, and now Ryan being falsely accused for Doctor Henson's death – it's all just very overwhelming."

Falsely accused? What was in Janet's coffee? Her lips parted and closed again while her heartbeat raced. "What do you mean falsely accused?"

Janet stepped out of ear shot from Brandon to spare him

from their conversation. "I haven't seen Ryan yet because I didn't want to leave Brandon, but we've talked on the phone and with our lawyer. He is adamant that he is innocent, that it's all just a misunderstanding."

"What?" The force of the word wasn't hidden within the whisper. "I was there Janet. I saw him shoot Scott – Doctor Henson."

Confusion clouded Janet's eyes. "You? You're the witness? Why? Why would you do this to Ryan? Haven't we suffered enough?"

Jules pursed her lips to keep from saying something she regretted. Inhaling a deep breath through her nose, she exhaled the same way before responding. "I was there, Janet. I saw the whole thing."

"No. I don't believe you. Sure, he was angry, but Ryan would never do something like that. You are just out to make him pay for the things he said. You said it wasn't a big deal, but obviously it was." Janet's arm flew out from her side, pointing to the door. "I think you need to leave."

Jules tightened her purse against her side. "I know the truth is hard to hear, but it's true."

Pointing again at the door, Janet's glare hardened. "I said, get out!"

With one last glance at Brandon, she turned and walked out, regretting that she had stepped foot into this room. Derek had been right. She never should have come.

CHAPTER TWELVE

JULES GRIPPED THE WET, AND NOW USELESS, TISSUE IN HER HAND. Five minutes ago she grabbed her last one and now the tears ran freely down her cheeks. The hard walnut pew in the church gave little comfort, but Derek's arm across her shoulders held the strength she needed. Guilt mixed into sadness with each tear, and she wondered how Derek was assessing her grief.

Throughout the memorial service for Scott, different aspects made her throat burn as she tried to keep her emotions hidden. What a pathetic job she was doing with that. Did it bother Derek that she hurt and cried from the loss of a man she'd once loved? When people died, it was easy to keep hold of the good memories, while letting go of the bad. She wanted to remember Scott not for the times he had hurt her, but for the times he made her life better. She missed him, his friendship. Would Derek understand that?

The large church seemed small from the masses of people stuffed inside. A portrait of Scott sat on an easel in the front of the sanctuary as a reminder of what he'd looked like while the pastor delivered a moving memorial about Scott's short life. Talking about his goodness, his accomplishments, and how he was in a better place now. She hoped with everything in her that he was. Despite their close relationship, she was never quite certain if he truly believed. He had mentioned God a few times, but there was a difference between knowing there is a God and believing that the way to eternal life was through the death and sacrifice of Jesus. It was more than living a good life, so much more. That was the beauty of God's grace. All we have to do is love Him and accept Him for what He has done for us. So simple, hopefully Scott had known that truth.

Whimpers bounced off the wall as a video began, starting with his childhood and showing the stages and seasons of his life. Jules jerked straight when a picture of Scott and her together flashed up on the screen. For a moment she held her breath, picturing their life at the time it was taken. It was from the night of her birthday party when Scott had taken her for a walk along the river and told her for the first time he loved her.

How had his family gotten the picture? Derek squeezed her shoulder but kept his eyes forward. She cast a look up to the front row where his parents and sister were sitting. She had met them once. Would they even remember her?

Once the service ended and they were dismissed, she turned to Derek. "I need to run to the bathroom to freshen up."

He slid his hand down her arm and squeezed her hand. "I'll meet you in the lobby."

In front of the mirror she wiped the mascara off from under her eyes. What was she thinking, wearing makeup? The door opened to a familiar face, Scott's sister, Meredith.

Recognition flashed across her eyes. "Julia, right?"

"Yes. Hi Meredith. It's nice to see you again." She leaned in and gave her a hug. "I'm so sorry for your loss."

"Thanks. He was a great guy and big brother. He always had my back." She leaned toward the mirror, wiping her own mascara away from her under eye skin. "How long has it been since I've seen you?"

Jules played back the last year, trying to keep her dates in order. "Memorial Day last year, I came with Scott to your family barbeque."

"That's right. He was so smitten with you, Julia. When I found the framed picture of the two of you on his home desk, I knew it needed to go into the video. You meant a lot to him. I always wished things had worked out between the two of you. You were good for him."

Tears welled in her eyes. Oh, how the road could have led differently had Scott not made the choices he had, and Derek had not walked into her life and made it all she hoped it could be.

"I'm just glad that through it all we remained friends."

"The detective said you were there when he died."

"Yes. I tried to save him, but there wasn't much I could do." Jules spared her the details.

"I'm sure you did all you could." Meredith placed a hand on her forearm. "I'm just glad he wasn't alone when he died. That he was with someone he cared for." She stepped away and then turned back. "Can I ask you a question?"

"Of course."

"What was he like that day? I know he was working on a hard case, but did he seem okay? Happy?"

Jules glanced down at the floor, not sure how to answer that question since she wasn't quite sure herself. "He seemed a little off, not himself. Quiet, like he had something on his mind. That's why we were together. He said he needed to talk to me about something."

"What do you think he wanted to talk about?"

"That's the thing, I'm not sure. But whatever it was, it was bothering him."

Meredith stared off into the distance, her eyes filling with tears. "The last few months we noticed Scott pulling away. His phone calls became shorter and fewer, he'd miss family things, and he seemed down, almost depressed. Maybe I should have tried harder to get him to talk to me, but I didn't want to push him away." She grabbed another paper towel and blotted her eyes. "Now I'll never get the chance."

Oh, how Jules understood the grip that regret and "what if's" could have over someone. "You can't blame yourself, Meredith."

She nodded. "I'm just glad he was finally ready to talk to someone. I wish he would have been given that chance."

So did Jules. She couldn't help but constantly think about what Scott wanted to talk to her about, but she had to let it go. There was nothing they could do now. Crushing the paper towel into a ball, Meredith threw it in the trash. "Well, I should probably get back to my parents."

"Of course." She stepped to the side. "Please give them my condolences in case I don't see them."

"I will. Take care, Julia."

"You, too."

CHAPTER THIRTEEN

JULES WIGGLED DOWN DEEPER INTO THE OVERSIZED LEATHER RE-cliner and pushed the blanket down further to cover her toes. After the memorial service, Derek brought her back to his house. He took the day off to be with her. She didn't take his devotion and purposeful care lightly. He had been pampering her since they arrived. Now he was in the kitchen making them chef salads for lunch.

When they arrived, he had given her a quick tour. Derek's house had an open concept. His front door opened into the living room, which then merged into the eating area with the kitchen to the side. Down the hallway, off of the living room were three bedrooms – a master and two that he'd converted into an office and workout room. He kept a modern feel throughout the house, which surprised her because of his country upbringing.

For the absurd amount of money his family had, he lived so normally. She had been expecting an outrageous bachelor pad, but his sense of style surprised her. Except for his manly recliner that was currently swallowing her whole. She was positive that if she searched for it, there would be a hidden flap that held a cooler and a stash of snacks.

Leaning her head to the side to face the kitchen, she called, "Are you sure you don't want any help?"

"Nope, and I meant it the other three times you asked, too."

"All right. It just feels weird to sit here while you slave away in the kitchen, for an hour, on salads."

He stopped chopping and caught her teasing gaze. "Hey, now. You're so impatient." He smiled back. "Don't you know the best things in life take time?" He added in a whisper that floated throughout the rooms, "Like us."

Whether it was his intention for her to hear or not, it touched her heart. He began cutting up the peppers again, and she gave herself a few minutes to appreciate the man before her. He hadn't changed out of his dress clothes yet. He wore a black shirt with sleeves rolled up to his elbows and khaki pants. His blond hair had slowly turned darker as winter set in. His strong features gave him a look of confidence. Why had she pushed him away for so long? Sure, she had baggage, and they came from two completely different lifestyles, but they could get past those encumbrances, right?

Wanting to be near him, she threw off the blanket, stood, and joined him in the kitchen. She pulled out the high-back stool at the counter and sat down. "Put me to work. I'll feel better if I stay busy."

"Since you are so good at following suggestions, I'll let you decide."

She laughed at the true statement. "I'll cut up the lettuce."

He held it out but retained his grip on to it, not letting go until she looked at him. "I'm really sorry about Scott. I know today couldn't have been easy." He released the lettuce but kept his concerned eyes on her.

"Thank you." She hesitated, hoping to say the next words correctly. "It was a hard day. I hope you understand that my grief over Scott doesn't diminish my feelings for you. Yes, at one time I loved him – and actually thought I might marry him – but my sadness isn't over my feelings for him. He was a friend, and that absence hurts."

Derek set down his knife and made his way around the

peninsula to her. He took hold of her hand and pulled her up into his embrace. "I understand the relationship you had with Scott." He whispered against her ear. "You have every right to grieve his loss."

He let go and leaned back, only to cup her face with his hands. For the first time, she noticed his blue eyes held gold flecks around the outside rim. Warm. Inviting. He leaned down and left his mark on her lips, tasting like sweet peppers. As sad as today was, being here with Derek gave her a glimmer of joy and hope for the days ahead. She leaned her head against his chest, listening to the rhythm of his heartbeat. He squeezed her tight and then plopped her back down on the stool. "Now, you better get working on that lettuce, because I have been waiting long enough to eat," he teased as he returned to his spot on the opposite side of the counter.

She obliged with a smile and began cutting the lettuce into small pieces and placing them in separate bowls. "I've been thinking –"

"Uh-oh."

"Quit," she smiled with tight lips belying her nerves as to how he would respond. "You know a lot about my past relationship with Scott, but I don't really know anything about your past relationships."

It was true, and it had been bothering her a little. She knew that he had been dating Chelsea when they met but really knew nothing about how they were together or why they didn't work out. It shouldn't matter. But it did.

He shot her a glance and looked at her a long time before answering, causing her chest to tighten. "Seems fair enough. Do I need to remove all cutting devices from the kitchen for this conversation?"

She couldn't help but laugh. "Depends."

"Well, lucky for me, there really isn't much to tell. I dated a few girls here and there at college, nothing serious. I started dating Chelsea, you know, the girl from the campfire –"

"Yes, I think I remember her," Jules said dryly. It didn't take long for her thoughts to drift back to the moment they first met at Matt and Ava's engagement party. Derek had sat down with her at the campfire and had begun to pursue her and even asked her out, only to have Chelsea show up and plant a kiss on him. "You mean the girl you were currently dating when you asked me out? The one you kissed right in front of me?" It was fun giving him a rough time over what happened. He had finally explained himself and apologized, but it didn't mean she couldn't tease him about it every now and then.

"I love that you have such a great memory."

"I'm sure you do. So Chelsea …"

He was slow to answer, and for an instant she wondered if he would. "I met Chelsea in Kentucky at a horse race last spring. She is originally from there but moved to the outskirts of Chicago for business a few years ago. We got serious pretty quick, but a few months into dating I realized that even though she was a great girl, she wasn't the one for me." A soft grin flirted across his face. "And then I met you." Her insides melted a little.

"So what made you realize she wasn't the one?"

"Besides the fact she wasn't you?"

"Flattery will get you everywhere."

"That's the plan."

"Seriously though, what was it?"

Derek leaned his forearms against the counter, keeping her under his weighty stare. "She reminded me too much of my family. I should have known better at the very beginning to start dating her, but I was attracted to her and hoped it would be different."

"So since you met her at a horse race, does your family know her?" She couldn't put her finger on it, but the thought of Chelsea knowing his family bothered her. Maybe because it had given Chelsea and Derek a connection that they didn't have? Or could it be the fear of not being accepted by his family? Either way, it didn't sit well with her.

Derek's phone started ringing. He wiped his hands off on the towel and picked it up. He checked the caller ID and then fastened his eyes on her as he answered, "Hey Trevor, what's up?"

Jules' stomach tightened into a fist. She watched Derek nod while he listened, waiting for him to give her a piece of information as to what they were discussing.

"Jules is actually with me at my house. Why don't you come over? We're getting ready to have a late lunch. You are welcome to join us." He paused and then said, "Okay, see you soon."

"What was that about?" Her words sailed out.

Derek cocked his head to the side, his eyes narrowing. "Trevor said the case is getting complicated, and he needs to ask you more questions. He said he'll be here in an hour and to go ahead and eat without him."

"Suddenly I'm not so hungry anymore."

"Neither am I."

§ § § §

DEREK WATCHED JULES LEAN BACK IN HER CHAIR AND PUSH HER half-eaten salad away. She looked drained and tired. Dark circles underlined her eyes. Their conversation became quieter and she wore a stressed smile when he could actually get her to laugh. And the worst was yet to come. His tight gut told him that the information Trevor had for them was not what they wanted to hear. There was no way to protect her from the news. He just hoped she'd allow him to be there for her.

"Are you sure you're done?" he asked, pointing to her un-eaten salad.

"Yes. Thank you. It was good. I just don't have much of an appetite."

"You didn't have any breakfast today and now only half a salad for lunch. I know we haven't talked much about your eating disorder, but I'm sensing some red flags here."

Jules sat staring at him. He was just as shocked by the words he spoke. Worry tightened his chest in fear he had overstepped and pushed. He wanted to be compassionate and understanding, but still toe a fine line of keeping her account-able. She bit her bottom lip and his heart sank. "I'm sorry, Jules. I didn't mean to –"

"No, you're fine." She waved her hand back and forth. "It's a valid question, and one I need to be challenged on. I just needed a second to check my intentions on not eating." Her chin sat on her fist. "To answer your question – I'm okay. Really. I'm just so nervous about the case and what Trevor has to tell us, I can't eat anymore. But I promise I'll eat din-ner."

He understood. His upset stomach came from the unknown of Trevor's visit as well. Despite the unease, he had every confidence that his friend would work this case to the best of his ability. That he wouldn't rest until the truth emerged and came to light. Reaching across the table, Jules grabbed his hand. "Thank you for asking. I know I dropped a bomb on you and didn't explain or give you a chance to ask questions."

He began rubbing her palms with his fingers as he spoke. "Jules, we don't have to do this now. You've had a long day already."

"I want to. I think it would be good for me …" she looked down, "and us if we talked about it." She retracted her hands and folded them on her lap. "When Scott cheated on me, I be-gan a downward spiral of losing who I was. My life felt out of control. I started losing weight from the stress," she shrugged, "and I liked it. It empowered me to stand on the scales and see the numbers drop. It became a calorie counting game – that turned into an obsession." Turning her eyes from him, she looked off to the side, as if collecting her thoughts. She had touched on the subject briefly in the past but today seemed more ready to talk and let him into her struggle. He kept quiet, waiting. Emerald eyes locked on him, and the sadness etched in her frown made him fight against the impulse to jump over the table and take her into his arms.

"I couldn't control the people in my life, my job, or my future, but I could control what I put in my mouth. It felt good to have people notice the weight loss, made me feel better about myself." She cleared her throat, sat back, and brushed her hair back with her fingers, tucking them behind her ears. "But then I couldn't stop. The ability to control consumed me. I didn't want people to know, because deep down I knew it was wrong. So, I began just eating overly healthy, exercising an insane amount while trying to burn more calories than what I consumed, and if I ate too much or if the scale started tipping the other direction, I started making myself throw up."

A soft smirk played against her lips, "Remember the night after your department Christmas party when you talked to me about how I wasn't allowing God to control my life?"

He nodded.

"I realized that night that I had a big problem, and I've been making huge steps since then. I'm still trying to eat healthy, but allow myself," she put her fingers up in air quotation marks, "'cheats' more often, and I'm really okay with that. I'm still exercising but in a healthy way." She paused. "I still battle the temptation to throw up sometimes. Not because of the fear of gaining weight, but the need to control something when my life feels out of control."

His fingers stroked his jawline, soaking in her words, her

heart, and her deepest secrets that she trusted him with. "I'm still a little in shock that no one caught on. To me, you don't look like you've had a problem. Sure, you've lost weight, but it doesn't look unhealthy. I guess when I think of eating disorders, I imagine someone getting down to skin and bones."

She nodded. "That's what is scary. Sometimes it can be easy to hide. It's a battle that rages on in my mind every single day. I'm gaining ground and feel such a freedom now. Some days I get frustrated and wonder if I'll struggle with this the rest of my life, but I have faith that God will never leave me and that He will walk me through this."

Without thinking first, he asked, "When was the last time you threw up?"

She looked away as she answered, "The night Scott died, after you left my house." Jules pushed her chair back, stood up, and left him sitting alone at the table. "This is so embarrassing."

He followed after, not letting her get far. Why had he asked her that question? He felt like a jerk. "Julia," he placed his hands on either side of her slim shoulders, "I'm sorry. I shouldn't have asked."

"Yes, you should have. You have the right to know – or to be warned."

Warned? Did she think admitting her faults would cause him to walk away? She obviously had no clue about the depths of his feelings for her. Or the fact that he had a long list of struggles, too.

"Pride."

She narrowed her eyes in confusion. "What?"

He lifted up his pointer finger, as a number one. "I struggle with pride." He lifted a second finger to join the first one. "I can lose my temper quickly." He held up a third finger. "I ignore my family even though I know I should make amends with them." Up went another. "I've been accused of being bullheaded on many occasions."

Out came his thumb to continue, but she grabbed his hand, "Stop," she said and then kissed his palm, sending shivers coursing throughout his body. "I get it."

"I hope you do." He leaned in and kissed her smile as the doorbell rang.

CHAPTER FOURTEEN

WHILE DEREK AND TREVOR TALKED SHOP, JULES FINISHED cleaning up the kitchen, washing the dishes and putting them away. Besides Scott's case, Trevor was also lead detective on another, draining his time and energy by the sound of things. When did the man ever sleep? It wasn't her place to say anything, but he sounded like he was being spread too thin.

She refilled their waters and added another glass for Trevor. With impressive skills from waitressing as a teenager, she collected the glasses within her hands and brought them to the table, handing them out. Taking a seat next to Derek, she slid into the crevice of his shoulder. He slipped his arm around her. Nestled against him gave her the confidence that she could handle what was to come. She had delayed the inevitable enough by changing into something more comfortable and making the kitchen spotless. Getting out of her navy dress made her appearance seem comfortable, but the jeans and sweater brought little comfort to her nerves.

Their conversation fizzled out. Trevor took a swig of his water before he began. "I'm sorry to have to meet with you today, of all days, Jules, but there are some details that are imperative for us to discuss."

"Not a problem. I want to get to the bottom of this as much as you do."

He gave a curt nod and pulled out a leather binder, opening it. He ran a hand through his thick brown hair, reading over the document on top. "In your statement, you said that Ryan Spencer discharged his gun twice. However, upon inspection of the gun, we have proof that it was only fired once. Are you still sticking to your original statement?"

She immediately felt the urge to defend herself. "Yes, I heard two shots."

"We've been over this plenty of times, Trevor. What's going on?" Derek asked, his words crisp. Jules patted his leg with her hand.

Trevor made eye contact with Derek but said nothing. Instead he turned his attention back on her. "Ballistics came back this morning. The bullet from Ryan's gun doesn't match the bullet that killed Scott, but it does match the bullet found in the cement wall."

"What?" She turned to Derek and then back to Trevor, confusion knitting her eyebrows closer. "I don't understand. I stood right there and watched him fire the gun."

Trevor pulled out a legal pad and clicked his pen on, scribbling down on the paper her response. "Did you see the second shot?"

She laid her face into her palms, concentrating on the playback of the shots. In slow motion, she saw Scott push her to the side, the first shot as Ryan stumbled forward, and then falling backwards against her vehicle as she heard the second. Her head snapped up, eyes wide. "I only heard it."

"Did you see anyone in the parking garage besides Ryan Spencer?"

Another quick run of her memories had her pulse pumping faster. "No, I don't think so."

Trevor frowned. Blinked twice and then asked, "Jules, do you own a gun?"

Before she could answer, Derek straightened in his

chair. "That's enough, Trevor," he said. His words crisp. Forewarning.

Trevor didn't stand down from the intense glare he received from across the table. "Derek, you know I have to ask."

"No, you don't."

"If you can't be impartial over this case, I'm going to have to ask you to leave."

"It's my home. I won't be the one leaving."

Jules looked back and forth between the two friends, both on edge. What had Derek so upset? He looked as if he could jump across the table and throttle Trevor. And why would it matter if she owned a gun? Oh.

"Wait." She placed a hand on Derek's chest to keep him back. His heartbeat pounded beneath her fingertips. "Are you asking me if I own a gun because you think I had something to do with Scott's murder?" She couldn't list how many ways that suggestion offended her. At this point, she was ready to release Derek on him.

Trevor broke eye contact before he answered. "I have to ask, Jules. It's my job."

She winced, hurt that he felt like he had to ask. "Well, you can rest easy. I don't own a gun, nor have I ever fired one. I wouldn't even know what to do with one. And no, before you ask, I did not murder Scott or have any part of his death except for the fact he bled out on me as I was trying to save his life!"

She leaned back against her chair, crossing her arms at her mid-section. Sick to her stomach as to where this conversation had headed. Everything in her wanted to go to the bathroom and lose her salad. Instead, she clamped her mouth shut and tried to regulate her breathing.

Trevor's lips parted and closed again. He breathed a defeated breath. "I'm sorry, Jules. I didn't mean to upset you. Let's move on."

"Good idea," Derek barked.

Jules hadn't expected Derek's anger. He usually held a relaxed disposition, but she couldn't help but feel appreciative by the way he strived to protect her, but she didn't want it to ruin their friendship. "It's okay, Trevor." She turned to Derek with a thankful grin, needing to reassure him, even if she needed to convince herself of it as well. "It's fine. We all want to get to the bottom of this and sometimes it takes hard questions to get there." Putting her focus back on Trevor, she asked, "What other questions do you have?"

Trevor waited a few beats before he continued, ignoring the tension between them all. "Let's go back to my earlier question of seeing anyone. Can you remember anything out of the ordinary? Did you notice something or someone when you stepped out of the elevator?"

She bit her lip, her eyes roaming the ceiling as she thought. "All I can remember is that a car drove out when I was working on Scott, but I couldn't get their attention because we were further back."

"Okay, you also mentioned that in your statement." He began writing again. "I'll see if there is any video feed from the parking garage that would give us a license plate number. See if this person saw anything. We have video feed at the elevator, but we can't see anything from the angle where you were standing."

The day just seemed to be going from bad to worse. "So you think some random person walked into the parking garage and shot Scott? Why?" As hard as she tried, she just couldn't wrap her mind around the fact that Ryan Spencer was not to blame for Scott's death.

Derek grasped her hand perched on the table, squeezing gently. Warmth soaked into her cool skin. "Not random, Jules."

Her eyes widened. Her mouth grew dry. She took a sip of her water, the cold liquid slipping down her throat. "So you think someone was after Scott?" Until this moment, she never realized how sheltered her life had been. The evil that was saturating her normal daily routine sucked the air from her lungs.

"I think there is a lot we don't know about Scott," Trevor stated. "You mentioned in your statement that he was on edge that day. It's time to find out why."

Adrenaline spiked through her veins and her pulse thumped in her ears. "Am I in danger? If there really is another person, I didn't see them. But they would have seen me."

Trevor held up his hand, patting the air down. "We don't know anything yet, Jules. Let me do some digging on Scott and see if I can get some information from the bystander that drove past you. Give me a couple days, and I'll have more pieces to this puzzle."

Jules stood in the living room as Derek let Trevor out, cold seeping into her bones. Dread engulfed her with what this new turn in the case would mean.

§ § § § §

"WHAT DO YOU MEAN THERE MIGHT BE A WITNESS?" Vince Deluca paced his high rise apartment, bourbon on the rocks in hand, wishing he could reach through the phone and strangle his cousin. He wondered why he hadn't heard from Frank the last couple days. Now it made sense. He should have known Frank would mess up the simple task he'd been given.

"I know you told me to take care of Scott Henson quick and easy, but I couldn't pass up the opportunity. The guy was already held at gunpoint, so I made a swift decision. It was perfect."

Vince grunted. "If by perfect, you mean stupid, then yes." He swirled his drink, the ice clanking against the sides. He finished it off and walked over to his liquor cabinet, pouring another glass. "This had better not come back to me, Frank."

"It won't. I'm taking care of her."

"Are you sure she even saw you?"

"Does it matter?"

Vince grinned. Frank might be more brute than brains, but at least he wasn't squeamish when it came to eliminations. You never, ever leave a trail or a witness. "How are you fixing this?" Frank paused. He rolled his eyes. This should be good.

"Well, I got into her house, took out her fire alarm batteries and then set her house on fire. I tried to make it look like an accident. She's dating a cop. I have to be careful."

Vince took a deep breath through gritted teeth. He never handled things himself, kept his hands clean, but there were times he regretted that strict rule. His next rule should be not to hire incompetent enforcers, even if they were family.

"So how did your brilliant plan turn out?"

"She escaped."

His glass flew across the room, nailing the wall. Glass shattered, spilling onto his marble floor. "Frank, so help me! Finish this!"

"I will. I will. I've got a new plan."

"You better. Don't call me again until it's done." He hung up, not waiting for a pathetic answer. He turned off the lights and headed to bed, leaving the mess for the maid in the morning.

CHAPTER FIFTEEN

JULES TIPTOED DOWN THE HALLWAY AND INTO THE KITCHEN, TRY-
ing not to wake up Lucy. The only noise breaking up
the silence was the ticking of the wall clock. She had been
awake for the last hour tossing and turning in bed and finally
decided to do something besides stare at the walls and let her
mind run laps. Like drink a hot cup of coffee. She put a new
filter in and filled it with coffee grounds. After pouring in the
water, she pushed the start button, already anticipating the
glorious aroma.

A big yawn escaped. She reached her hands up in the air,
giving her body a good stretch. She just wanted to sleep, especially with her big day of returning to work. But she couldn't
calm her mind and the worry that tangled her thoughts.
Someone else had been in that parking garage with them.
Someone had seen her, but after hours of retracing her steps
and trying to visualize what happened, she just couldn't remember seeing anyone.

She could tell Derek was worried, but he didn't say anything. He just continued to reassure her that even though
Trevor lacked tact while questioning, he was an excellent
detective. If he could have anyone on the force working this
case, it would be Trevor.

As the coffee finished brewing, she pulled out a mug from
the cabinet. Maybe she was on edge because she wasn't in

her own house. She was thankful to Lucy for letting her stay here, but it didn't feel like home yet. It was hard to be totally comfortable when she still felt like a guest.

After pouring her coffee, she padded into the living room and took a seat in the corner chair. She clicked on the lamp and grabbed her Bible she had placed on the floor last night. If she couldn't turn her mind off, then she needed to turn her thoughts to God.

Halfway through reading a chapter in Proverbs, a vehicle pulled into the driveway and turned off. She checked the time. 5:35. Who would be here this early in the morning? Panic spread as she looked around the room for something to use as a weapon. She spotted nothing but a picture frame or lamp that was heavy enough to do any damage. Setting her Bible back on the floor, she stood up and crept up to the front window, peeking out slowly behind the curtain.

Her muscles relaxed when she spotted Lucy walking up the sidewalk. She returned to the chair just as Lucy made her way into the house. "Hey, Luce."

Lucy stopped short and gasped, putting her hand over her heart. "Jules, you scared me. What are you doing up so early?"

"Couldn't sleep. Are you just getting home?" When she had returned from Derek's yesterday, Lucy wasn't home. Nor had she returned by the time she went to bed.

Lucy dropped her purse and bag at the door. "Oh, um, yeah. After working at the restaurant I headed over to the art studio to work on a project. Time just got away from me."

Not only was Lucy a chef at the restaurant Riverside, but she had been pursuing her art career on the side as well by working a second job at the local art studio. Jules didn't know where she found the time to do both and still function. Lucy had always struggled with finding her way, always jumping from different careers and jobs, searching for her place in life. She understood that. Probably more than anyone in Lucy's family could.

"What project are you working on?"

Lucy slipped off her coat and put it in the closet. "My boss at the art studio, Dillon, is giving me my first showing in a couple months. I'm working on building my collection."

Jules noticed how much more this Dillon guy had come up in conversations lately. Against her nosy desire, she decided to let her curiosity pass for now. "That's great! I can't wait to see it."

Lucy stepped into the room and found a seat on the couch across from her. Jules wasn't sure if it was the lack of sleep or the shadows cast across her face, but Lucy looked different. Sad even. "Thanks. I appreciate it." Leaning her head back against the headrest, she asked, "So how was Scott's memorial service?"

The service hadn't even been twenty-four hours ago, but it felt like days. "It went well. Despite the sadness, the pastor presented a beautiful service. Derek took the day off to attend with me, and then I spent the rest of the day at his house. It helped having him with me."

"I heard the two of you are together now."

Jules couldn't read Lucy's reaction. She didn't seem upset but also not happy. It was too early in the morning to decipher people's thoughts. "We are. I feel badly starting a relationship with him during the turmoil of Scott's case, but I can't imagine going through this without him, especially yesterday afternoon."

"What happened yesterday?" Lucy asked, leaning forward with her arms resting on her knees.

"Ballistics came back. Ryan Spencer didn't kill Scott. They are going with the lead that someone else was in the parking garage and killed him."

Lucy's eyes widened. "What? That is crazy ... and scary."

"Tell me about it. And to top it all off, Trevor Hudson had

to re-question me. Let's just say it got a little intense."

Lucy's face scrunched up in disgust. "That's the detective that helped find Ava when she was kidnapped, right?"

"Yep."

"I know Matt really respects the guy, but he just rubs me wrong. When we first met that day as we started the search for Ava, remember I tried to give my opinion and he shot it down without any consideration. He seems a little full of himself, arrogant even."

"Tell me how you really feel."

Lucy smirked. "Sorry, I'm too tired to control my tongue."

"Derek thinks pretty highly of him, even if he disagrees with his approach at times. He explained it to me by pointing out that Trevor likes to follow things by the book, and sometimes that just comes across as insensitive. I know your first impression of him wasn't ideal, but I think you should give him another shot."

She snorted. "Well, I don't plan on ever being around him again, but if I do, I'll keep that in mind. So what is happening now on the case?"

"I'm not sure. Trevor said he's going to do some digging into Scott's past. For now, it's just a waiting game." She wished her heart felt as confident as her words sounded. Wrapping her hands around her mug, she asked, "Want some coffee? I made a full pot."

"No, thanks. I'm going to try and get a little sleep before I have to get back to the restaurant." She stood, rubbing her red lined eyes. Her body betrayed the weight of the world that looked to be resting on her shoulders.

"Hey, Luce. I'm praying for you." She wasn't sure what made her say it. Maybe the Holy Spirit nudging her to give her friend the encouragement she needed to hear.

Lucy paused, forming a smile that looked strained. With a hand running through her dark pixie cut hair, she said,

"Thanks."

After she left the room, Jules did just what she said, she prayed for Lucy. There was something going on with Lucy, but she couldn't put her finger on it. Maybe she understood living a life with a secret all too well, because she had a strong suspicion that Lucy was hiding something.

CHAPTER SIXTEEN

"OVER HERE, JAKE!" DEREK WAVED HIS HAND TO GET JAKE'S attention.

Jake nodded and made his trek to the back of the breakfast diner, smiling and saying hello to a few people he knew along the way. He took a seat opposite Derek, setting his briefcase on the floor. "How did you know I love this place?"

Derek set down his menu, "I didn't. It's purely selfish intentions. I'm a sucker for their biscuits and gravy."

"Have you tried their French Toast? Trust me, you'll never turn back to your old ways again. Is Matt coming?"

"No, he picked up an earlier shift today. I guess he's surprising Ava with concert tickets tonight and needed more leeway." He reached across the table to shake hands with him. "Thanks for meeting with me."

Knowing there was a chance the person who shot Scott could still be walking around looking for Jules didn't sit well with him at all. Derek had total confidence that Trevor would handle the case. Together they decided since Trevor already had a full plate with another case, it might be good to have an extra person digging up Scott's past. After he took Jules home yesterday, he made the call immediately.

Enter in the hound dog of investigating, Jake Williams.

"Glad to help. Jules is like a sister to me. I'm happy she took me up on my offer to look into Scott."

Guilt crept up Derek's neck and squeezed him tight. "Well, she doesn't know yet that you're helping. I wanted to get an idea of what we are up against before I bring her into it." He wasn't trying to hide it from her per se. He just didn't want to worry her unless it was necessary.

The waitress reached their table and took their orders. They handed back their unneeded menus, and she promised to be back shortly with their drinks. Jake unzipped his briefcase and pulled out a folder. Pushing his utensils aside, he laid it on the table. "From what I understand, she's already involved, Derek. Hiding things from her might save you worry, but it won't gain her trust."

Derek chewed on that truth for a moment. "You're right. Once we have new information, I'll tell her."

They had lost precious time in the investigation with their assumption that this was an open and shut case with Ryan Spencer. The new information revealed caught them extremely unprepared and pushed them back to square one, while their assailant could already be many steps ahead of them. He didn't like to lose. He couldn't this time – not with Jules' life as the cost.

"That might be sooner than you think." Jake opened his folder. "I haven't had a lot of time to dig too deep, but I've uncovered a few things you might find interesting. I already called Trevor this morning, and he is working off these leads."

Derek leaned forward. "I'm listening."

"Scott Henson has been very busy over the last year. It looks like he has been taking short trips a couple times a month."

"Do you know where he was going?"

"Not exactly, but we have a close proximity of the destinations and what airlines he used. That is what Trevor is looking into."

Jake passed over sheets of paper stapled together. Derek

took it from his hand, reading the top. Scott's bank statements from the last eight months. "How did you get these?"

"You don't want to know."

Derek laughed. He probably didn't.

Jake leaned forward, passing over another stack of papers that held Scott's credit card statements. Using his pen, Jake pointed out certain dates. "Look at how his bank records fluctuate with the times he travels."

Scanning the records back and forth, he could see what Jake was talking about. Back in April, Scott began his multiple trips. On June 17th his credit card statement showed his flight, and then on his bank statement a few days later, he deposited fifty thousand dollars. Derek continued matching up the dates. Most of the time his bank statements showed a hefty deposit, with only a few that had withdrawals instead. However, starting in September, that began to change and the scale began to tip into the negative direction.

"Look at this." Derek turned the sheet around, pointing. "On September 25th, he withdrew until all his accounts were empty. Then without the flights, he began depositing money into his account, but then the next day withdrawing that same amount."

Jake nodded. "I saw that. Look at October 8th."

Derek flipped the sheet over to bring up October. He scanned down until he found the date. "Whoa. He deposited a hundred and ten thousand dollars." Running a hand down his face, he sighed. "What was this guy up to?"

Jake leaned back against his seat. "I have a few ideas."

Lifting his coffee to his mouth, he said, "Enlighten me," and then swallowed. The liquid burned his tongue.

"With that kind of cash, I'm guessing something illegal was going on. My first assumption, since he was a doctor that could have had connections all over the world, is something along the lines of selling drugs or working with the black market. Maybe with organs or getting medicine that isn't approved yet by the FDA into the hands of people that are desperate."

Derek's heart dropped. This would devastate Jules. Jake's speculations made sense, except for … "What I don't understand is the drop in his account. Why would he be losing money?"

"Maybe he was stashing the money in an off-shore account so it didn't come back on him. Do you know if he had been making any big purchases?" Jake asked. "That could explain where the money went."

"No, but that would be a good question for Jules. I'll stop by Lucy's place and see if she has any answers for us."

Anything to do with that large amount of money couldn't be good. Whether Jake had the right idea or not, Derek was certain the answers they sought wouldn't be any better, especially if the person who'd killed Scott had also seen Jules which at this point, he was a hundred percent sure he had.

While passing back the papers, the waitress arrived with their food. Derek appreciated it when Jake changed the subject to the NFL football play-off games that weekend. He didn't want to waste his food on an upset stomach.

Chapter Seventeen

THE DOORBELL RANG. ITS SHRILLNESS SMOTHERED THE SILENCE. Jules rushed from her room to answer the door, hoping it didn't wake up Lucy. She opened the door to find Derek standing on the front porch.

"Derek." It took a second for her to find more words. He looked amazingly good in his dark uniform that accentuated his strong and tall physique. He had been trying out a new hair cut with it longer on top. She wanted to reach out and run her fingers through it. Instead, she refrained and with a simple smile. "Come in."

She opened the door further to give him more room to walk through and closed it behind him. She rubbed her arms to generate heat from the cool air that slipped in with him. Winter had reared its ugly head, and the temperatures had dropped drastically in the last few days.

He tugged on her jungle animal scrubs. "Are you working today?"

"I am. When I got back yesterday, a co-worker called and asked if I could cover for her a few hours this afternoon. I thought that would be a good adjustment back to work. I'm not sure if I'm ready for a full shift."

She stepped into him, tracing her fingers along his buttons. She couldn't help herself. The surprise of seeing him made her realize how much she enjoyed his company, his closeness.

He seemed to sense that by lifting her chin up and bringing his lips to meet hers. Pressing his forehead against hers, he sighed. "As much as I'd like to spend the rest of the day doing this, I'm here for other reasons."

She could tell by his strained features that he had come here for other reasons. She put her bet on the case, but that was the last thing she wanted to discuss right now. For just a moment, she didn't want it running through her mind, controlling her every thought.

"Are you sure I can't change your mind?" she asked, looking up at him through her lashes. Heat flushed her cheeks from her flirtatious question.

Embarrassed, she stepped away, but he didn't let her go far. He grabbed hold of her hand and drew her back into his chest. His blue eyes turned to laser, slicing right into her thoughts. "Julia," he whispered against her lips. She loved when he spoke her name – the sweetness and desire twisting within his deep voice. His lips settled on hers. He held back, keeping a tight rein on his self-control, honoring her with respect. With a reluctant groan, he ended the kiss.

Sliding her hands up his arms and resting on his shoulders, she noticed the tightness in his neck muscles. She took her right thumb and began rubbing it in small circles. Eyes closed, he smiled. "Keep that up, and I will forget why I came here."

She couldn't push off the reason he'd come by kissing him all day. Although, that idea did sound more appealing. "Liar. So tell me what's causing these tense muscles."

He frowned, opening his eyes. "I asked Jake to do a little digging into Scott's past."

"Okay. He had mentioned earlier about wanting to help," she pointed out. "I take it by the look on your face, he found something?"

Derek took a strand of her hair, twisting it around his finger. "Jake was able to get his bank and credit card records.

112

Over the last year Scott has been taking a lot of trips out of state and making large amounts of deposits and withdrawals that fluctuated in his accounts. Do you know anything about that?"

She threaded their fingers together and led him into the living room, taking a seat on the couch. "I knew he was traveling, but I'm not sure how much help I can be. We broke up in the summer and I really didn't have much contact with him after that unless we were at work —" she paused. Why hadn't she thought of this sooner? "Wait here."

Jumping off the couch, she made her way into her room. Against the wall sat the boxes she had packed from her house. She slid the top two down onto the floor and began rifling through the third one until she came across the blue leather book. Walking back into the living room, she held it up. "My journal, I can't believe I forgot about this."

His eyebrows arched. "I really don't think I want to read all about your romance with Scott."

She lightly punched his shoulder as she took a seat next to him. "It's not that type of journal." Opening the book, she flipped through the pages, scanning the dates. "I mostly write in here about prayer requests, blessings, and the things I did that day. I'm sure I wrote in here when Scott traveled. Or maybe I will re-read something that will trigger a memory."

Together they speed-read through the journal, keeping an eye out for the times she mentioned Scott. Derek traced his finger along the page and said, "Look here. April 5th, you wrote, '*Today Scott left on a weekend trip with some friends to Las Vegas. Praying he has a safe flight and good time. I miss him so much already.*'" He made a gagging noise from her last sentence.

Her laughter evaporated. Why didn't she realize earlier the trap she had just set up for herself? Sure, she had written about Scott, but she had also written about Derek. In fact, a lot about Derek. In heartfelt details and prayer requests. Details that made her want to go out to the backyard, dig a hole and bury herself in it. Heat soaked her cheeks and worked its way down to her toes.

He turned a few more pages. "Here's another. May 23rd, you wrote, '*This weekend we were going to celebrate our six-month anniversary, but Scott had an unexpected business trip come up. Instead, I spent the weekend at Ava's. She is starting to date again. I'm so proud of her. Praying that God continues to heal her heart and show her what a great catch she is*'." Derek smiled. "You're a good friend."

She shrugged. "Thanks." She tapped the book, "I do remember that trip, though. He never did business trips, and then all of a sudden, he started having them frequently, and at the last minute, too."

"Did he ever talk about them? Say what they were about?" Derek asked.

"No. I asked once, and it seemed to upset him. I didn't ask again."

"What about big purchases? Did he mention anything about investing or his increasing bank account?"

She shook her head. "No. He was a very private person." Their parking garage discussion came to mind. "One thing I thought was weird. He sold his treasured BMW car and bought some old rust bucket."

Derek rubbed his hand over his chin, looking as perplexed as she. "Did he say why?"

"Just that he didn't want the payment anymore. Like he couldn't afford it? He was the head of pediatrics."

Derek looked off in the distance, his mind at work. "Okay. Let's get back to his traveling. How did he seem when he returned from these trips?"

"Hmm ... usually good. Upbeat. Overly happy for his calm demeanor. Although there was one time I remember he came home very upset." She took the journal from him and scanned the dates, trying to jog her memory. "Here. July 22nd. I remember after that trip, things seemed different between us. More tense. Then after his next trip, I found out about him cheating on me, and we broke up."

"Do you think those trips had something to do with this other woman?"

Once she'd found out, she often wondered that very thing. She had never asked him, and deep down she didn't want to know. It hurt enough that she wasn't enough for him, but to add months of deception and lies seemed too much to handle at the time. Now she wished she had. The unanswered questions were driving her crazy. "I don't know. Maybe? You'd have to ask her."

"I'm sorry, I didn't mean to –"

Jules placed her hand on his forearm. "It's fine. Really. She might have some answers we are looking for." She bent down and tore out a piece of paper from Lucy's sketchbook. With pen in hand, she began writing. "Her name is Emma Zentz. She works in ICU." Finished, she handed Derek the paper.

"Thanks. I'll get this to Trevor and let him contact her."

Thankful that Derek wouldn't be meeting with this woman that had helped cause such horrible heartbreak, her muscles relaxed until Derek began flipping pages again. Her throat began to tighten, straining her breaths. He was getting too close to the entries written when they had met. He would begin seeing his name soon. She placed a hand on his, causing him to stop. "Wait." She took a deep breath. "There … there is going to be –"

"I promise I won't read any pages that have my name on it." He leaned into her, bumping their shoulders together. "Although, my imagination can be very descriptive."

"Why does that not surprise me?" she said dryly, biting the

inside of her cheek to keep from smiling. "Go ahead and read about the night we met at the campfire. I'm sure you'll find a few things there that are very descriptive."

He chuckled, soothing her anxiousness. "I can only imagine. However, I'm more interested in the thoughts over the last month." He caught her glare. He slipped his arm around her lower back, dipping his mouth down to her ear. "Don't worry, I'll just wait. I'd rather hear you share your feelings than read them."

Share her feelings with him. Why did that excite her and yet scare her to her core? Her feelings ran so much deeper than finding him attractive and enjoying his company. She was falling in love with Derek Brown and had been for awhile. Even though she had pushed him away, he continually worked himself into her heart – as her prayer journal would announce to him very quickly. In fact, if she was truly honest with herself, she was no longer falling.

He went out of his way to protect her. He gave when she had nothing to give in return. When she went through her mental check-list of what she wanted in a man, Derek surpassed them all. For the first time ever with a guy, she could completely be herself. She loved him.

What scared her most wasn't the realization of her feelings, but how he felt about her. She saw it in his eyes. When he smiled. By the way he took care of her. Through his kisses. She had always struggled with being loved, allowing those around her to love her. She didn't understand it. Especially God. How could He love her after she failed Him over and over again?

No. She couldn't – wouldn't – share her feelings with Derek. Not yet, at least. Slipping from his embrace, she turned back to her journal. She couldn't bear to look at him, see the disappointment that marred his gorgeous features. "I think the only other time I wrote about Scott would have been back in

December after we talked and repaired our friendship."

She turned the pages, her nerves like hot wires, wondering what she had written about Scott – and Derek. "Here, on December 14th." She picked the book up, turning so he couldn't read along with her. "'*Scott and I went out tonight. He apologized for what happened between us. I'm worried about him. He admitted that he had been going through some really hard stuff and getting mixed up in bad decisions. He mentioned that it seemed easier to keep his darkness hidden than to share. If only he knew how much I understood that. Praying that God takes hold of his heart and helps Scott break free from whatever is keeping him in bondage.*'" Her vision became cloudy from the tears that pooled in her eyes. She had to stop reading anyway, the next paragraph she wrote about Derek.

"Oh Jules, come here." Derek wrapped his arms around her and pulled her into his chest. He stroked her hair while she cried. The grief rolled back like a wave with vengeance. He didn't try to talk and comfort her with words, relying instead on his quiet strength that wrapped her up in a cocoon. She stayed in his arms until she breathed normally again. Pulling back, she swiped her hands over her face, pushing the moisture off her cheeks. Derek used his thumb to wipe away a lone tear in the corner of her eye. "From the things Scott said to me in the parking garage, I don't think he ever broke free."

Sadness gripped her heart for him and the freedom he never had. The fear in his eyes that told her he was in trouble. Scott had wanted her help, and now it was too late. "We have to find out what happened, Derek. For Scott, we need to find his killer."

"And for you." He rubbed a hand down his face. "I should get this journal to Trevor. Let him take a look at it, see if there is anything he can use."

Jules stilled. Seriously? Why had she even brought the

stupid thing out? Trevor might as well take copies of it and hang them up all over the station. A sigh leaked out. "Sure, why not."

"He'll be discreet. I promise." He stood up and straightened out his uniform with a quick brush of his hands. "Why don't I swing by later and give you a ride to work? When your shift is over I can pick you up, take you to dinner?" He wiggled his eyebrows, enticing her.

She smiled while rising. "You have sacrificed enough for me this week." She caught him in a hug. "And as much as I would enjoy spending the evening with you, I'm going to pass. I think I'm just going to come back, put on pajamas, and finally take some time to unpack."

He started toward the door with her on his heels, answering over his shoulder, "Alright, but if you change your mind, I'm just a call away." With one hand on the door handle, he used his free hand to pull her into him, leaving with a kiss that already had her changing her mind.

CHAPTER EIGHTEEN

THURSDAY LATE AFTERNOON, JULES SLIPPED INTO THE EMPTY patient room to catch the last of the day and a moment to herself. The sun began its descent, causing the shadows to shift inside the sterile room. Facing the west windows, she watched the heavy snow clouds move in. By the time her shift ended, it would be dark and snowing, the two things she despised while driving. If the local meteorologist was correct, the city of Rockford would be under a thick blanket of white by morning.

She should have agreed to Derek's suggestion of picking her up. At times she felt the need to pinch herself that they were really together as a couple. Checking the clock on the wall, she debated calling him. She could always unpack tomorrow. Weighing her options, she decided against it. She didn't want to be the needy girlfriend that selfishly consumed all his time. He deserved a night off from the drama. Plus, it wouldn't hurt to have him miss her a little. After this morning, she could only imagine the kiss he would give her after not seeing her for a couple days. Her fingers lightly traced her lips as she smiled.

"There you are."

Jules dropped her hand to her side and turned to find Becky standing in the doorway. She couldn't hide forever. With a final glace outside, the last of light falling behind the tall buildings, she admitted, "Sorry, just needed a breather."

Becky kept her stance at the doorway, blocking her exit. Concern gathered her eyebrows together. "You doing okay?"

"I am." She meant the words. She was doing okay. It helped that today had been a slow day. Only two patients on the floor. The shift hadn't been as emotional as she thought it would be. But after sitting at the nurses' station for the last hour next to the empty chair Scott used to claim, she began replaying her last moments working alongside Scott. She just needed a couple solitary moments to let the sorrow pass.

Becky nodded. "Is it true?" she asked.

"Is what true?" Did she not believe her answer?

"That they don't know who killed Scott?"

Leave it to the news and word of mouth to so quickly expose and make public a very sensitive case. "As of now … no."

"You were there. Did you see someone?" Jules appreciated Becky's concern and friendship in wanting to check on her, but she didn't want to talk about it or be a source of new information on the grapevine. Rumors spread like wildfire among the staff. She learned early on it was best to give as little details as possible.

She shook her head while working her way around Becky into the deserted hallway. "I'm sure they will find a suspect soon." She gave the best smile she could muster up. "I'm going to go check in on Room 310 before I leave for the day," she added before Becky could ask another question.

§ § § § §

DEREK WORKED HIS WAY THROUGH THE PRECINCT, FUMBLING through his bag for his keys. A low whistle brought his head up. He scanned the room and found Trevor with his phone up to his ear, waving a hand at him to come over. He diverted his original path and zig-zagged through a cluster of officers to arrive at Trevor's desk as he finished up the call.

"What was the pick-up date?" he asked, scribbling down January 7th on a pad of paper. "And the return date?" Trevor's eyes widened slightly before they narrowed. "Okay, thank you. I'll be in touch." He slid the receiver into the cradle and then finished up his notes.

"Long day?" Derek asked when he laid his pen down.

"Long week." Trevor's eyes met his and he saw trouble brewing.

"Hate to break it to you, but it's only Thursday."

"Thanks for being the bearer of bad news." He sat down on his chair and leaned back with his arms crossed over his chest. "Now it's my turn."

Derek's legs went numb. He perched his hip on Trevor's desk. "What is it? Please tell me you have some good news to go with it."

"It goes hand in hand." He bent over his desk, sifting through papers. Within the pile, he pulled out a picture and laid it out for him to see. "We found the car Jules mentioned seeing. The time stamp on the video feed matches up to the time Scott was shot. We can't make out a face, but it looks to be a guy."

"That's good, right? Have you been able to question the driver?"

"No." He pulled out another picture of the license plate up close. It was grainy from zooming in so close, but the letters and numbers were still visible. "We ran the plate. It's a fake."

Derek's throat closed. Had they just stumbled across the shooter? His gut told him, yes. Why would someone have a fake plate unless they were trying to hide something? The idea mixed a sense of fear and drive into him. He looked over the picture again. "It's a Nevada state plate. Why would someone get a fake plate from another state? It would stand out more here," he pointed out.

"That's what I thought which made me think he isn't from here."

"Have you tried the airlines? Car rental companies?"

"One step ahead of you, my friend." He picked up the first picture and turned it to him. "In the passenger side seat, the guy had his receipt from the Enterprise Company on top. That was the phone conversation I just had."

Derek braced himself for the bad news. "Did you get a name?"

Trevor read off his paper, "Nick Ortega."

"That's a start. Did you get a driver's license picture?"

He nodded. "They are faxing it over." He paused. "The thing is, Derek, if the plate is a fake, why wouldn't the license be fake, too? I don't want to waste my resources and energy chasing after a ghost."

He didn't wish for Trevor's job. "So what is your plan?" He had one. The sheer determination laced his tired eyes.

"Everything about this guy is fake. I need to find the man that boarded the plane, not the man who landed. I'll see if a Nick Ortega has flown into Rockford, but I think we are going to come up empty. I don't even know if this is our guy. I'm going purely with my gut on this."

Derek didn't take his words lightly. Trevor followed the rules without abandonment. Hearing he followed these leads without much evidence made him realize the step he was taking for their friendship. "Please tell me that is the bad news."

"I wish I could." He ran a hand down his face. "The rental has not been returned."

The implications of that sentence made Derek's heart drop to his knees. "Maybe the guy ditched the car and already left town?" Derek hoped with everything in him, for Jules' safety, that was the case.

"The worker at the car company said they got a call a few

days ago, and the rental was extended a few more days. He's still in Rockford. I'll get an APB out for the car and both license plates. Until the dust settles and we find this guy, I think –"

"Jules will need eyes on her at all times," he finished Trevor's thought for him.

Trevor nodded his agreement. "There is a reason this guy has extended his stay in our city. And I think it has everything to do with Jules."

§ § § § §

JULES PULLED HER GLOVES ON AND BUTTONED HER COAT ALL THE way to the top. The gust of cold air lifted the back of her coat and sent shivers up her spine. She shuffled her feet along the sidewalk, taking each step with ease. A thin layer of ice had been covered up with snow, making her trek to the car quite the balancing act. Once again she couldn't bring herself to park in the parking garage. After today, that might need to change. Her CR-V sat parked in the same spot a few blocks down from the hospital, but now it was covered in ice and snow. Starting up her car, she placed her purse on the passenger seat and pulled the scraper out from under the seat. She started with the windshield and worked her way around the vehicle. By the time she was done, sweat had pooled between her shoulder blades and began its trail down her back.

Lights on, she merged into the slow moving traffic. The windshield wipers grated across the glass. They needed replacing. She adjusted her rear view mirror to block out the lights from the cars behind her.

Keeping her speed under thirty miles per hour, she stayed with a group of vehicles. At the next road she turned right. Her back tires fish-tailed until she worked the brakes to get control. Her hands tightened around the steering wheel, knuckles white. She hated driving in this weather. She needed to run by the market and grab a few groceries but instead made the decision to just go home and get off of the roads. Another fifteen minutes and she'd be at Lucy's place with hot tea, snuggled under a blanket, and watching her favorite television show which sounded better by the second.

The next turn put her on the road that led her away from the city and into the country. She had always been surprised that Lucy had picked a place away from the city life. When she thought of Lucy, she pictured her in an apartment overlooking downtown, not along a deserted road, out in no man's land.

Her phone began to ring. She looked down to see it was Derek. As much as she wanted to talk to him, there was no way she would remove her hands from the steering wheel. In fact, she gripped tighter as the open field pushed snow drifts along the road. Behind her, vehicle lights grew brighter, closer. She pumped her breaks. Winter drivers irritated her. They were always in a hurry despite the bad conditions. "Slow down, speedy, this is as fast as I'm going," she said out loud, as if the driver could hear her warning.

Ahead, the road veered around a wooded area. She never liked this road because of its deep ditches on both sides that made the road almost feel like a bridge. The car behind her grew even closer. With the turn approaching, she tapped on her brakes again. The driver didn't slow.

A few seconds later she felt the slam. That's all it took for her vehicle to catch on the ice, turning out of control. She spun once, then again. She took her foot off the brake, pulling the steering wheel to the left. It didn't work. She pumped her brakes again, getting dizzy from the turns. She couldn't see where she was headed next, until the ditch came upon her. Her scream filled the air as she slipped over the side of the road, tumbling straight for a tree.

§ § § § §

"**S**HE'S NOT PICKING UP," DEREK GROWLED. HE SHOULD HAVE tried harder to convince her to let him drive her to and from work. He probably shouldn't have let her out of his sight from the moment they knew the shooter was still on the loose.

"Try the hospital. Maybe she stayed later?" Trevor suggested.

"Good idea." He punched in the number and asked for the pediatrics floor.

"Pediatrics. This is Becky."

"Hi, Becky." The name sounded familiar. Jules had talked about her before. "This is Sergeant Brown with the Rockford Police. I'm looking for Julia Anderson." Sometimes it was easier to get what he wanted quicker by throwing his profession in the mix. He wasn't proud of it at times, but at this moment, fully necessary.

"I'm sorry, Sergeant, but she already left for the day."

He squeezed his eyes shut. "Can you tell me when she left?"

"Let's see." She paused. "Her shift ended at five o'clock. She left shortly after that."

He checked his watch. It was a quarter to six. "Okay. Thank you. If you happen to hear from her, please have her call me. She has my number."

"Sure will."

Derek ended the call even more frustrated. He looked up at Trevor. "She already left for the day." He called her number and got voicemail again. Her sweet voice played a chord of fear that drizzled worry throughout his body. Where was she? He called Lucy and Ava. Neither had heard from her.

"I'm sure the roads are getting bad with the storm. Maybe she is driving and can't answer. Let's give it a few minutes before you send out the dogs."

Derek laughed at Trevor's accurate assessment. The concern wouldn't have been so fierce if he hadn't just heard that the shooter could still be in town. He needed to know she was okay and then keep it that way.

Twenty minutes later and still no contact, he decided it was time for action. "I'm going to head to the hospital and retrace the roads she would have taken home." He'd rather be on the move than sitting around waiting. He was tired of feeling two steps behind.

"Sounds good." Trevor swiveled in his chair and brought his leg to rest up on his opposite knee. "I'm going to keep working on these leads. I'd like to know how Scott Henson and our mystery man know each other. Once you find Jules, keep her with you until we come up with a plan. I know I don't have to tell you this – but she is probably in danger. We all know she didn't see this guy, but as far as he's concerned, she's a witness."

While driving, Trevor's words throbbed through his head with each heartbeat. She's in trouble. She's a witness. She's in danger. He called her phone again. When it flipped over to voicemail, he threw his phone down onto the passenger seat with a frustrated grunt. "Julia, where are you?" His plea filled his squad car.

Up ahead, flashing lights caught his attention. He pulled up behind the ambulance, fire truck, two squad cars and a couple bystanders trying to get in on the action. The cold air burned his lungs as he jogged up to the site. He took off in a sprint when he found a black CR-V on its side up against a tree.

CHAPTER NINETEEN

D EREK PACED THE SMALL ER EXAMINING ROOM, UNABLE TO burn off any steam in only four short strides. He sucked in a deep breath. The disinfectant tingled in his nose. Mid-turn, he stopped as Ava and Matt rushed into the room.

"Is she okay?" Ava asked with wet eyes.

Standing in front of her, Derek placed his hands on her shoulders. "Jules is fine." Alive. *Thank you, God, she is alive.* "She's having tests done now. X-rays and a CT scan. She was awake and her ornery self when they wheeled her away."

When he had arrived on the scene, they already had her loaded up into the ambulance. The EMTs didn't let him see her, not wanting to waste any time since they weren't sure the extent of her injuries. He followed behind the ambulance to the hospital. The longest ten minutes of his life. Once she was settled in the room, they allowed him back to be at her side. Red hair against her ghostly pale skin, bruising along her arms and a gash above her left eyebrow about did him in. He had leaned down, letting his lips settle on her forehead.

"That doesn't surprise me. She is an excellent nurse, but a horrible patient," Ava disclosed, having the most history with her between the three of them.

"How did you guys get back here?" he asked. "I was told they only allow one person at a time in the room."

Ava crossed her arms. "I *informed* the front desk receptionist that we were coming back no matter what."

Matt smirked. "And after that didn't work, I asked her nicely."

Lifting her chin, Ava tilted her face to him, "You mean, flirted."

Matt shrugged his shoulders. "Hey, we're in here, aren't we?" He leaned down and kissed her scrunched up nose. They shared a smile that Derek envied. Derek wanted to be married. He wanted a wife, the intimacy, nights where he didn't have to leave her side, a partner in life, a helpmate. He desired someone to grow old with, raise children alongside, and give his heart completely to without reservation. He wanted to share *that* smile with someone. And he wanted it with Jules.

Derek covered his grin with his hand and cleared his throat. "All right, break it up."

Matt cradled Ava from behind, placing his chin on the top of her head. "Was Jules able to tell you what happened?"

"Not yet. I only had a few minutes with her before they took her for tests, but we need to find out soon." The time had come to share the new developments on the case with them. "I called Trevor. He's on his way here. The case has taken a turn, and we think it's for the worse." Within a few minutes he had Matt and Ava caught up on what he knew. "Jules doesn't know any of this, so let's wait for Trevor."

"Why are you waiting for me?" Trevor asked as he stepped into the room.

"To pay for dinner later, we're all starved." Matt teased.

"Not a problem. McDonalds is on me," he retorted.

"Trevor, you look exhausted. Have you been sleeping?" Ava asked.

"Of course."

"More than four hours a night?"

He smirked. "I plead the fifth."

Derek could see a reprimand forming on her lips, but she

deterred her focus when the glass door slid open. The nurse and orderly rolled Jules back to her spot and re-hung her IV. "Once the radiologist gets the results to the doctor, he'll be in to see you." The nurse lightly squeezed Jules' knee. "Let me know if you need anything. However," she looked around the room, "I think you will be taken care of just fine."

"Thanks, Connie," her weak voice answered as Connie excused herself. Jules then turned to the group. "Had I known you were throwing a party, I would have dressed for the occasion. Hospital gowns are totally last season."

Ava giggled, making her way to the side of the bed. She pulled a chair over and took a seat. The two friends slipped into their normal rhythm. "How are you feeling?"

"My lower back and neck are sore." She touched her gash, now covered with bandages, and cringed. "My head hurts." She caught everyone's eyes on her. "But by the looks on your grim faces, I should be close to death."

Ava handed over a cup of ice chips the nurse had left. "We're just concerned, Jules."

Jules shoved a few into her mouth. "I'm fine. My vehicle on the other hand, is not. I'm sure it's totaled. But really, who needs a car or a house? Obviously, not me."

Derek caught her strain to smile and saw the hurt in her eyes. And unfortunately, it was about to get worse for her. He wanted to be next to her, holding her hand, reassuring her, but he had to think in cop mode. His feelings couldn't shape his reactions.

Trevor stepped forward. "Can you tell me about your accident?"

"I was heading to Lucy's house after my shift. The roads were slick so I kept a slow speed. A car came up behind too fast and bumped me, sending my vehicle out of control. The next thing I knew, my vehicle was on its side up against a tree."

"Did you call 911, or did the driver?"

She pursed her lips. "The driver never stopped. I couldn't find my phone, so I had to wait until someone drove by to help me."

Derek tensed and shot a quick look at Trevor, meeting his eyes. "Jules, do you know what the car looked like that hit you?" he asked.

She shook her head. "No. It was too dark and it all happened so fast." She turned to Ava. "I mean, who does that? It was freezing outside. What if I had had a child with me?"

"I know, I know." She patted her arm. "But you're safe now."

And Derek would make sure she stayed that way.

Trevor pulled a chair up to the foot of the bed and took a seat. Leaning his elbows against his knees, he steepled his hands, resting his chin on his fingertips. "We need to talk about Scott's case, Jules."

"Okay," she replied in a shaky voice.

"I have a few updates for you on leads. I know Derek shared some with you this morning, but I have more now. We have identified the car you saw in the parking garage, but unfortunately the license plate is a fake. At this point, we are still trying to identify the driver."

"Do you think this driver is the one who killed Scott?"

"Not sure yet, but he is our top suspect."

Matt crossed his arms over his chest, a scowl replacing his ease. "What do you know about him?"

"Nothing, really. The car rental has his name as Nick Ortega, but over the last month, no one with that name has flown into Rockford. His license plate is from Nevada, so our lead is that he's not from here and arrived under a different name."

"So he came here to kill Scott and then left?" Jules couldn't hide her fear as her voice held a high pitch.

"That's the thing, Jules. We don't think he left," Trevor admitted.

Her eyes widened and then fastened on his. "Derek?"

"Right now, all the evidence is developing. Nothing is for sure," he noted.

Hurt flashed across her emerald eyes. "Did you know about this and not tell me?"

"No, it's not like that." He rounded the bed and knelt by her head. Ava stood up and made her way to Matt's side. "I found out about it right before your accident. I tried to call you." Ever since Jake's words at breakfast, he had made a vow to always be up front and honest with her. He would never gain her trust if he kept things from her.

"This … this guy saw me," she turned to Trevor, "but I didn't see him." She slid her clammy hand into Derek's. He held on tight. "What does that mean?"

"That's what we are trying to figure out, Jules."

A knock at the glass door turned everyone's attention to the doctor entering. Derek eased off the floor and stood against the perimeter to give him more space. "Hi, Julia. I'm Doctor Stone. I hear you work here in Pediatrics?" He reached out and shook her hand. "Wish we could have met under different circumstances. How are you feeling?"

"Sore."

"After what you've just been through, I don't doubt that. What is your pain level?"

"Maybe a six? The medicine is helping."

"Good. That will be your best friend the next couple days. Your x-rays and scan came back clear. It looks like you'll just be dealing with some bumps and bruises and mild whiplash. I know it doesn't sound like much, but you'll be sore for a few days. And I hate to tell you this, but the worst is yet to come. I'll write you a prescription for pain meds. Keep on top of it through tomorrow and then use as needed. Otherwise, just take it easy." He looked around the room. "Make sure she listens. Medical personnel are the worst at following instructions."

An uneasy quietness settled in the room after Doctor Stone left. The accident changed things drastically for Derek. Did everyone else in the room agree? Someone ran her off the road. Until they found out who did it, things would be different. They had been going off 'what if's' for the past week. Today they would be on alert and react with caution. He would make sure of it.

Trevor opened up the folder he had tucked on his lap and pulled out a copy of a driver's license. "Jules, have you seen this man before?"

Without a word, Jules took it from him. The paper wiggled slightly in her hands. For a good minute she did nothing but study the picture. Derek didn't have to see it to know it was Nick Ortega. His five-foot-eleven, two hundred and forty pounds, bald head, olive skin and dark eyes had been imbedded in his mind since he first saw the picture at the station.

Finally, she broke the stare, finding his eyes before she placed her hand on Trevor's. "No, I don't think so," she admitted. "I'm sorry."

"There's no right or wrong answer here."

"But that's who you think shot Scott, isn't it?" She tapped the picture.

"We're not sure," Trevor leaned forward in his chair, "and until we know exactly what's going on, I would like to put you under protection."

"You think this guy is after me now," Jules concluded.

"Someone just ran you off the road, Jules. We aren't going to take chances," Matt pointed out and everyone nodded in agreement.

"So I just stay at Lucy's house like a sitting duck until you find this guy?"

"I'll have an officer with you at all times. You'll be safe. This is going to be over soon. I've got guys working around the clock. Jake is working on this full time alongside me. We're going to find this guy, Jules."

Derek leaned back against the wall, listening as they talked about options, while coming up with a plan himself. She had to get out of Rockford. It was the only way he would be able to sleep at night. Jules even said it. She would be a sitting duck if she stayed here. They could heighten protection, but if they removed her first this guy would lose his edge on them.

"I can put a female officer with you to stay at the house at night and then —"

"No." Derek spoke up, without time to finalize his plan. "I have a better idea." He broke off from the wall and crouched down in front of her. "Run away with me."

"What? Did you steal some of my meds?" Her smiled faded as she began to realize his seriousness.

"I have some vacation time coming up. I know a safe place. I would feel better if you were out of the city."

"I can't ask you to put your life on hold for me."

He smiled. "You didn't. I volunteered, remember?"

"It's a good idea, Jules. Knowing you're safe takes a huge burden off the rest of us. It might even throw this guy off enough to make a mistake," Trevor suggested.

She palmed the sides of her face. "When would we leave?" she directed her question to him. He took it as a good vibe that she was caving.

"First thing tomorrow morning." It would give them time to get packed and for him to finalize a few details to make his plan work.

"You can stay with us tonight," Matt offered.

Derek nodded his thanks. He could breathe easier knowing she was under Matt's protection until he could get her out of the city. "Jules, please." He didn't want to beg, but he would if it came down to it.

For an instant, he thought she would refuse, but he watched her resolve vanish. "All right. I guess I could handle a few days of vacation with my own personal bodyguard." The smirk she gave him melted his insides. "Where is this mysterious place you're sweeping me off to?"

He paused, not sure either of them was ready for where they were going. "My parents' cabin."

CHAPTER TWENTY

E VERY BUMP ON THE ROUGH ROAD JOSTLED JULES' SORE MUS-cles. She adjusted Derek's coat she had rolled into a ball and stuffed it against the window. A pot hole dipped her head, banging it into the glass. Enough was enough. She sat up and wiped the sleep that refused to come from her eyes along with a soft growl.

"Can't sleep?" Derek asked from the driver's seat.

"No. It's impossible to get comfortable." She had never been able to sleep while traveling, whether by car or airplane. She rearranged his coat to drape over her lap and leaned her head gently back against the seat.

"Sorry. Welcome to the back roads of Galena."

It was Friday morning, and she still couldn't believe she was on her way to the Brown estate to stay until they captured the man assumed to be after her. The entire situation seemed outlandish.

On top of that, being back in Galena stirred many emotions and memories. Besides her life possibly being in danger … so was her heart. Last fall Derek had brought her, Matt, and Ava to his family's ranch to go horseback riding. Her horse had gotten spooked by a storm coming in and sent her on a wild ride until she got dumped in the creek. Derek had found her wet, limping and miserable. Their relationship had taken a turn that day. Within those short hours, she finally realized

– or let's be honest, admitted – that she wanted more than just a friendship with him.

She leaned her head to the side, drawing in his strong profile. His straight nose and rigid jaw gave him a tough exterior. But she knew better. Underneath all the muscle and power he displayed was a man with compassion, a pure heart, and an unwavering character. And he chose her. It didn't add up. She came from a broken home with baggage that piled up to the ceiling. He came from a prestigious family and seemed to have it all together. Coming back to Galena ushered in a new fear. When she was last here, they were just friends. Now they were back as a couple. Would their differences be more highlighted now?

"Jules," Derek waved a hand in front of her face, "what are you thinking about?"

"Nothing," she lied. She shifted her gaze to look out the window. If he saw her eyes, he'd know. "The snow is so pretty."

Over the last twelve hours the clouds had dumped up to six inches – beautiful to admire, stressful to drive in. Even under a blanket of white, the landmarks became familiar. They passed a house with a large rock in the front drive, etched with "The Miller's." Next, a farm with a large, red barn amongst a cluster of silos. She folded her shaking hands together. They were almost there.

"It is, but I'm looking forward to seeing it from inside the cabin, snuggled up with you."

She returned his smile. "Me, too, along with a cup of coffee that wards off my growing headache."

"Did you take your meds before we left?"

"Yes, doctor."

They passed the vinyl fence that lined the Brown's property. Derek slowed when they reached the paved driveway. He rolled down his window and punched in the code. The gates opened, releasing butterflies in her stomach. Accelerating slowly, they continued. First they passed the massive two-story, brick-fronted main house. Taking a left as the driveway split, they drove along the fence that led them into a small wooded area. The asphalt turned to gravel as they pulled into a clearing. A log cabin with a wrap-around porch and stone entry sat surrounded by the trees. It looked as if it had come straight out of a magazine. The morning sun filtered through the pine trees that lined the premises, causing a soft glow to reflect on the windows.

She slowly closed her mouth, not realizing it had gaped open. "Wow. This is ... this is beautiful."

"It's my hidden paradise." He parked in front of the entrance and shut off the truck. "Didn't you see this when you came last fall?"

"If you recall, as I passed by, I was holding on for dear life as your horse tried to kill me. I didn't really have time to stop and admire."

Derek pursed his lips to keep from smiling. "How could I forget?"

"Don't worry. I won't let you."

A smirk slid across his lips. "I'm sure you won't." He pulled the keys out of the ignition.

"C'mon, I'll give you a tour before we unload." He rounded the truck, opening her door. With his hand on the small of her back, he led her up the short steps. Walking into the cabin, she spun around, soaking it all in. Straight ahead through the grand entrance was the living room. A stone fireplace ran up the wall with two large windows on each side, from floor to ceiling. Outside the windows stretched a deck that overlooked a small pond. An enormous half-circle leather couch faced the television mounted above the rock fireplace. In the center sat a circular ottoman big enough for her to nap on comfortably. "Over here is the kitchen and dining room area."

She turned. Pine cabinets ran across the wall. A large island stood between with stools lining one side. It was exquisite with the perfect mix of pine wood, contemporary and a hint of modern.

"How often does your family use this place?" she asked, stepping closer to the kitchen.

"I'm not sure. They use the house on the east side with the pool for guests in the summer, and this for guests in the winter. This is where I always stay when I visit."

Her head wanted to explode. She couldn't fathom this lifestyle that included building a home they only used a couple times a year. Derek seemed to sense her shock. He slid his hand into hers. "Let's go pick out which bedroom you want." He walked her to the opposite side of the cabin. Cabin. That word didn't really do this place justice. A cabin in the woods in her vocabulary meant small and cozy with one big room and a loft that looked down over the living quarters. Not this ginormous, posh residence.

Down the hallway were three bedrooms, each with their own bathroom. She chose the bedroom at the end of the hall, overlooking the pond. It had a splash of hunter green and maroon that highlighted the light pine. An elegant landscaped painting hung over the four post bed. She guessed it cost her monthly salary. A small fireplace sat to the left with two wing backed chairs and a side table smooched between.

While Derek ran out to the truck to retrieve her suitcase, she took a few minutes to freshen up. When she stepped out of the bathroom, he was placing her suitcase on the bed.

"Are you sure it's okay if I take this room?" she asked, not wanting to choose the room he usually stayed in.

"Yes. I stay in the first room. I like the sunrise as my alarm clock."

He could have his sunrise. She planned to sleep in every day they were here. When in Rome. If she had to be forced into taking a *vacation* – and she used that word loosely – by golly, she was going to enjoy every minute of it.

He came toe to toe with her. "Are you sure you're okay with me staying here?"

"Of course."

He had explained to her on the drive that while he could stay at the main house, he didn't feel comfortable having her stay somewhere alone. She had no protest. She didn't want to be alone either.

"Listen, I know this is an uncommon situation we're in, but I promise to respect and honor you while we stay here."

Never once did she think he'd ever be anything less than a gentleman. "Derek, I've never felt safer than I do right now." She meant every word.

He drew her in, placing a quick kiss on her forehead. She soaked in his closeness and strength before he stepped away. She could already see the restraint he exercised during their physical touch. While they stayed here, she'd be lucky if he ever allowed himself to kiss her.

"Why don't you unpack and then rest while I unload the truck?" Derek suggested.

Before they left the city they had stopped at a grocery store and picked up a week's worth of food. "I don't mind helping," she offered.

"No need, just take it easy. I can put you to work later." He turned, throwing a smile over his shoulder. "Before I forget, I have something for you." He bent down and unzipped the bag he had on the floor.

"Oh, yeah?"

He pulled out her blue journal. "Trevor made copies of the pages he needed." He handed it to her. "Said you could have it back."

"Thanks." She ran a hand over it and then crushed it against her chest, relieved to have it back, her personal thoughts no longer laying around for all to read.

"I figured you have some time on your hands if you want-ed to write some lovey-dovey stuff about your amazing boy-friend." He winked at her. She rolled her eyes in return.

Through a smile, she said, "You're impossible –"

"To live without?" he interrupted. "I was hoping you'd say that." He reached out and ran a hand gently down her cheek. "Unpack. Get settled. Lunch is in an hour." He scooped up his bag and disappeared down the hallway. After unpacking, Jules followed orders and stretched out on the bed, letting much needed sleep overcome her.

§ § § § §

DEREK HEARD JULES COMING BEFORE HE SAW HER. SHE AP-peared from the hallway, padding along the dark hardwood floor. "Why didn't you wake me up?" she asked, taking a seat at one of the stools.

He slid a mug of coffee across the granite counter to her. "You needed sleep." He had checked on her a few times dur-ing the hours of sleep. He couldn't bring himself to wake her.

"Please tell me you had lunch without me."

"I did." He opened the fridge and pulled out a blue Tupperware container. "I made grilled chicken sandwiches. I'll get this warmed up for you if you want to grab what condi-ments you want on it."

She slid off the stool and rounded the island. She pulled out lite mayo, lettuce, tomato and a whole-grain wrap while he warmed up the chicken in the microwave.

"How are you feeling?" he asked.

"Better. Still sore, but my headache is gone."

"You should be able to take another round of pain pills with your food."

She shook her head, "I might wait until this evening. They

make me drowsy. Hence my two hour nap." She pulled out a bag of carrots and tossed them next to her sandwich. With bright eyes that no longer held exhaustion, she caught his gaze. "So what should we do today?"

He figured she couldn't just sit around and rest. "I was thinking we could go horseback riding. I'm sure Gracie misses you," he teased, mentioning the horse she rode during her last visit. Laughter came from deep within his chest in response to her glare. He put his hands up in surrender. "Okay, okay. How about a walk through the woods?"

"As long as my feet are on the ground, I don't care what we do."

"All right, why don't you finish up eating while I go through my sisters' snow clothes." In the walk-out basement was a mudroom filled with extra gear for the winter weather. "What shoe size are you?"

"Eight. But I brought boots."

"Those cute leather boots you brought would keep your feet warm for about two minutes. I'm sure I can find something around that size." He tousled her hair as he walked by her and headed to the lower level.

A half hour later, decked out in heavy coats and boots, they trudged out through the woods, ankle deep in snow. He took her gloved hand in his and led her down the path that circled the pond and headed into the woods. By the time they reached the back of the woods, they had touched on the subjects of work, old comedy movies, and how he could convince her to get back on a horse. The trail turned, leading them back to the cabin, when she asked, "Have you heard from Trevor yet?"

He nodded. "He called earlier. He's meeting with Emma Zentz tomorrow afternoon, and Jake is working on finding out who this Nick Ortega guy really is. He said he'd call us tonight if he had any more updates."

"Do you think Trevor will find him?" she asked while he

helped her step over a fallen log.

"Absolutely." Given enough time, he was totally confident that Trevor would find the shooter. Getting Jules out of the city had hopefully bought them the extra time they needed. "I trust him with my life – and more importantly, yours."

A few minutes later, the sky opened up again. Snowflakes fluttered to the ground. The sunlight peeked out from behind the clouds, reflecting off the large flakes and causing them to appear as diamonds. Jules stopped, stuck her tongue out, and spun around slowly.

"What are you doing?" he asked with a chuckle.

"Catching snowflakes. You should try it," she giggled, leaning to the left and then the right.

He could, but he didn't want to take his eyes off her for a second. With her rosy nose from the cold, bright emerald eyes and the joy in her smile, she became a kid again. His heartbeat accelerated. He loved this woman. Should he tell her and risk that it was too soon and push her away? With the case, he vowed to always be honest with her. Should that include his heart as well?

Jules stopped and caught him staring. "What?" she laughed, grabbing hold of his hands, pulling him. "Try it."

He yielded to her wish. Leaning his head back, he stuck out his tongue. Large flakes, so big he could almost see their unique detail, landed on his cheeks and forehead, with a few finding his mouth. He joined in with her laughter, enjoying the memory forever embedded in his mind. Adjusting her stocking hat, he let his hands slip down her hair and onto her shoulders. With his nerves exploding like fireworks, his smile faded.

"What's wrong?" Jules asked, her eyebrows smashing together.

"Nothing's wrong. In fact, everything feels right." He brushed away a snowflake that landed on her eyelash. *Deep breath.* "I'm in love with you, Jules."

She blinked twice before a slow grin stretched her lips. Reading her reaction was nearly impossible. She didn't slap him or turn around and run away. He took that as a good sign.

Without warning, she crashed into his chest and wrapped her padded arms around his neck. Placing her mouth up against his ear, she whispered, "Thank you for loving me."

He couldn't deny the rejection that came from not hearing it back. It might have been a little early in their relationship to declare it, but he had thought maybe she felt the same way. It hurt to be mistaken. He had to remember that over the last couple months his feelings had been developing, while she had been stuck in a holding pattern. A chill ran through him from her cold cheek pressed against his. "C'mon, let's get you back inside before you freeze to death and then all my efforts in keeping you safe will have been in vain."

CHAPTER TWENTY-ONE

JULES BURIED HERSELF DEEPER UNDER THE RED FLEECE BLANKET. Her muscles melted into the leather couch. It had been a wonderful day. After their walk, they spent a couple hours downstairs in the game room playing ping pong and billiards. As if the place wasn't big enough, he had to show her the entire bottom level that consisted of the family room and small kitchenette, game room, mudroom, workout room, and an office. This place was ridiculously, over the top ... awesome. She understood why Derek called it his hidden paradise. She just tried not to think about the fact that her entire house could fit inside the basement. For dinner they made homemade pizzas and ate on the floor in front of the crackling fire. Now, they were getting ready to watch a movie. The best part of her day, the part that kept a smile on her face and her heart beating wildly, was when Derek told her he was in love with her.

She wished she could rewind that moment. Her heart wanted to say, "*I love you*" back to him, but instead her mouth said, "*Thank you for loving me.*" Seriously. How pathetic. *Thank you?* She might as well have shaken his hand or fist bumped him to go along with her lame reply. *I'll take, 'You're an idiot' for two-hundred, Alex.* Oh, why didn't life come with a few do-overs? Despite trying to hide his disappointment, she saw straight through his cover up, right there in his blue eyes that lost their sparkle when he smiled. She had to fix this, but how? Especially when she wasn't ready to share the depth of her feelings yet.

"Jules, do you want a Diet Coke?" he asked from the kitchen.

With an arm over the back of the couch, she placed her chin on her shoulder. "I better not. With a nap and coffee, I'm already going to have a hard time going to sleep tonight."

The microwave beeped. He pulled out the bag of popcorn and filled two bowls. He shoved a Coke and a water bottle under his arm, picked up the bowls and met her on the couch.

"I can't believe you've never seen this movie before," she said with a hint of disbelief.

"You're *surprised* I haven't seen, "While You Were Sleeping"? What do you think I do in my spare time?"

She grabbed her bowl and drink from him. "It's a classic."

"It's a chick-flick."

"Well, someone needs to educate you on a good romance movie."

He cracked open the tab on his can. "Let me guess. They meet. Fall in love. Have conflict and a misunderstanding. And then they end up together." He lifted his eyebrows. "Am I close?"

"Men. You don't get it." She popped a kernel in her mouth. "It's all about the journey."

"I guess I just have a problem with how most romance movies, and books for that matter, portray love. They make it look so magical and effortless. We poor guys don't have a chance to live up to the expectations it sets."

She shook her head. "I'm pretty sure our view of love has mostly been skewed from past relationships and hurts."

"Everyone is human." He propped an elbow up on the back of the couch. "We're going to mess up. That's why we need God's love for us to be the foundation. The best thing about God's love is that it's unconditional. We do nothing to gain it, and we can do nothing to lose it. It's just there for the taking." He paused. "We love, because He first loved us."

"You make it sound so easy."

"That's because it is."

"Not for someone who has experienced, first hand, love at its worst. Abandonment. Unfaithfulness. Feeling like a burden." She shrugged and played with the edge of the blanket. "It's hard not to see God that way, too."

His fingertips slid gently across the surface of her cheek. His eyes reached down to her barren soul. "I'm sorry you've been hurt. God can cover those hurts. He's the author of redeeming love."

"I guess it's just hard for me to accept it. It's easier to leave the barriers up."

"You don't have to leave the barriers up for God. He will never fail you."

"My head knows that's true. I just haven't convinced my heart of it yet." She wished to be released in this area. To be able to break down the barriers that held her captive. To accept God's love – or even Derek's – for that matter.

Derek's cell phone rang. He lifted it up off the ottoman. Shoulders sagging, he said, "Excuse me, Jules. I need to take this."

"Sure. No problem."

He walked down the hallway to get some privacy, but she still overheard a few seconds of him saying, "Hey, dad."

She waited on the couch for a short couple minutes before he rejoined her. His body language had changed. His shoulders were now rigid. His soft blue eyes had turned to ice. His lips pursed. His focus on her was removed.

"Hey," she cocked her head, "everything okay?"

It took him a few beats to respond. "I'm sorry, what did you say?"

Laying a hand on his, she pulled his attention to her. "Is

everything okay?"

"Yeah … sorry … everything's fine." He ran a hand through his tousled blond hair. "That was my dad."

Not new information to her. "Just checking in with you?" she prodded. What could have been discussed in their short two minute conversation to cause this change in him?

"You could say that," he crossed his arms over his chest, "but keeping his thumb on me is more like it."

"What does that mean?" She had no clue of the dynamics he had with his family, let alone his father. Over conversations she had gotten the hint that they weren't close and that his father didn't like that Derek had decided to become a cop, but something seemed deeper than that.

"It means that my parents are here."

Jules' eyes widened from his admission. He had told her that his parents wouldn't be here while they stayed. "I thought they were in Kentucky?"

"They were until they learned I was coming home. They flew in about an hour ago."

"Well, you haven't seen them in months. I'm sure they've missed you, especially since you didn't come home for Christmas. Maybe this is a good thing?" Her words and tone didn't come out as encouraging as she had hoped.

"My dad isn't here because he misses me, Jules." He rubbed the back of his neck with his palm. "Everything he does has ulterior motives." Derek practically growled the words.

"What did he say?"

"Wants me to head up to the main house so we can talk."

Disappointment weaved throughout her. She didn't like the idea of him leaving her alone. And it went deeper than her safety. She liked being with him as much as possible. "And what did you say?"

"I told him I'd be there in a couple hours, that I was in the middle of something." She breathed lighter, seeing his smile return.

"I don't mind if you need to go now." She did her best to make it sound believable.

"But I do. He can wait. I have a sappy love story to watch with my beautiful girlfriend."

He leaned over and surprised her with a kiss, ending the discussion. She took advantage of his light-hearted mood and deepened the kiss. Without giving her enough time to savor the moment, he pulled back with complete control.

Remote in hand, he started the DVD and turned up the volume. As the main menu popped up, he grabbed a handful of popcorn and shoved it in his mouth. He chewed. Frowned. Chewed some more. Then scrunched up his handsome face. "What is this?" He coughed and took a swig of his drink.

"Popcorn," she responded defensively.

"No. This is cardboard reincarnated as popcorn."

She threw a kernel at him. He batted it away and sent one back. It hit her square on the nose. His laugh warmed her more than the blanket ever could. "It's good for you. Lite popcorn with no butter or salt –"

"Or taste. Next time, I get to shop for the snacks."

She giggled as he pulled her into his side and pushed play on the movie menu. With an arm draped over her shoulder, she snuggled into his chest. A smile of contentment danced across her lips.

§ § § § §

FRANKLIN DELUCA SLAMMED HIS FIST DOWN ON THE CENTER console of his rental car. Where was Julia Anderson? He thought for sure that when he ran her off the road and she flipped and crashed into the tree, she'd be dead and his problems solved. No such luck.

Packed and ready to leave the city that morning, he stopped when he realized the news never covered a deadly car accident. With further digging, he found the report of her minor injuries. Since he had already checked out of his hotel room, he decided to choose a different place to stay while he remained in the city. Staying in one place too long wasn't smart. It's what would get him caught. In fact, he had already delayed long enough in Rockford.

He sat parked forty yards away from the house she was currently living in. With only the full moon to use as light, he scanned the dark house. No light leaked out from behind the drawn curtains during the long hours as he watched. She had been discharged from the hospital. He'd checked. Where would she have gone? If she had returned and then left, he missed it. Time was no longer on his side. He had to eliminate her. The creative attempts to make it look like an accident didn't work. It was time to just finish the job. But first he had to find her.

CHAPTER TWENTY-TWO

"Dad?" Derek called out while he made his way through his parent's house, down the marble hallway that led to his dad's office. The grandfather clock chimed, echoing throughout the quiet house that the eleven o'clock hour had arrived. Light spilled out underneath the closed office door. His knuckles rapped on the wood. "Dad?" He pushed the door open to find David Brown at the desk, papers covering the glass top.

"Come on in." His brown hair had turned a frosted gray near the temples since Derek had seen him last. With his pointer finger, he pushed up his glasses which perched half-way down upon his nose. "Good to see you, Son."

Derek stepped forward and shook his dad's outstretched hand, "Thank you, Sir. I hope you had a good flight."

"We were able to charter a last minute flight which made for a quick and easy trip." He pointed to the chair. "Please, sit down."

Derek lowered himself onto the chair, muscles stiff just like their greeting. Awkwardness hung between them like body odor in a high school boy's locker room. Heavy. Hard to breathe. A connection didn't come easy with his dad since Derek had left for college. His decision to become a police officer had created a barricade that neither could work around to repair the lost relationship.

For years he had bent over backwards to get his dad's approval. He worked hard and became a Sergeant. He joined the SWAT team. Mostly for himself and his dreams, but there had always been a part of him that hoped his dad would be proud of him. To love him just because he was his son. Instead, he lived each day knowing he was a huge disappointment.

"Sorry I'm here so late." He hated to leave Jules, but she finally convinced him to go. They compromised with him waiting until she had gone to bed to make the trip over.

"No problem. Care to tell me why you came to the cabin?" His dad didn't waste a moment of surface conversation. Would it kill him to ask a few normal father-son questions? *How are you? Can you believe this weather? Did you see the Bulls basketball game this week and the last second shot that won the game?* Derek swallowed his pride and took a deep breath.

"It's a long story."

"I've got time."

Over the next five minutes Derek gave his dad, without too many details, the quick version of what had happened over the last week until he brought him up to date on the latest incident. "Then last night as Jules headed home from work, she was run off the road. We think that the shooter may be after her. Getting her out of the city seemed like the best idea."

"So you decided to come here and put your family in danger as well?"

Derek bit back a few words. "In my defense, you weren't supposed to be here, Dad," he pointed out. "How did I know you would make a last minute trip?"

"Who is this Julia Anderson girl? She seems more than just a victim to you," he noted.

He really had no interest in sharing his relationship with Jules, but he decided to offer an olive branch and see what would happen. "Up until a week ago, we were just friends, but

I've been pursuing her for months." He smiled, picturing the feisty redhead that claimed his heart. "Now we're together. I'm in love with her, Dad. I had to make sure she was safe." He paused, speaking with courage and a sincere spirit. "I hope you know I would never intentionally endanger you, mom, Lauren or Claire."

The powerful David Brown eased back in his leather office chair, rested his elbows on the side arms and did something foreign … he smiled. "Derek, I trust you. If you say we aren't in danger, then we aren't in danger. You think with your head, not your emotions. You see things that others don't. You take your work seriously and give it everything you have."

Derek blinked in disbelief. His dad just gave him a compliment. "Thank you, Sir."

"Speaking of your sisters, Lauren and Claire will both be here tomorrow. Your mother would like to have you all here for a family dinner."

Despite his family drama, he cherished his younger sisters. For years he had pulled away from them even though they didn't share their parents' negative feelings towards his life choices. Excitement filled him at the thought of seeing them. "Sure. I'll be bringing Julia, if she agrees." He didn't ask it as a question. If Jules wanted to come with him, that would be her choice, not his dad's.

He paused, ever so slight, but Derek caught it. "That's fine. We would like to meet her."

The only girlfriend his dad had ever liked was Chelsea. On the few occasions that they talked, he would always comment about how great it was that Derek had found a woman that fit so perfectly with the family. Wouldn't his dad be ticked to know that was the exact reason he had broken things off with her? How would his dad handle meeting Jules? On the flip side, how would Jules handle meeting his family? He could sense it overwhelmed her to be here and see firsthand his family's wealth and worldly treasures. Did he just make a mistake by accepting the invitation? Derek checked his watch. He needed to get back to the cabin. "So is that why you asked me here? To invite me for dinner?"

His dad swiveled his chair around, stood tall, and walked over to the bar. He poured himself a drink. He offered one to Derek, but he declined. "No, that's not why I asked you to come here." He took a long swig. "I have a proposition for you."

§ § § § §

Jules pushed the LL button on the elevator. A few moments later the doors opened, exposing the shadowy cement parking garage with only a few lights above to guide their way. She and Scott turned left, arriving at the row that held their vehicles. Although Jules had parked further away, Scott insisted on walking her to her vehicle. As their footsteps pounded along the cement, his stride quickened, and Jules had to work hard to keep up. A car door slammed shut. Scott jumped, pushing her to the side. "I'm sorry, Julia." He grabbed her arm, bringing her close to him again.

"Are you all right?"

Putting his hands on his hips, he looked down at his shoes, scuffing his toes against the floor. "No, I'm not." He let out a defeated breath, bringing his eyes up to reach hers. "I've got some things going on right now. That's why I wanted to have coffee with you. I could use a friend right now."

She reached a hand up, squeezing his bicep. "Of course, and I'm happy to be that friend. I'm worried about you, Scott."

He placed his hand on his arm, covering over her hand. "Thanks. I knew I could trust you." Looking around the garage, he pulled her toward her car that was parked four spaces down. "We should get going. It's not safe."

"Safe? What are you talking about?" She tried to slow down their pace, but he wouldn't slow, even with her resistance. "Scott, what is going on?" She finally worked out of his grasp and stopped short of her car.

Scott turned, "Julia, please just trust me and get in the car," he pleaded.

"No. Not until you tell me what is going on," she demanded, while straightening her stance. Determination laced her words.

"I promise I will tell you everything over coffee, just get in the car."

They began their stare down, neither budging. Suddenly, she felt the hair on the back of her neck prickle from the unease of being watched. She scanned the parking garage. Empty. They were alone.

No. Wait. From the shadows a figured appeared. Burly. Dark hair combed over. Olive skin. A thin mustache. Dark eyes. And his right hand raised horizontal with a gun pointed at them.

"Scott!!! Watch out! He has a gun!"

In slow motion she tried to cover Scott, protect him, but he pushed her to the side. "Let her go," Scott spoke to the man. "This doesn't concern her."

"It does now!" The man belched in return.

The blast from the shot immediately caused Jules' ears to ring. She screamed, falling back against her vehicle. Jules covered her ears, hoping to stop the ringing. She looked behind her to find Scott on the ground, a pool of blood growing on his chest.

"Scott!" she screamed, the sound ricocheting off the cement walls.

Looking up, she found the barrel of the gun pointed at her. "Now it's your turn."

The shot jerked Jules awake. Her body shook uncontrollably. Her pajamas clung to her wet body from the sweat. Adrenaline pulsed through her as her eyes adjusted to the dark room. Pulling the sheets tighter against her, she tried to regulate her breathing. It was just a dream.

But that's not what scared her to her core. It was the realization that she'd seen that man before.

§ § § § §

"WHAT KIND OF PROPOSITION?" DEREK ASKED, HIS TONE betraying the turmoil inside. He should have known his dad had lured him into the lion's den for a reason.

"Just hear me out before you get all defensive."

"Fine." He leaned back in the chair, with an ankle resting on his opposite knee. "I'm listening."

"Over the last few months, your mother and I have been talking about making Lexington our permanent home. We love Galena, but let's be honest, it doesn't hold the social aspect of our lifestyle. And as I get older, the stress of handling both estates is beginning to wear on me." David walked over to the wall that held an arrangement of pictures. "Your great grandfather built this company, our legacy, from the ground up." He turned on his heels, gripping Derek with the intensity of his eyes. "And now it's time for you to step up and take part in that legacy."

"Dad," Derek interrupted with a warning.

"Let me finish!"

Derek didn't even flinch from the reprimand. Instead, he crossed his arms against his chest and gave a curt nod for his dad to continue.

"Now, I understand that you needed to go off into the world to find yourself. And I commend you for your hard work and all that you've achieved. But you're thirty years old. It's time to come back to your roots. I need to leave the Galena ranch in someone's hands that I trust and have full confidence in. That's you, Derek."

Mixed within the patronizing comments, Derek caught a couple compliments. "Dad, I appreciate your confidence in me, but –"

David held a hand up. "Stop. Just hear me out. I know you don't want this, but sometimes we have to make sacrifices. Let's compromise. Give me a couple years. Help me figure out all the dynamics that go with changing of hands. If, after those years, you still want to do this cop thing," he flicked his fingers as if swatting a fly, "then you have my blessing."

Derek rubbed his hands over his face and let out a quiet growl. His dad's blessing. There wasn't much more in life he wanted than that, but to deny what God had called him to do didn't sit well either. Why couldn't his dad just accept him for who he was and not for whom he wanted him to be?

"What about Henry, dad? He has been your right-hand man for years. He knows more about this business from the inside out than I ever could." Henry Shaw had become like family. There had never been a time that Derek didn't know him. If anyone deserved this position, it was Henry.

"No. This legacy belongs to our family."

"What about Claire?" His youngest sister traveled with them between Galena and Lexington, training the horses.

"Derek, don't you get it? You are my firstborn," he pounded his chest, "my son. I have worked my entire life to hand this over to you one day."

Guilt constricted his breathing. His head began to spin. He loved being a cop. It was in his DNA. But was he being self-ish? The commandment said to honor your father and mother – and all he'd done was despise them and run in the opposite direction. He bent over, his elbows braced on his knees, his head resting in his palms. "I don't know what to say, Dad."

"Then don't say anything yet. Just promise me you'll think
156

about it."

He sat up, meeting the hope that flashed in his dad's eyes. He surrendered with a nod. "I'll think about it."

David clapped his hands together. "Excellent!"

Peeling himself off the chair, Derek stood, feeling a few inches shorter from the weight that had just been placed on his shoulders. He pulled his ringing phone from his pocket, panic shooting through him as he answered, "Jules?"

"Derek." She was crying.

"What's wrong?"

"I … need … you." She hiccupped between each word.

That was enough for him. "I'll be right there." He ran out the door, not giving his dad a proper goodbye, and not in the least bit sorry about it.

§ § § § §

SLOWLY, JULES MADE HER WAY OVER TO ONE OF THE CHAIRS IN her room. Derek would be here soon. She took relief in knowing that she wouldn't be alone much longer. Each creak and groan from inside the cabin sent her heart beating even faster.

Gravel crunched outside as his truck approached and then skidded to a stop. The door slammed shut. Within seconds the front door lock clicked open. "Jules?"

"Back here, Derek." The words came out so faint, she wondered if he'd even heard her.

Quick footsteps approached. From the only light in the room that came from the lamp on the side table by the bed, she caught the panic in his eyes. He came around the chair, offered his hands, and pulled her into his arms. She had just managed to stop crying, but being with him, secure in the strength wrapped around her, caused a new unleashing of tears. He palmed the back of her head, resting it on his chest.

His sweatshirt grew damp, but he didn't seem to care. Once settled down, she apologized. "I'm sorry I called you." She didn't like the weakness that made her interrupt his time with his dad. She wasn't giving a very good first impression.

Gently he pulled her away, "Don't be sorry, okay?" He crouched to see into her eyes. His eyes trailed over the length of her body, as if checking for himself that she was really all right. "What happened?"

She shuddered, having to explain the nightmare. "I fell asleep shortly after you left." She twirled her finger around the strings hanging from his hooded sweatshirt. "I had a dream." Now she just felt silly. Like a five-year-old that came crying to her mother's bedside because a monster had chased her. "I replayed the night Scott got shot, which has happened before, but this time it was different."

"How so?"

"This time a man came out from the shadows and shot Scott and then shot me."

Derek lightly gripped both of her arms. "Are you telling me you saw who shot Scott?"

"No. I still don't remember seeing anyone in the parking garage. But with that man's face embedded in my mind, I realized I'd seen him before. Take away the hairpiece and the mustache, and I am almost certain that is the picture of the man Trevor asked me about.

"Nick Ortega?"

"I think so."

"When did you see him?"

"Earlier that day. Maybe a couple hours before Scott and I left? I had gone to the storage closet to grab a couple of things, and I saw Scott talking with this guy in one of the alcoves down the hallway. The picture Trevor showed me threw me off because of the bald head and hairless face, but I'm pretty sure that was him."

He massaged her shoulders. "This helps, Jules. Every detail you can tell us brings us one step closer to finding this guy."

She couldn't shake the fear that this man could possibly be after her. For the first time, she fully grasped the severity of the situation. "I just keep thinking about the gun in my face and that this guy might actually want me dead! I'm scared Derek. For me. For you ... if anything happened to you because of me, I could never forgive myself."

"Hey, hey." He cupped her face, giving her no choice but to look at him. "Nothing is going to happen to me, or you. We're going to be fine."

Not trusting her voice, she nodded. With a hand covering her mouth, she tried to stifle a yawn. Her eyes grew heavy, but she didn't want to sleep. She didn't want to close her eyes and see that man again and relive the pain and fear of watching Scott get shot. She didn't want to once again be left alone in this room.

"C'mon, let's get you back in bed."

She resisted when he grasped her elbow. "Don't leave me." She sucked in a shaky breath.

His lip curved up a little on one side. "I won't."

This time she allowed him to escort her back to bed. He flipped back the sheets while she slid inside. After tucking her in, he bent down and kissed her hair. He then proceeded to walk across the room, turn the chair around and scoot it up to the bed and shut off the lamp. Grabbing a blanket, he slipped off his shoes, sat down and rested his feet on the end of the bed.

"You're going to sleep there?"

"Yep."

"That can't be comfortable."

"Mind over matter. I bet I'll be asleep before you are." He leaned back, pulled the blanket up to his neck, and closed his eyes.

"I'll take that bet."

"I hoped you would. See you in the morning."

Jules turned to lie on her side, facing him. Even in the still of night, by the twilight that shone across his face, she saw deep grooves of worry.

CHAPTER TWENTY-THREE

DEREK CRACKED OPEN THREE EGGS INTO THE WHITE TUPPERWARE bowl and added a splash of water. With a whisk, he scrambled the egg mixture until completely blended. Once the butter ceased foaming over the hot skillet, he poured the contents into it. For a few seconds he let the egg settle along the edges. Using a spatula, he carefully pulled eggs in from all sides, allowing the liquid eggs to flow underneath the cooked ones. Towel over his shoulder, he whistled as he added a dash of salt and pepper, mushrooms, tomatoes, and green peppers.

"How are you so chipper on a Saturday morning?"

He looked over his shoulder to see Jules approaching … and he couldn't help but stare. She braided her hair over to the side. She wore her glasses and not a lick of make-up. Complete with an oversized gray sweatshirt that swallowed her whole. And she was, without a doubt, breathtakingly beautiful.

"Breakfast isn't going to make itself." He turned back to the stove, hoping his hormones hadn't cost him a burnt omelet. Using the spatula, he folded over half of the omelet. With a plate in one hand and the skillet in the other, he flipped the omelet onto the plate. And from years of practice, with perfection, he got the folded side facing down. He placed it in front of her. "I made this for you, but I can make an egg white only one, if you'd prefer."

"This is perfect. Thank you."

"Orange juice?"

"I'll get it. You're making me feel lazy." Pulling two glasses from the cabinet, she said, "I didn't think you could cook."

His mention of multiple frozen dinners must have stuck with her. "I don't. But I can make an omelet." He broke four more eggs, starting the process over again for himself. "I lived off of these in college."

She filled the glasses with orange juice and placed them in front of their seats at the island. "I lived off Ramen noodles and bananas. This looks way better." After putting the container back in the fridge, she sat at the stool, grabbed her fork and took a bite. Her eyes widened. "Wow. This is really good."

"Thanks." He turned back to the stove and got to work on his omelet. A few minutes later, he grabbed another plate and slid his omelet onto it with ease. He rounded the island and took a seat next to her. He noticed she had taken the bandage off from over her left eye and the gash was held together with a butterfly Band-Aid. "Your cut looks better today."

"It must be healing, it's starting to itch. I thought it would be good to air it out for awhile."

"Did you sleep okay?"

"Yes. Not sure if it was from being so tired, or the fact you stayed three feet away from me. But I'm pretty sure it had more to do with the latter." Tears misted her eyes. "Thanks for staying with me."

He caught her stool and tugged it closer to him. "It wasn't the worst night of my life," he teased. "By the way, you're adorable when you sleep."

"You watched me sleep?"

"For like an hour this morning. Pulled over a chair and just stared at you." Her mouth dropped open. He tried to stop the smile but failed. "I'm kidding, Jules. I checked on you when

162

I got up, that's all."

"Derek!" Palm against his chest, she playfully pushed him. He laughed, keeping her hand prisoner. "What time did you wake up?" she asked, squeezing his hand.

"Before sunrise. I wanted to get a workout in and call Trevor." Lifting weights this morning had been therapeutic for him. He burned off the hormones from being in the same room all night with Jules and not being able to touch her, as well as burning off steam from his talk with his dad last night, which had all exhausted him. After a quick shower and quiet time reading his Bible, he felt more able to handle the day.

"Did Trevor have any updates?"

"Not yet, but he will take the information you gave and work off the new description. Trevor said they will go back through surveillance tapes and see if this guy sticks out."

He watched her process the information while she played with her food. "It just feels like it's never going to end."

"From my experience," he said, shifting her body to look at him square on, "we are just waiting for a piece of information to fall in our lap. I think with a good lead, Trevor is going to break this case wide open, and our heads will spin with how quickly it comes to a resolution." At least that is what he hoped and prayed for.

Her gazed shifted over his shoulder, as if watching the sunrise begin to melt the snow outside could also melt away her worry. Emerald eyes found his again "You're right. I guess we should just take advantage of our time here together." She leaned in, only inches away, "You know, since it hasn't been the worst couple days of my life," she smiled, playing back his words.

Everything in him wanted to grab her and kiss her senseless. Instead, he yanked gently on her side-ponytail. "Well, I have a request that might dampen our time together."

"When you put it that way, how can I refuse?"

His gut swirled with dread. He wanted Jules to meet his family, but he just wasn't sure if she was ready. He had already proclaimed his love to her, with nothing in return. Now he was asking her to meet his family. Why did it feel like he was piling a heap of burning coals onto firewood soaked in kerosene – as if everything was about to explode in his face?

"I guess my entire family will be in town tonight, and my mom wants to host a family dinner. I'd like for you to join me." He left off the part where if she declined, he wouldn't be going either. There was no way he would leave her side again tonight.

Jules tilted her head, studied him. Her slow smile unwound all the knots inside. "I'd love to meet your family." She took another bite of her omelet, laid her fork down, and pushed her plate aside. "Listen, about last night. I'm sorry I interrupted time with your dad."

"It's okay, really. You saved me."

"Did it not go well?"

"It went exactly like I thought it would," he rubbed his hands together, "but enough about my family. I have a plan for us today." After seeing the fear in her eyes last night, he decided something needed to be done. The idea came to him during his workout.

"I'm intrigued. What kind of plan?"

"You'll find out soon enough. But I need some time to get it ready." He stood up and carried his dishes to the sink filled with soapy water. He turned and shoved his hands in his jean pockets. "Give me an hour?"

"Sure."

"You'll need to dress warm."

"Why does that not surprise me?"

§ § § § §

"YOU'VE GOT TO BE KIDDING ME!" JULES STOOD WITH HANDS on her hips.

"Just trust me."

"Said the man before he lost an arm, or leg, or toe. I don't know what I'm doing!"

"Exactly." His voice softened. Behind her, he adjusted her shoulders to face forward.

In the middle of the woods, he had built his own shooting range. Between two trees, he had a string tied with five paper silhouettes hanging from it. Behind the targets, an earth-made dirt embankment sat in the background.

"So your plan for the day is a shooting lesson?" she said, her voice slowly reaching the next octave.

He stepped in front of her. Hands on her shoulders, he tried to calm her panic. "Jules, you've had a very traumatic experience happen with a gun," he pointed out. "Plus, I'm a cop. I carry a gun at all times. I think it would be a good idea for you to face your fears, know how to handle a gun, and realize it's not as intimating as you think."

His explanation made sense, but it didn't magically soothe the tremors vibrating throughout her body. "Ahhhh, just give me a second."

"Take all the time you need."

She turned and paced to the nearest tree and back. Finding her spot next to him again, she shook her hands out to the side and jumped up and down. "Okay, I'm ready." And by ready, she meant sick to her stomach, hands drenched in sweat, heart thumping so hard it had to be audible.

"Let's start with some basic training. Never point a gun at something you don't want to shoot at. Never rely on a gun's safety. Be aware of your target, and what is behind and around it. Never put your finger on the trigger unless you plan on firing."

Were her eyes as wide as they felt? She blinked. "Okay, makes sense."

He lifted up his shirt and unhooked his gun from his side holster. "This is a nine-millimeter Glock. This is my personal gun, and the one you will most likely see me carry." He handed it to her. "It's not loaded."

Hand extended, she took it from him. It felt weird, foreign. Sliding in behind her, he pressed his chest against her back. He began to explain with his hands covering hers instead of just verbal instruction. "Your right hand is going to grab hold of the handle. The groove between your thumb and pointer finger is going to slide up until it reaches this lip." He gently positioned her hand. "Keep your pointer finger straight along the outside of the trigger. When you're ready to shoot, that's when you'll bring it in. Now, with your left hand you are going to cup the bottom of the handle and cover some of your right hand. That will help you keep control." He leaned around her head and she could feel him smiling in her ear. "Breathe, Jules."

His hot breath slid down her neck and into the collar of her coat. She exhaled slowly, not realizing she was holding it. "Okay, what's next?"

"Your stance. Bend your knees slightly. Keep them a shoulder length apart."

"Can I keep my left foot a little in front? I think it goes back to my basketball days at the free throw line."

"Whatever is comfortable. Now, slowly extend your arms out." She did. "Good. On the top of the gun there are dots with grooves in the front and rear. These are called sights. You need to make sure your targets are lined up with those."

Closing her left eye, she focused, putting the target right in the middle. "Got it."

"All right, the gun is semi-automatic, so you will need to

let go of the trigger and pull back again if you want further shots. Place your pointer finger against the trigger."

"Okay."

"When you pull back, you will feel the safety trigger first. Keep squeezing and you will finish out your shot."

The gun wasn't even loaded, and her nerves had formed a ball in her throat, constricting her airway. She followed his instructions. The click made her jump. She did it!

"Great job, Jules. Let's try it loaded now."

He took the gun back and released the thingy-bobber to put the bullets into. She was so clueless when it came to guns. "What's that called?"

"A magazine."

"It looks like a clip."

"Chicks usually call it a clip."

"I should be offended."

He handed back to her the loaded gun and placed orange ear protectants in her ears. "Show me what you got. Put a hole in the chest of the target. Prove me wrong for calling you a chick." Then he put the ear protectants in his own ears.

Gun in hand, she mentally – and then physically – walked through his earlier instructions. Right hand wrapped around the handle. Pointer finger straight along the outside. Left hand cupped under the handle. Arms extended out. Knees slightly bent. Target lined up through the sights. Deep breath.

Bam!

The gun recoiled. Jumping up and back, she let out a scream. Then a laugh. What a rush! She turned to look at him, swinging around. He grabbed her arms, pushing the gun toward the ground and not himself. "Oops, sorry."

He laughed. "That's okay. Great shot. You hit the target in the stomach. Not too bad for your first shot."

"Not too bad? Let me do it again."

"That's my girl."

Once again she walked through his instructions, but with a higher level of comfort. She aimed for the second target, ready for the kick back this time. She hit the target's right shoulder.

"Nice!" Derek reassured. She loved his encouragement. Shifting, she focused on the third target. She hit the head. The fourth target she hit the outside circle. The final target, the same. Bringing the gun to her side, she couldn't help the smile that widened. "That was by far the coolest thing I've done in a long time. *That* could get addictive."

Derek took the gun from her and wrapped his arm around her waist, pulling her into him. "This could, too," and kissed her.

Both hands on his chest, she pushed him away. "All right, hot shot. It's your turn."

With a smile, he released the clip – "magazine" – and added more bullets. "What do I get if I hit all the targets, right in the bull's-eye?"

The bet seemed to wager more on his side, and she didn't doubt for a second he could do it, but she took the bet anyway. "You get to pick out our movie and snack every night."

He nodded with a smirk. Legs spread apart, he drew up the weapon and within seconds fired along the targets. Confidence protruded from his swift movements. Quick, but with control. Focused, with no waiver. He shot each bullet right through the bull's-eye.

CHAPTER TWENTY-FOUR

I N ONE HOUR JULES WOULD BE INTRODUCED TO DEREK'S FAMILY.
She felt unprepared both emotionally and physically for
the meeting, so she began her pep talk.

Emotionally: points easily came to mind. She didn't fit in.
Derek will be there as a buffer. Would they even like her? *It
doesn't matter what they think. Derek likes you.* What kind of
conversation could she have with them when they had nothing in common? "*Hey, Mr. and Mrs. Brown, I am terrified of
horses and nearly killed myself last time I rode one of yours.
Do you watch "Castle"? To save money, I clip coupons.*"
Without a doubt she was in love with Derek. *Do I rush out
into the living room and share my feelings with him now ...
or wait?*

Physically: she groaned at her appearance in the full-
length mirror. When packing, she hadn't thought to bring a
"meet the folks" outfit. She packed for a comfortable vacation
in the woods, holed up in a cabin. She glanced down at her
black leggings. They seemed tighter than usual. *A little added
weight is fine, Jules. Don't panic.* Her plum sweater dress
clung to areas she wasn't used to in the last couple months. *It
was only a piece of pizza for dinner yesterday ... and an omelet for breakfast ... and a hamburger with no bun and salad
for lunch.* She gripped her throat as she added up the calories.

She turned, no longer able to look at herself in the mirror.

A Rescued Love

Slipping her gray leather boots on, she made her way out to find Derek and stopped instantly in her tracks when she found him waiting for her in the entryway. He wore a gray sports jacket over a charcoal dress shirt, dark jeans and black boots. Tall, smooth, gorgeous, and hers.

"Wow, Jules!" He stepped forward with a goofy smile. "You look … well … wow!"

"Thanks. You don't look too shabby yourself."

He smoothed his hands over his jacket. "This old thing?"

"You seriously packed that for our stay?"

"No, I keep a few things in the closet so I don't have to bring clothes back and forth. My mom is picky on what we wear to dinner."

She wrinkled her nose at him. "I feel underdressed."

"You look amazing. You're lucky I'm even letting you leave this cabin. If it were my choice, we'd just spend the evening here together." He pulled her into his chest. "I don't really feel like sharing tonight."

A giggle bubbled. "Since we are stuck being social, you need to prep me for your family. I really don't know much about them."

He ran a hand over his two-day facial growth and released her. "Where to start?" He tapped his chin. "My parents, David and Kathleen, were high school sweethearts. Their families were close friends growing up. Equestrian lifestyle has always been a part of both their lives. They really don't know much different.

"Lauren is a couple years younger than I am and lives in Chicago. She received her MBA from Harvard and is a financial advisor. Her company handles our estate's stocks and funds. Lauren heads up the department. Claire is the youngest and travels between Galena and Lexington. Not only does she help train the horses, but she just finished her degree in equine veterinary medicine at Michigan State University."

"That's quite the list of accomplishments," she noted.

He rubbed the back of his neck, then finally nodded. "Now you can see why my parents are disappointed in my profession." She soaked up the hurt etched in his eyes from years of feeling like a failure and the black sheep of the family.

"Derek," she tugged on his jacket sleeve, "your job is noble, selfless and takes such incredible skill and determination. And you're excellent at it. Don't diminish who you are and who God created you to be, just because that wasn't in your parents' plan."

He raised his hand and gently, with his fingertips calloused from playing the guitar, brushed her cheek. He worked his hand to the back of her neck and pulled her close. "Thank you for saying that." The look in his eyes made her nerves sizzle. "I love you."

Her throat clogged with emotion. Her pulse misfired. This was the moment. It felt right, perfect even. "I love you, too."

His smile almost brought her to her knees. With a further pull on her neck, he brought their faces closer. A moment later his mouth brushed against her trembling lips. He kissed her tenderly at first, then came slightly untamed, a groan escaping from the back of his throat. Deepening the kiss, he nudged her lips open for more. She ran her hands from his waist up to the middle of his back, drawing him closer, if that was possible. Arm around her waist, he walked her backwards until her body bumped into resistance. He pinned her arms back against the wall as his kisses made their way down her neck, rendering her speechless.

When he stopped, his breath came out in ragged gulps. He brought his palms to rest on the sides of her head, kissed her forehead and then laid his forehead against hers. "Woman, you drive me wild." He shook his head. "I'm sorry if I crossed some boundaries. Hearing that you love me, just ... well ... no excuses, I won't let it get that heated again."

He stepped back, creating an unwanted distance between them. She desired to pull him back but respected his limitations. A battle raged in his demeanor. His eyes beckoned her even as he slid his hands into his back pockets.

The regard he held for her emotions and purity didn't go unnoticed, but he was right. If they were going to be able to stay here together, they needed boundaries. And what just happened couldn't happen again, because they might not be strong enough next time.

She held out her hand, a peace offering. "I'm sorry, too." He threaded his fingers into hers. "Let's get to dinner. I have a family to impress."

CHAPTER TWENTY-FIVE

TREVOR RAPPED HIS KNUCKLES AGAINST THE DOOR AND THEN stepped back, creating a little distance for him to be seen clearer through the peep hole. He checked his watch. Only an hour left until he had to meet Jake at the station. This would need to be a quick interview. And one he hoped would be very beneficial to the case. The door swung open, revealing a short, curvy, unnatural blonde with too much red lipstick for his liking. "Emma Zentz?"

"Yes."

"Hi, I'm Detective Trevor Hudson with the Rockford Police Department." Badge lifted for her to see, she nodded. "Thanks for taking the time to meet with me." He extended his hand.

After shaking his hand, she stepped back and opened the door further. "Come on in." She directed him to the living room and ushered him to the couch. "Can I get you something to drink? Water or coffee?"

"Coffee would be great, if it's not too much trouble."

"Not at all. I just made a pot. I'm working the night shift tonight and need the caffeine. How do you like it?"

"With just a little creamer."

She started towards the hallway but snuck a look over her shoulder. "Make yourself comfortable, I'll be right back."

Trevor pulled out his notebook from the inside pocket of

his jacket and clicked on his pen, scribbling on the corner of the page to make sure it worked. He needed this interview to go well. Pressure was high, and he needed a break in the case. Thankfully Derek's plan of getting Jules out of the city seemed to be working. It was late Saturday afternoon, and since Thursday night, there seemed to be no contact or sense that she had been found by their mystery shooter. And he wanted to keep it that way.

Emma sauntered in and handed him a mug of coffee. "Let me know if I need to add more creamer."

"I'm sure this is great." He took a sip. "Yep, perfect. Thank you."

She took a seat at the other end of the couch. Crossing her legs, she leaned back against the arm rest. "What can I do for you, Detective? I know you wanted to discuss Scott, but I'm just not sure how much help I can be."

After another sip of his coffee, he grabbed a coaster from the middle of the coffee table and set his mug down. "I'm not sure if you can help either. At this point in our investigation, we are just meeting with people that were close to Scott to get a better idea of what had been going on in his life over the last year."

She looked at him over the rim of her coffee cup. He couldn't see it, but her eyes gave away her smile. "I'm an open book, Detective. You can ask me anything," she said with a wink.

Oh brother. Was this her attempt at flirting? He hadn't flirted with a woman in over three years. He wouldn't even know how to start. But one thing for sure, he wouldn't be starting now.

"Miss Zentz, how –"

"Emma."

"Okay, Emma, how long have you been an Intensive Care nurse at Rockford Memorial Hospital?"

"This is my fourth year. I started there right after college."

"Tell me about your relationship with Scott." Derek had given him a heads up about her affair with Scott. He was interested as to how Emma would explain it to him.

"We were introduced at a work party in early June and a few weeks later started seeing each other."

"Exclusively?" he baited her.

The look she gave him told him she wasn't stupid. "I'm sure you've been told he was already dating Julia Anderson up on Peds."

"So you started dating him in secret since he was already with someone?"

Her spine straightened as she sat up. "Who are you, my priest?"

"No, but I guess your earlier comment of being an open book doesn't include your relationship with Scott."

Shoulders relaxing, her voice softened. "Listen, I'm not proud of what I did, but it just happened. But who could blame him? She wasn't giving him what he wanted," and then she winked again, "or needed."

Trevor couldn't end this interview fast enough. Time to move away from this subject. "Over the past few days, it has come to our attention that Scott had started taking business trips. Do you know what they were about?"

"Business?" she laughed. "The trip I went on with him had nothing to do with business. And it would surprise me if any of the others did."

Finally he was getting somewhere. "What do you think the trips were about?"

"Gambling," she said matter of factly, "and from what I understood, it was a common thing."

Gambling? How had he not seen this? It was the puzzle piece that made everything fall into place and make sense. Scott's financial roller coaster. His life falling apart. The change in his personality. The code words he had said to Jules about going through some really hard stuff and getting mixed up in bad decisions. How he mentioned that it seemed easier to keep his darkness hidden than to share. Trevor wanted to kick himself for missing the crucial information right in front of him. "Tell me about the trip you took with him." He got his pen ready, not wanting to miss a word she said.

"After Julia broke things off with him, we went public with our relationship. To celebrate, he took me along on one of his trips to Las Vegas. One night I went down on the casino floor with him, but usually he just gave me cash and sent me shopping or to the spa." Eyes closed, she sighed. "Let me tell you, there is nothing better than a *free* Swedish massage."

There was no way he was going down that road with questioning. "Did Scott always go to Las Vegas for his gambling?"

Bottom lip tucked into her top teeth, she took a couple seconds to think about her answer. "No, I think he traveled a lot of different places, but I know he liked Vegas best because he could meet up with an old college friend."

"Did you meet this friend while you were there?" Saliva built up in his mouth over the hope that there could be another person in whom Scott had confided.

"Yeah, he's some plastics doctor with a practice outside the city limits. We met him for dinner one night, and then I went back to the hotel while they went to the casinos." She took a sip of drink. "He didn't make it back to the room until I was getting ready to head for breakfast the next morning."

"Can you remember his name?"

"Randall Masterson – no, McGill – no, hang on." She stood up and walked over to the table next to the front door to retrieve her purse. "He had the audacity to give me his card and say he'd give me a deal if I ever wanted him to work on my nose." She returned, sorting through her overstuffed wallet. "Aha, here it is." She held up a white business card with black lettering. "Randall McGuire." She handed the card to him. "Here, you can have it."

He thanked her. Randall McGuire would be hearing from him soon. "Did Scott ever talk to you about the gambling?"

Emma ran her hands up her arms and shrugged. "Not really. He kept that part of his life to himself. But if you want my opinion, from watching him that weekend, he had a problem – an addiction."

Over the years, Trevor had seen his fair share of gamblers and the destruction it caused. They didn't just ruin their own lives, but also the lives around them. Everyone was affected by the lies and deception, the power of greed, the ache of hopelessness, and the mountain of debt.

He checked his watch. He needed to go if he was going to meet Jake on time. "When and why did you and Scott break up?" He didn't know why, but he felt like the question mattered. Any insight into the man Scott had become over the last year might be helpful.

Hurt flashed across her blue eyes. It didn't take a genius to see that she had also become damaged goods from Scott Henson.

"He broke things off with me about the middle of November." She looked down at the floor and then back at him. "He got all self-righteous on me and said he didn't want the lifestyle he was living anymore. That I just reminded him of the life he wanted to change." She leaned forward, "If you ask me, I think he was trying to win back Julia." She rolled her eyes. "I don't know what he ever saw in that Goody Two Shoes."

The short time he had spent with Jules, he couldn't fault Scott's determination to win her back. Jules was a sweet, attractive, and respectable woman. She deserved a better man than Scott. And in his opinion, Derek appeared to be that great guy for her.

"One last question, Emma. Where were you last Friday around five thirty when Scott was shot in the parking garage?" He didn't think Emma could have done it, but he had to cover all his bases. Just like when he had to ask Jules about owning a gun. Not intended, the question had offended her and really ticked Derek off. He didn't regret doing his job, but sometimes it came at a price when work mingled with friendships.

"I was in the ICU working on a patient that had coded. After the patient stabilized, I exited the room and heard everyone talking about what had happened. You have no idea how fast news can spread through the hospital."

"Thank you for your time, Emma." He slipped his card out of his pocket. "If you think of anything else, please don't hesitate to call." He hoped his statement wouldn't backfire on him later. The last thing he needed was to get a call from Emma in the middle of the night asking what he was wearing.

Emma leaned on the door as she let him out. "You know where to find me, Detective, if you have any more questions."

Waving as he walked away, Trevor already made the decision that a phone call would be sufficient enough if any further questions needed to be asked. Or send Jake. He laughed to himself, imagining the chewing out he'd get from Jake if he let that happen. He got in his car and headed to the station. Twenty minutes later he sat at the conference table across from Jake, folders scattered between them. Jake booted up his laptop.

"You want me to go first, or do you want the honors?" Jake asked.

"I'll go first," Trevor decided. He pulled out his notepad even though he was certain he wouldn't need it, having the interview so fresh in his mind. "I crammed my day full of interviews with people that knew Scott or had worked with him the day he was shot. I really didn't get any helpful information until I interviewed Emma Zentz."

"The woman Scott had an affair with?"

"Yep. Let me tell you, night and day difference to Jules. However, she gave really good insight into Scott's life."

"Like the kind of insight that's going to blow this case wide open?"

"It just might."

Jake leaned forward, eyes tense. "I'm listening."

"Gambling. Scott Henson got caught up in gambling. I don't know how severe it was, but by the looks of his financial statements and Emma's testimony, he was in pretty deep." For the next ten minutes, he went over the interview with Jake, careful not to miss any details.

Jake leaned back against his chair. "Wow. Knowing all that helps make a little more sense of what I found." He grabbed a paper lying on top of the stack. "I was able to pinpoint more directly where he traveled on these trips. Emma was right. He spent a lot of time in Vegas, but he also went to Reno, Los Angeles, Atlantic City, and a couple months ago he even made it to San Jose, Costa Rica."

Trevor leaned his elbows on the table. "Those are all big gambling cities." Chin on his steepled fingers, he continued, "Scott Henson didn't just love gambling, he loved the life-style of gambling. Knowing he traveled to gamble, instead of playing online or in a poker game around here, tells me he didn't play for chump change. He played for stakes so high that when he lost, even a doctor couldn't afford it."

Jake nodded, "His financial records tell us the same."

"So if you're playing for that kind of money, you're going to need help and make some enemies along the way," Trevor rubbed his hands together. "This is good. We have a new angle for the case. And now we might have the motive for our mystery shooter."

"I think I can add even more," Jake offered. "I've also been working on finding out who this Nick Ortega guy really is. Besides the driver's license he gave the car company, he doesn't exist."

"That doesn't surprise me."

"It didn't me either, so I decided to trace back from where Nick came from." He turned his computer for Trevor to see. "Since we assumed he flew in from somewhere, I was able to get the video feed from the Chicago Rockford International Airport." He pushed play. "Here is Nick Ortega exiting Allegiant flight 3747 from Las Vegas to Rockford."

Trevor leaned forward and watched the burly man walk out through the door, throw his carry-on over his shoulder, and set off in a steady pace out of the screen shot. "Can you play it again?" They only had about ten seconds of camera time on him, but he wanted to know every detail. Jake played it two more times as he wrote down his appearance, and anything else he found noteworthy. "So we know he came from Las Vegas, but without his name, it will be nearly impossible to find out who he is."

"Maybe not." Jake shifted through his pile of papers, scanning quickly over the information until he found what he was looking for. "The video shows Nick Ortega coming off the plane, but no Nick Ortega boarded the plane."

"So he checked in under his real identity, but when he landed in Rockford he assumed his fake identity?"

"That's my guess. I was able to get hold of the manifest for Flight 3747. Through process of elimination I got the list of names down to about twenty." He handed Trevor the manifest. "We know it's a male, so I removed all the women. We know the guy is between thirty and fifty years old, so I removed the men outside that age group." He picked up another paper off the table and handed it to him. "Here are the names I came up with. Now, we start the grunt work of eliminating this list down to one."

Trevor couldn't stop the smile that spread over his face.

"I'm really glad you're on my side, Jake."

"Yeah, it's more enjoyable to use my powers for good and not evil."

Trevor laughed. If only everyone in the world would do the same. But because they didn't, that's why he had a job. "Anything stick out to you about any of these names?"

"No. A few of them sat together on the plane, so that makes me think they were probably traveling together and not our guy."

Starting at the top, Trevor scanned the names. Jonathan Rauch. Zachery Worthman. Mark Goertz. Rickardo Yoder. Matthew Wyman. Larry Jon White. Franklin DeLuca. Wait. Franklin DeLuca. Why did that name sound familiar and make his heart beat in overtime? He cracked open the tab on his energy drink and took a sip as he mulled over the name.

"I've seen that look before. What's eating you?" Jake asked.

Trevor stood up. He could think better when he paced. "Franklin DeLuca. The name sounds familiar, but I just can't place why." Legs extended, he walked along the table, wearing down a path in the carpet.

"Maybe you know someone with a name close to his," Jake suggested, "or maybe from an old case?"

Trevor stopped in his tracks from the memory that flooded back. Palms on the table, he met Jake's gaze. "That's it." Pacing again, he continued. "Have you heard of Vince DeLuca?"

"No."

"A couple years back I used to work in St. Louis. We had a case come through on this guy that had been beaten up within an inch of his life. We connected him to the loan shark, Vince DeLuca. However, we were never able to get a conviction because the victim refused to press any charges."

Jake tapped his pen against the table. "I see where you are

going with this, and it all makes sense except for one thing. Let's say Scott needed money and used this DeLuca guy to get it. But why would he turn around and kill Scott? He'd never get his money that way."

Phone in hand, Trevor started dialing. "I don't know, but I'm going to find out." While waiting for the other end to pick up, he started collecting his papers. "Hey Brenda, this is Trevor. I need to be on the next flight to Las Vegas."

CHAPTER TWENTY-SIX

HAND IN HAND, DEREK ESCORTED JULES INTO HIS PARENTS' house. He couldn't believe all that had happened in the last fifteen minutes. Jules had admitted that she loved him. He thought he'd seen it in her smile, in her vulnerability when she shared about her past, in the way she said his name. It was one thing to hope for it, and another to hear it. Like she had breathed life into him.

He'd never felt more alive than he did right now, or conflicted by the crazy hormones rushing through him. He'd always known it, but tonight confirmed it. Julia Anderson was his kryptonite!

Having her in his arms back at the cabin, desire flowed through him like molten lava, slow, steady, covering all his senses ... and his conscience. Sure, what they did wasn't sinful, but the thoughts penetrating his mind were. He had to keep a level head and boundaries in place, or they wouldn't be able to stay at the cabin together.

"We're a little early. I want to show you something."

Her quietness gave him an inkling of her nervousness in meeting his family. An ice breaker might be just what she needed. He led her up the grand staircase, turned left into the west wing and walked to the second door on the right. A long squeak echoed down the hallway as he opened the door.

"Where are we?" she asked.

He flipped on the lights. "My old bedroom." It hadn't changed at all since he left for college. Navy and brown filled the immaculate room, dotted with a western theme. The bed sat in the middle between two night stands. On the adjacent wall above his desk was an arrangement of photos from his years of riding competitions.

Jules' boots clipped along the hardwood floor as she made her way over to his desk. She picked up one of the many trophies sitting on top that he'd left behind. "You didn't tell me you participated in competitions." She bent down and scanned the other trophies. "And by the look of things, you must have been really good."

"I enjoyed it." His fingertips traveled along the photos, bringing back the memories of yesteryears. He stopped at the picture that had him in the middle with his arms around Lauren and Claire. The three musketeers growing up. It was the world against them. Oh, how things had changed. Why hadn't he stayed in better touch with them? Sure, he had called them a few times over the last year, made sure to send them birthday presents, and visited when in the area, but he hadn't gone out of his way to invest in their lives. Too scared to be roped back into his father's grip, he kept his sisters at arm's length.

"Why did you stop?"

He turned to face her. "It started to not be fun anymore. My dad pushed too hard and set expectations I couldn't fulfill. Plus, I started college, and once I got away from here, it was just easier to stay away."

Trophy back in place, she walked along the photos with a soft smile in place. A few times she looked over her shoulder at him as she soaked in his memories. She pointed to the picture at the far right. "Tell me about this one."

He smiled, remembering that day. "That was my fourteenth birthday, and my parents gave me my horse, Captain." Eyes locked on the photo, he thought back to the years he had

184

with Captain. Some people couldn't understand the connection a person could have with an animal. For years, Captain had been his best friend. Whenever he had a bad day or just needed a break, he'd jump on his back and ride for hours.

Jules stepped closer and laid her head on his shoulder. "Do you miss it?"

"Miss what?"

"This." She pointed to the wall. "The horses, the riding, the lifestyle. Is there a part of you that wishes you could have it back?"

That was the million dollar question – literally. The question that kept him restless all last night as he mulled over his dad's proposition. He had the opportunity to trade in his life now and come back. The issue he struggled with was, *should* he come back whether he wanted to or not? "I miss the horses and riding." He wrapped his arm around her. "My dream would be to find my own place out in the country with a couple horses of my own. Nothing big, just something for enjoyment. A place for my kids to grow up and share the love of horses with me."

She turned into him and placed her hands on his chest. "I think that's a great dream."

He looked over the pictures again and then caught her gaze. "Yeah, but sometimes dreams can't always become a reality." Pulling her in for a hug, he placed his chin on the top of her head, drawing in a deep breath of her clean smell. He needed to tell her about his talk with his dad, but he couldn't bring himself to say the words. Already overwhelmed with being here, how would she respond if she knew he had been considering moving back? Could their relationship survive the distance? Would she ever be willing to move here if he chose to return?

"C'mon, we better get downstairs." He hooked an arm around her waist and led her out of the room.

At the main level, they followed the voices coming from the dining room. Derek slipped his hand into Jules' and squeezed as they crossed the threshold. He couldn't believe the changes that had been made in the room since he had been here last. A dark, rectangular wooden table sat in the middle of the room surrounded by eight high-back chairs. A glass chandelier and taupe-colored walls lightened the once-darkened room. His dad stood at the bar pouring a drink, listening to Claire as she spoke.

"I know you don't agree, Dad, but I think it would be good for Hugo to skip the race next weekend. His leg hasn't completely healed yet, and if you want him to have a chance to win next –" Claire stopped mid-sentence when they walked in. "Derek!" she shrieked, moving around their dad and running full bore into his chest.

He laughed, picked her up and spun her around. "Hey, squirt! Good to see you," he spoke the endearment as he placed her feet back down on the ground. He soaked in the sight of her. She still had the same short, curly brunette hair, button nose and sparkling eyes that radiated the fullness of life.

Claire kept him in a tight hug around his waist, refusing to let him go. "I've missed you."

Arms around her slim shoulders, he agreed, "Me, too."

His mom pushed through the swinging door that stood between the dining room and kitchen. "Derek."

"Hi, Mom." He left Claire's side and met his mom halfway.

Reaching up, she placed both hands on the sides of his face. "You look handsome as always. Thanks for taking the time to join us for dinner." He paused, not expecting the amiable words. Maybe his sisters had been right and their mom had mellowed some over the last couple of years. Her eyes shifted over his shoulder. "Are you going to introduce us to your guest?"

Jules! He had left her standing alone at the doorway. Quickly he moved back to her side. Her stance was rigid with her shoulders back and arms tight to her sides. He put an arm around her, "This is my girlfriend, Julia Anderson." He had never, in all his life, been prouder than he was at this moment. With Jules by his side, he felt like he could conquer the world. "This is my dad, David, my mom, Kathleen and my sister, Claire."

Muscles relaxed under his touch as Jules flashed the smile that had stolen his heart. She stepped forward, shaking each of their hands. "It's so nice to meet you all." She turned to Kathleen. "Your home is so beautiful, and I love what you've done with this room. You have quite the touch to take such a big room and make it feel so homey."

"Thank you, Julia. I see you have good taste in decorating, and men."

Jules grabbed hold of the crook of his arm. "I seem to think so." She looked up at him and smiled.

Maybe he had been overreacting with introducing her to his family. So far, so good.

"Derek told me you were in an accident this week. How are you feeling?" David asked before he took a swig of his drink.

"I'm feeling better. A little sore, but that's to be expected."

"Is that what the cut above your eye is from?" Claire asked.

"Yes." She touched the spot. "It looks worse than it feels. I figured I'd wear purple to match the bruise. Go big or go home, right?"

Claire laughed and hugged Jules. "I like her, Derek. She's a keeper."

He had to agree.

"Hello?" Lauren's voice beckoned from the entryway.

"We're in the dining room!" Claire shouted as she pulled

on Jules' arm. "C'mon, let's grab our seats. I want to make sure I get to sit by you."

Derek gave his sister a wink as she gave Jules no other option but to follow. Claire had a way of making everyone feel comfortable. She was the baby of the family – everyone's favorite she would claim – and in honesty, probably the truth. Full of love and laughter. When Claire entered a room, the party started.

"Hey, everyone!" Lauren called as she stepped into the room. "Look who I brought."

Dread engulfed him as the familiar tall blonde walked in behind Lauren. "Chelsea." Saying her name sucked all the air from his lungs. Everyone paused. Eyes darted around the room. He turned to find Jules staring down their new, unexpected guest.

Chelsea didn't seem to catch on to the awkward situation. She stepped forward, invading his space. "Hey Derek, it's really good to see you." Her fingers played with the top of his hair. "You're growing your hair longer. I like it."

He stepped back. "I didn't realize you were coming."

Kathleen stepped in between them. "I didn't either, but we're so glad you're here." She gave Chelsea a hug. "Take a seat at the table, and I'll get another place setting. Our chef, Annabelle, made enough for an army. We'll have plenty!"

Derek caught the confused look Lauren gave their dad.

"Yes, let's all have a seat," David said, gesturing for them to make their way to the table. Derek gave Lauren a quick hug and then took his seat next to Jules, who had Claire on her left. Lauren sat across the table from him, and Chelsea in the middle, across from Jules. His dad took a seat at the far end of the table. His mom made her way back into the room with an extra plate, utensils and glass filled with water for Chelsea. Annabelle followed right on her heels with the first course of salad.

"Lauren, this is my girlfriend, Julia." He looked to Chelsea. "Chelsea, do you remember Julia?" He put his arm on the back of her chair. He didn't want to be a jerk, but a line needed to be drawn in the sand immediately before anything got out of hand.

Chelsea nodded. "Yes, I met you at Matt and Ava's engagement party, right? It's nice to see you again." Her southern drawl curled around her words.

Jules folded her hands into her lap, knuckles white. "Nice to see you, too." She paused.

"So how do you all know each other?" Only he would recognize the rise in her voice that betrayed her lack of confidence.

Did someone turn up the heat? Sweat trickled between his shoulder blades. Of course he had to wear a jacket that turned into an inferno during stressful situations. Why did Lauren bring Chelsea? He intended to ask that very question when they had no ears listening.

Lauren took the lead on the explanation. "Chelsea grew up in Lexington. We spent every summer during high school together at a riding camp. When I started working in Chicago as a financial advisor, I was able to get Chelsea a job there also. I introduced Derek and Chelsea last spring when we all headed down to watch the Kentucky Derby together."

"Hmm, small world," Jules squeaked out.

Derek swallowed. And getting smaller.

"Julia," Claire interrupted. "Tell us about yourself."

She finished her bite of salad and took a drink. "Oh, well, there isn't much to tell. I grew up in Rockford and still live there. I'm a pediatric nurse at Rockford Memorial Hospital."

"That's so cool you work with kids. I don't know you well, but I'm sure you're great with them. You have a sweet smile that probably puts them at ease," Claire chirped. He wanted to hug Claire.

"Derek, how did you and Julia meet?" The question came from his mom.

They looked at each other and smiled. He'd leave out the minor detail of pursing her while still "technically" with Chelsea. "Through our mutual friends, Matt and Ava. I had been trying to get Jules to date me for months, and just last week I finally wore her down." Jules jabbed her shoulder into his. Everyone laughed, except for Chelsea and his dad.

Annabelle brought out the main course of roast, carrots, potatoes and homemade rolls. Derek noticed Jules squint and rub her temple. He leaned in, hoping not to draw attention. "Are you getting another headache?"

"Yes, but I left my pain killers back at the cabin." She patted his hand. "I'm fine, really."

"Let me see if I can find you something in the kitchen." He stood up, excusing himself before she could protest. Inside the empty kitchen, he opened the cupboard by the sink, hoping his mom still kept the pain reliever medication there. The door swung open behind him. Lauren stood with her hands on her hips, clearly distraught.

"Derek, I'm so sorry. I had no idea you were bringing someone to dinner. I never would have brought Chelsea if I'd known."

Bottle in hand, he pressed his fingers on the lid and twisted. "It's okay, Lauren." He took out two pills and returned the bottle. Leaning back against the counter, he folded his arms across his chest. "Can I ask you something, though?"

She approached. "Sure."

"Why did you bring her? Was it an attempt to try and get us back together?" He didn't want to be annoyed with her, but he couldn't hide his irritation over the situation. As if he wasn't loaded down enough with the case, keeping Jules safe, and making a huge life-altering decision, he had to add an uncomfortable dinner with his ex into the mix. Maybe he needed

190

a couple pills for himself.

"Derek. That's the thing." She stepped closer and he caught fire in her eyes. "It wasn't my idea to bring her. Dad called me this morning and asked me to bring Chelsea along."

What? His blood pressure spiked. Heat flooded his face. "Unbelievable!" He hissed through a clenched jaw. He turned and gripped the counter with his hands and hung his head. His dad had finally crept to an all-time low in trying to dictate his life. David Brown held no regard for anyone but himself. He wanted to pick up the three layer chocolate cake perched on the counter and throw it across the room.

"You believe me, right?" she asked, uncertain of the direction of his anger.

He straightened and laid his hand on her shoulder. "Of course."

"Did Dad know Julia would be here tonight?" He heard the hope, the wanting to believe this had all been a misunderstanding. Except the reality of it smothered all wishful possibilities. They had both been played.

"Yes, I told him last night." Along with his foolish mistake of announcing his feelings for Jules to the one person that would use that vulnerability against him. His dad knew how he felt for Jules, but that obviously hadn't stopped him from setting this trap. "Let's keep this between us for now, okay? I don't want Jules to find out. That would crush her."

"I won't say anything." She turned to leave, but stopped. "For what it's worth, I like Julia. I can tell she makes you happy."

"Thanks, Ren."

Lauren cocked her head to the side. "I hate when you call me that."

He laughed. "I know. What kind of older brother would I be if I didn't annoy you every once in a while?"

Lauren stood facing him for a moment, a slight frown

damping her features. "Can I be honest with you?"

"Would it matter if I said no?"

She smirked. "Probably not." After a deep breath, she continued. "I know things didn't work out with you and Chelsea, but selfishly I wish they had."

The admission confused him. "I thought you said you liked Julia?"

"I do!" She held up a hand when he tried to further question her. "It's just … It was nice having you back in my life again. When you dated Chelsea I saw you more. I know we didn't get together every time you came to Chicago to see her, but I haven't seen you since the two of you broke up." A sigh escaped. "I guess all I'm saying is I miss you."

The admission sucked the air from his lungs and crushed his heart. He'd failed her. Selfishness over his need for space had hurt her. No excuses, he had to make it right. He stepped up to Lauren and pulled her into a hug. "I'm sorry. Things will be different from now on. I promise." He leaned back to look her in the eyes. "How about Jules and I come some Saturday next month and take you out for dinner?"

Tension in his neck eased from her smile. "Sure. But my town, my treat. A new Indian restaurant just opened down the street from my condo. It's amazing."

"Sounds great." Once the case wrapped up with the shooter in custody, a weekend in Chicago with Jules sounded pretty amazing.

Derek plastered a smile on his face as he followed Lauren out of the kitchen and returned to the table, catching Jules in the middle of a story.

"… then Ava never showed up. We had no idea where she was. Scariest time of my life until she was found. From the beginning we assumed she had been kidnapped by that Chad Taylor guy I told you about that had threatened her, but –"

"When I talked with Ava," Chelsea interrupted and continued as if Jules didn't matter, "over the course of our conversation, she told me about Chad Taylor, but I didn't know she had been kidnapped." Chelsea exclaimed. "How scary!"

Leave it to Chelsea to control the conversation and make digs against Jules whenever possible. Derek hadn't known that Ava and Chelsea stayed in touch, and it didn't matter to him, but by Jules' wide eyes, she didn't seem aware of that piece of information either. He held out his hand and slipped the pills over to Jules, figuring she needed them even more now.

She leaned in and whispered, "What's wrong?"

"Nothing." He pressed a smile.

"That's your fake smile."

"I'm fine," he falsely reassured and kissed her cheek. He couldn't even look in his dad's direction. They would definitely be having a little talk about what he did, but now wasn't the place or time.

Chelsea cleared her throat and with her attention turned on Derek, she asked, "What part did you play in finding Ava? I've seen you in work mode, Sergeant. I don't imagine you stayed on the sidelines." Maybe he was reading into it, granted he was on edge, but the smile Chelsea gave made him feel like her intentions in that statement were solely to remind Jules of their past relationship.

"I was on the team that took down Chad Taylor and joined the team that searched for Ava."

Jules gripped his bicep. "What he's not telling you is he chased down Chad Taylor through the woods and apprehended him."

Out of the corner of his eye, he caught her mischievous grin. Two could play at this game. "And what Jules isn't telling you, is that when Ava was found, Jules gave her medical treatment that spared her extra days of recovery."

"Sounds to me like the two of you make a pretty good

team," Claire assessed.

"Derek, I'll be honest, and I'm a little embarrassed to say this, but I just figured you wrote tickets and covered accidents," his mom confessed. A guilty look clouded her dark brown eyes. It didn't surprise him. No one in the family had really taken the time to ask and he never felt the need to defend his profession.

"Same for me," Claire added. "What does a day entail for you?"

"Well, I'm a Sergeant now. I have a team of officers under me that I train. Every morning I make out duty assignments, prepare a shift briefing and make preparations to relieve the officers currently working. I get information from the previous shift Sergeant on his shift's occurrences. From then on, every day is different, depending on the calls we get."

"He is also on the SWAT team," Jules interjected.

"I remember when we were together and the calls I'd get from you after you'd been on a SWAT mission and the stories you'd tell me," Chelsea smiled and lifted her eyebrows. "It was so hard knowing the danger you put yourself in every day."

Seriously, Chelsea? Was she on his dad's payroll now? He remembered those calls as well. He'd come home, take a shower, and depending on the time, call Chelsea. Excitement laced with exhaustion made him on edge. Having someone to talk to at the end of the day and process what happened had calmed him. He had yet to have one of those phone calls with Jules, but he looked forward to it.

"Are you in a lot of danger when you go on these SWAT calls?" his mom asked with a hint of worry in her voice. This was the most his family had ever asked about his job. Maybe after this conversation his family would see how much he loved his profession and fully support him.

"Depends on the call. Last week I went because we had a

high profile case that needed a warrant. I was just there as a precaution in case things got out of hand. However, there are times I'm put in danger, but that's what I train for, and I take that training very seriously."

"Kind of like the case you're on now?" His dad gave him a questioning eye.

"Dad." Derek's tone gave a warning.

"You see, Derek isn't just here to see his long lost family, he's here on a case to protect Julia."

All eyes beamed in Derek's direction.

"David, what are you talking about?" Kathleen's eyes darted between the two men.

"Julia is a witness to a murder, and Derek brought her here to the cabin to keep her safe from the shooter they assume is after her." His dad cocked his head with a look of dissension. "How trained are you if this shooter walked into this room right now?"

"That's enough, Dad!" Derek blinked twice and breathed in through his nose a few times to settle his anger. Leave it to his dad to ruin a nice family dinner. Jules squeezed his hand. Eyes full of panic searched his.

"Derek? Julia? Is this true?" Lauren asked, worry knotting her brows.

He never should have told his dad – mistake number two. Number one was when he talked himself into trusting him. He wouldn't make that error in judgment again. But right now, he had to put out the fire his father started.

"Listen, I didn't say anything because this is a sensitive case and there was no need to worry all of you. Without going into many details … yes, Jules did witness a doctor at the hospital getting shot. We don't know who the shooter is, and until we do, I wanted to take every precaution to keep her safe."

"Wait. Did your accident have something to do with this, Julia?" Claire asked.

Jules gave a slow shrug. "Maybe? Someone ran me off the road Thursday night."

"Derek, if this shooter is after Julia, how do you know he didn't follow you here?" His mom closed a hand around her throat.

When they left Rockford, he had kept an eye out for anyone that could be trailing them. He even had Matt keep a distance behind them at least an hour out of the city to make sure. He had complete confidence that he had all his bases covered.

"Mom, everyone is safe." He turned to give his dad a glare that could melt rock. "There is no reason to get upset. I've got everything under control." Except for the anger that brewed in his heart. "Jules and I are staying at the cabin, and if anything seems off, we'll leave, or I'll get you out of here."

His mom looked between him and Jules. "I didn't realize that the two of you are staying at the cabin together. Alone." Her lips thinned and gave him the disapproving look she mastered during his teenage years.

"Mom, it's not like that. We aren't here for a romantic getaway. We're here to keep her alive, nothing more." He hated how he felt like he'd been caught with his hand in the cookie jar. He didn't feel the need to defend himself, but he didn't want assumptions to shadow Jules' integrity. He'd defend her until his last breath.

"Are you two even together, or is this a pretext for an undercover story?" Chelsea asked, a hopeful look in her eyes.

"Of course we're together." Quick to answer, Jules slipped her hand into his. "I'm sure this is all very overwhelming and confusing. Derek never meant to deceive you. If anyone should be fearful of danger here, it would be me," she looked at him and smiled, "and I'm not. Derek is an excellent cop with superb instincts and skills, with a rare passion for serving others. As for us staying in the cabin, he has been nothing but respectful." Head swiveling between his parents, she added,

"You raised an amazing man who deserves your praise."

Silence spread across the table. He wanted to hug Jules for sticking up for him, but Claire beat him to it. "You're right, Julia. I'm pretty proud of my big brother. So proud, I think he deserves some chocolate cake." Claire jumped up from her chair, disappeared into the kitchen and returned seconds later with the cake.

Dessert went cautiously well with small talk of everyone's plans they had over New Year's Eve. During his second to last bite his cell phone rang. Trevor's name popped up in the ID. He leaned over, speaking quietly into Jules' ear, "It's Trevor. I'll be right back." He stood and excused himself.

"Derek, we don't take phone calls during dinner," his dad reprimanded.

"Sorry, but I have to take this." He rushed out of the room, down the hallway and into his dad's office to ensure privacy. "Hey, Trevor. What do you have?"

CHAPTER TWENTY-SEVEN

JULES SAT AT THE DINING ROOM TABLE SIPPING HER COFFEE, TRYING to keep a calm demeanor after Derek left the room. Sitting here without him felt like living out her old teenage nightmare of walking into school and realizing she still had on pajamas with no bra – uneasy with herself, uncomfortable, and out of place with all eyes on her. Now if only she could wake up and be in the safety of her bed. The pleasant evening had unraveled quickly, starting with Chelsea and ending with the blow-up over why they were here. Tension sparked, igniting uneasiness around the table.

"So Julia, do you have any siblings?" Claire asked.

"I had a younger sister, Jenna. But she passed away when I was eight."

"Oh, I'm sorry to hear that. I'm sure that was very difficult for your family."

"Yes, it was devastating." *Please don't ask me about my parents,* she mentally begged, hoping they wouldn't uncover her past.

"Even though I haven't found my perfect guy doesn't mean I don't like a good love story. I love to hear how people met. So you and Derek met through mutual friends. How did your parents meet?" Claire inquired, an innocent smile spreading.

Maybe she could strategically push the subject away from her family. "From what Derek tells me, we have something in common. My parents were high school sweethearts as well."

"Oh, so your parents knew a good thing when they saw it, too?" Kathleen laughed, her eyebrows wiggled at David. The man produced the softest smile. David Brown might be headstrong, but there was no denying the love he had for his wife. "We've been married for thirty-two years!" Kathleen said proudly. "How about your parents?"

And backfire.

Jules quickly took a bite of her chocolate cake to give her a few minutes of chew time before having to answer. Oh wow, she couldn't remember the last time she'd splurged and had chocolate. The soft cake melted in her mouth. *Focus, Jules!* How could she dodge this question? Thoughts of pretending to pass out unashamedly flooded her mind. If she leaned forward and fell to the right, her head shouldn't hit anything…

She took a sip of her drink and faced the inevitable. "My dad left us when I was nine. My parents divorced shortly after. They couldn't get past Jenna's death."

David tapped his fork on the plate. "So, not really much in common with us after all." He turned to the gorgeous blonde Barbie doll that sat across the table from her. "Chelsea, how are your parents doing? We haven't seen them since their thirtieth anniversary party last month."

Jules sat in shock as Chelsea updated him on how great they were doing and the house they just bought on the beach in Hilton Head. In his subtle way, David Brown had put her in her place. She got the message loud and clear.

"Before I forget, I have an announcement." David lifted up his glass. "After a year of uncertainty, Kathleen and I have decided to move permanently to Lexington."

"What!" Lauren exclaimed. "When did you decide?"

"Last week." Kathleen answered. "I can't believe we're actually going to do it. I've wanted to move for years. I'll miss this place, but at our age, Lexington fits us better, and your dad needs to relieve some stress."

"My parents will be so happy to have you around more," Chelsea added.

Jules tuned out the voices around her, wondering if Derek knew about this information. Probably not. He wasn't close to his parents or a part of their daily lives. If his sisters didn't know, surely he didn't either. Claire cleared her throat, pulling Jules out of her cloud of thoughts.

"Who are you going to have run the Galena estate?" Claire asked. Jules noted a trace of hope in her question as she inched to the edge of her seat, eyes focused on her father.

"That's the best news of all. I've asked Derek to take over. I should have waited to give him the honors of giving us his answer, but I'm certain he will accept."

Jules' head swam. It didn't make sense. Why would Derek not have told her? Had he realized the same thing she had long ago, that she didn't belong here? That she wasn't good enough for the Brown family? Surveying the table, Jules took in everyone's different responses.

Kathleen clapped her hands over her mouth. "Oh, that is exciting news!"

Claire simply sat back against the back of the chair, eyes filling with tears. Chelsea shared a smile with David.

Lauren drew her brows together, "This is a surprise. I thought he loved his job?"

Reaching out, Kathleen grabbed hold of Lauren's hand. "Maybe he's finally realized this is where he belongs."

David checked his watch. "In fact, I'll go find Derek and let him do the honors." Abruptly he left the room, leaving the women to process their own emotions from the grenade he just threw.

§ § § § §

"**T**REVOR, THIS IS GREAT NEWS!" DEREK PUMPED HIS FIST IN the air. A Nevada license picture matched the same picture they had of Nick Ortega. They had a name. They had their man.

Franklin DeLuca.

"I thought you might like that. Called you the second I had any free time," he said, sounding out of breath.

"So you're on your way to Vegas?"

"Yes. I'm jogging into the airport as we speak, trying not to miss my flight. I have a couple interviews scheduled tomorrow. One is with an old college buddy of Scott Henson and the other is with Vince DeLuca, cousin of Franklin."

"How can I help?" Missing all the action wasn't his preference. He wished he could tag along on the trip to Las Vegas, but he wasn't trusting Jules' safety to anyone else. Despite having a good idea who the shooter was, they unfortunately didn't have a clue where to find him. No, top priority had to stay with keeping Jules safe. Despite his offer, Trevor would agree.

"You're doing it! We're moving fast here, my friend. Sit tight, I'll keep you updated."

Derek ended the call and took a seat in his dad's leather wing back chair. Elbows on his knees, he dipped his head to rest into his open palm. *Thank you, God.* Trevor had a lead. A good one. At least something was going well tonight.

Backtracking through the evening, his anger emerged with a vengeance, thinking about what his father had done. He deliberately had Chelsea come to dinner when he knew Jules would be here with no regard of what Derek wanted or had chosen for himself. Of course, David Brown had overstepped the boundaries many times in the past. This time was different, unforgivable. He had been taught early on that his father demanded respect. You only shared your opinion when asked. Well, his father would be hearing his opinion tonight, whether he wanted to or not.

He needed to get back to dinner and relieve Jules, but that meant he had to be in the same room as his father. He leaned back against the chair, unable to leave this spot. He just needed a minute. Or two. His eyes roamed the ceiling. If only God would write the answer in the white paint as to what his decision should be. After what his dad just pulled, he should refuse the job offer, but he knew better than to make a decision out of pure anger. A knock at the door interrupted his thoughts. His dad took a step inside the office and shut the door.

"Dad, I could use a minute alone."

"If case you forgot, you're in my office."

Derek pushed up tall. "Fine. Whatever. I'm going to head back."

"Wait." His dad placed a hand on his arm as he tried to walk past. Derek shrugged it off. "We need to talk first."

"Trust me, Dad. You don't want to talk to me right now."

"While you were off taking your phone call, I told every-one about your mother and I moving and the offer I made you. I think tonight would be a great time to share the good news of you taking over the Galena ranch."

Derek stepped back, processing the ridiculous string of words his dad had just spoken. He had told the entire table about the offer. Had probably gotten his mom's hopes up and confused Jules in the process. He knew he should have told her. The last thing he wanted was for her to hear it from his dad.

"Dad, you shouldn't have done that. I told you I would think about it."

"Well, time is up."

"It hasn't even been twenty-four hours. I'm in the middle

of a huge case. I can't make a decision like this right now."

"What more is there to think about, Derek? This is your inheritance, what you were born to do."

"Don't pressure me to make a decision right now, or you won't like my answer. I need time to think about it."

"You're so stubborn. Why can't you see that this," David swung his arms around, "this is where you are supposed to be?"

"You think you know everything don't you, Dad? Especially about *my* life."

"When it comes to what is best for you, yes."

"Like bringing Chelsea here?" He caught the surprise flash across David's face. "Lauren told me you called and asked her to bring Chelsea tonight." The deception caused his throat to tighten. "How could you do that, Dad?"

"I just wanted you to see her again. To see how Chelsea is a better fit for you."

"No, Dad. You just see Chelsea as a better fit for this family."

§ § § § §

WHAT WAS TAKING DEREK SO LONG ON THE PHONE? DID Trevor have more information for them or was he just breaking the news that the case continued to stagnate? While waiting for him to return, Jules tried to appear current on the latest fashions Lauren and Chelsea were discussing, sitting in their size two, tight-as-skin designer jeans with shirts her salary could never afford. She was pretty sure Claire had on a cashmere cardigan. Cashmere. How crazy would she look if she rubbed her cheek along Claire's arm? She, of course, would draw the line at purring. She wasn't being shallow. Seriously, she wasn't. Okay, maybe a little, but she was certain her awkwardness at the table went much farther than clothes and her lack of fashion sense. It was the conversations. The inside jokes. The fact that she sat amongst a table of extroverts, and all she wanted to do was crawl back to the cabin for a little alone time. Now, if she had been sitting around with a bunch of her pediatric patients, she would have nailed it and probably been asked for autographs at the end. But no. She sat mute as the women talked around her in circles, reminding her of how out of place she was here.

She wished Ava was here. Ava knew how to work a crowd and could, at the very least, handle these women and help move the conversation to something neutral. She longed to have someone on her side with their own inside jokes and their own familiar brand of comfort. Now they were talking about Chelsea's apartment and all the remodels she had been doing on it.

"Lauren, remember when Derek and I met you at Tinley Park this past summer to watch the Maroon 5 concert?" Jules' ears perked up to Chelsea's question.

"Yeah."

"It was that weekend I decided to redecorate my apartment. I can't believe it has taken me so long to finish," Chelsea whined. Well, she didn't really whine. But anything that came out of the woman's mouth just annoyed Jules.

"Wait, you went to a Maroon 5 concert without me?" Claire piped in. "You know that is my favorite band."

"It was totally last minute," Lauren assured. "Derek had a high school friend that worked there and scored us some amazing tickets."

"And backstage passes," Chelsea added a bit too enthusiastically.

Claire clasped her hand over her heart. "You are kidding me! Derek always has a way of orchestrating the best things."

Finally, something she could chime into. "I agree. When Matt and Ava's wedding plans had to be postponed, he took it upon himself to make sure they ended up having an amazing wedding. He coordinated and helped finance the ceremony on the beach in Key West."

"Oh, I love the beach!" Chelsea revealed in her southern drawl. At first Jules had liked her accent, now it just sounded nasally, like she needed to blow her nose. Would it be rude if she offered her a tissue?

"One weekend Derek surprised me and planned an entire day of riding horses on the beach at Lake Michigan. It was so thoughtful and romantic."

Forget the Kleenex, now Jules wanted to give her a throat punch. Chelsea's comment silenced the room. No one made eye contact. No one offered a transition into another subject. Maybe now would be a good time to excuse herself and find Derek. Before she could, Claire turned to her. "Speaking of horses, do you enjoy riding?"

Oh, you know. I'm only terrified of them. The first and only time I've ridden a horse, I fell off and nearly killed myself. Had I been the one Derek took to the beach, I'm sure my horse would have taken off into the water and drowned me. How on earth did she answer that question without sounding like an idiot? She twisted her cloth napkin in her hands to release some pent up energy. "I have only gone horseback riding once. I don't have much of an opinion about it yet." *Besides that, I hate it, and it makes me panic thinking about getting on a horse again.*

"Where did you ride?" Lauren asked.

"Here, actually. In the fall Derek brought me, Ava, and Matt on a Saturday to ride."

"Oh, fun!" Claire clapped her hands. "Which horse did you pick?"

This conversation needed to come to a halt soon. "Derek picked Gracie for me."

Claire's face softened at the name. "Oh, Gracie is such a

great mare and trail rider. How did it go?"

She could lie. Wanted to, all the while staring down Chelsea. *Oh, it went great. Derek and I talked and laughed as we rode along, holding hands into the sunset.* "Well, it could have gone better. Gracie got spooked and threw me off. I ended up twisting my ankle, and we had to head home."

"I remember Henry telling me about that. I'm glad you were okay," Kathleen interjected.

Of course Henry told Derek's parents. And probably the rest of the staff. Chances were good she had been the source of conversation for days.

"Wait, isn't Gracie old as dirt? How could you fall off her?" Chelsea eyed her.

Jules took a deep breath before she responded. "A storm was coming in, and Gracie got spooked. She took off running and I couldn't hold on."

Claire placed her hand on Jules' forearm. "I'm so sorry. I'm sure Derek picked her because she is super easy to ride, but she does have a flaw when it comes to storms," she smiled. "It could have happened to anyone."

"I hope you give riding another chance, Julia." Kathleen said. "When Derek returns here, horses will once again be his life. *If* your relationship makes it, horses will be a part of yours also."

Thanks for the vote of confidence, Kathleen. But her remark held some bitter truth. What if Derek decided to come back here? What place would she have in his life? Anxiety clawed its way into her chest. Her heart pounded. Her breathing constricted. Her skin crawled. Her stomach lurched. She had to get out of this room.

"Thanks, Kathleen. I'll keep that in mind." She stood on shaking legs and pressed a smile upon her face. "Excuse me. I need to use the restroom."

"Yes, of course." Kathleen pointed to the dining room's

French doors. "Turn right, go down the hallway, third door on your right."

Jules swiped the sweat off her brow and paused outside the doors for a moment to catch her breath. She couldn't go back into that room. She just couldn't. Following the directions she'd been given, she started down the hallway. Halfway down the hall, she overheard Derek's voice coming from behind a closed door. Thank goodness. Maybe she could sit in on the rest of his conversation with Trevor and then ask him to take her back to the cabin. With her fist raised to knock, she stopped short when she heard David's voice.

"You're so stubborn. Why can't you see that this – this is where you are supposed to be?"

"You think you know everything, don't you, Dad? Especially about *my* life!" Derek snapped back.

"When it comes to what is best for you, yes."

Jules needed to leave. It wasn't right to eavesdrop on their conversation.

"Like bringing Chelsea here?" Lead filled her shoes from Derek's comment and rendered her unable to move. "Yep, Lauren told me you called and asked her to bring Chelsea tonight." She leaned into the door, pressing her ear against the wood. "How could you do that, Dad?"

"I just wanted you to see her again. To see how Chelsea is a better fit for you."

"No, Dad. You just see Chelsea as a better fit for this family."

"Oh course Chelsea is a better fit for this family – and you! And the sooner you see it, the better. Sure, Julia is attractive and nice, but if you think some poor girl from a broken home is going to marry my son and inherit this estate, you're wrong. The two of you will never last. Mark my words."

She couldn't listen anymore. Hot tears pricked behind her eyes, blurring her vision as she stumbled to find the bathroom.

Once inside, she shut the door, locked it, and dropped to her knees. With her back pressed against the door, she drew her legs up and encircled her arms around them. Her cry erupted into the crevice of her chest from the disappointment of how the night had gone. The realization that she didn't belong here. The awareness that everyone, especially David Brown, felt the same way. The understanding that at some point, whether Derek knew it now or not, he would see that they were too different. The sadness of no longer allowing Derek in her life. The end of something beautiful. All of it caused the demon inside her to crawl over to the toilet and stick her finger down her throat. A sense of control strengthened her with each gag.

CHAPTER TWENTY-EIGHT

DEREK BALLED HIS FISTS TO HIS SIDES, WILLING HIMSELF NOT TO hit his father. He was a bigger man than to allow violence to get his point across – but not big enough to stop the thoughts of losing a fist in that smug facial expression.

"Dad, don't speak of Jules that way." He turned, stepping towards the door. He knew his limitations and he couldn't hold the rein of his tongue much longer.

"Where are you going? I'm not finished with this conversation."

Derek turned on his heels, glaring in his dad's direction. "But I am." With that he exited the office, slamming the door behind him. Palm extended against the wall in front of him, he laid his head on his arm. He needed to collect himself before returning to the dining room. Jules would sense his tension and ask what was wrong. How would he explain to her what had happened without pushing her away and making her feel badly about herself? He pushed those thoughts aside. For now, he just had to get through the rest of this evening. Straightening tall, the sound of crying led him further down the hallway. He stopped in front of the bathroom door.

His pulse quickened. Jules? Desire to protect her swelled in his chest. What had happened to make her cry? Then a sound that dropped his stomach to his knees trickled through the door. Gagging.

He pounded on the door. "Jules, are you okay?" Only silence met him in return. His voice softened. "Jules?" Another gag.

"Go away, Derek," Jules said without much conviction, as if giving up a fight before even fighting.

He turned the knob. Locked. He palmed the door, whispering into the crack. "Jules, please let me in."

Nothing but coughing and gagging, and then, "Derek, just leave me alone."

She obviously didn't know him well. He jogged to the kitchen to retrieve the tool his mom had used in their growing up years when one of them locked a door. He found it in the battery drawer, where it had probably sat for the last fifteen years. He rushed back to the bathroom to hear her crying even harder. The toilet flushed. He waited a moment and then knocked on the door. "Jules, I'm coming in."

As he opened the door, she protested, "No."

Too late. He locked the door behind him. Jules sat with her back against the vanity, her shoulders slumped forward, head down. Crouched down on the balls of his feet, he placed his hands on her shoulders. Maybe she had eaten something that didn't settle well? That had to be it, right? "Jules, Honey, are you sick?"

She looked up at him; face swollen, eyes rimmed in red, cheeks wet with tears. He pulled away a strand of hair matted to her face.

"No." Jules turned her head away.

What had happened in the last half hour to cause this? He stood, plucked a tissue from the box, and laid it in her hand. His chest tightened as he took a washcloth and dampened it with cold water. Something was wrong. It didn't take cop instincts to determine he wouldn't like the reason behind her tears. She took the washcloth he offered and held it over her eyes. Hiccups punctuated her deep breaths. Jules wanted to be alone, she made that very clear. But he couldn't leave her. Not like this.

"Babe, what's wrong?"

She waited so long to respond, he wondered if she would. "I don't think we should be together anymore."

Derek rocked back on his heels from the utter shock of her words. His mind buzzed with panic over her admission. "What are you talking about?" She seemed fine when he left to take the call from Trevor. "Did someone say something that upset you?"

He'd put all his money on his dad. He couldn't see Lauren or Claire betraying him by saying something to upset Jules this much. Maybe his mom, but she seemed somewhat supportive of their relationship. Chelsea?

"It doesn't matter." Her tight words sliced right through the thick air between them.

Frustration from her nonchalant response burst through him, pushing him to his feet. "Of course it matters!" He stepped away, thrusting a hand through his hair. "Something happened in the last half hour to change your thoughts of wanting to be with me. I think I deserve to know!" He needed to keep a tight rein on his anger. Yelling at her wouldn't make the situation any better.

Mute, she remained on the floor. In his mind, he ran through the evening, trying to guess at the reason for its downfall. He remembered his dad telling him about announcing the offer for him to come run the Galena estate. Was she mad and hurt that he didn't tell her?

Hands in his back pockets, he softened his stance and voice. "Jules, I know my dad announced that he offered me the position of running the estate here." He paused, making sure he formed the right words. "I'm sorry I didn't tell you myself. The offer came as a shock. I'll be honest; I'm confused as to what to do. With everything going on with the case and the amount of stress you are already under, I just didn't want to add to it." She finally looked up at him and his face melted. "No excuses, I should have told you. I'm sorry."

Glassy emerald eyes lacked emotion as she stared at him. "I'm not upset that you didn't tell me. We've dated for a week. You don't owe me anything."

She was drawing away and shutting down. Everything in him wanted to claw and beg his way back. "Jules, do you not understand the depth of my feelings for you?"

"We're just too different, Derek. I'm doing you a favor by ending our relationship now."

Mouth gaping open, he grunted. "Doing me a favor? Jules, I'm in love with you!" He sank to his knees, with his hands on his hips. "I know you love me, too." He pleaded with his eyes and words. "Why won't you let me love you?"

A single tear slid down her flushed cheek. Misery clouded her eyes. "Because sometimes love just isn't enough."

The woman was talking crazy. And she never fully answered his earlier question. Something happened, and they weren't leaving this blasted bathroom until he found out what it was. He scanned the room and landed on the toilet. It seemed fitting to have this conversation here as all his hopes and dreams were getting flushed away.

Wait. Outside the door he'd heard her throwing up, but she said she wasn't sick. His chest constricted and dread left a sour knot in the pit of his stomach. "Jules." He cupped her chin, demanding her attention. "Did you make yourself throw up?"

Her chin quivered within his hand. She didn't even need to voice the answer. The guilt in her eyes and the slack of her shoulders told him the truth.

Leaning forward, he drew her into his arms, resting his chin on her head. "Please tell me what happened?"

She stiffened in his embrace and wiggled herself free. He

didn't protest. Just rocked backwards to sit on the floor, his hands extended behind him to brace him upright. He didn't time her silence, but after what felt like five minutes he finally caved. If it took twenty questions, he was going to get to the bottom of her sudden change of heart.

"Is this about Chelsea?" he asked. "You have to know I had no idea she was coming."

"I know."

"And that I no longer have feelings for her."

"Maybe you should. She seems to be a better fit for you than I ever will."

Okay, he sensed he was getting warmer. "I think you're a perfect fit for me."

"Your dad doesn't." Her lips thinned into a frown. "I heard the two of you talking. I know he invited Chelsea here and thinks that I'm not good enough for you."

He closed his eyes. He opened them to see her features tighten with resolve. He was losing. "Listen, my dad is a jerk and if I return, I will make sure there are huge boundaries set up. He will respect you ... and us."

"That's just it. I don't belong here! I don't like horses, your family doesn't think I'm good enough for you, I'm like the Faded Glory brand mixed in with the Banana Republic, and I'm a damaged woman who just forced herself to throw up." Her feet shuffled as she pushed to a standing position. "You deserve better."

He stood up behind her. At the mirror she ran a finger under her eyes to remove the smudged mascara. She turned to face him, arms crossed over her chest.

"I don't care about any of those things, Jules."

"But I do."

"What can I say to change your mind?"

"Nothing." She walked past him. "I'm going to head back to the cabin. Please stay with your family."

Saying anything more would be wasted breath. He had to let her go, for now. "Wait." He dug into his right front pocket and pulled out his keys, handing them to her. "Take the truck. I'll find another way back later. Call if you need anything." He knew she wouldn't.

She walked out of the room, leaving him to drown in his suffering. He was a fixer, and he couldn't fix this. After hearing the last couple days about her issues with love, this shouldn't really surprise him. Until she could fully understand how much God loved her, she wouldn't be able to accept the love of others – or especially his love. He pulled his cell phone out of his sports coat pocket and made a call. "Ava, it's Derek. I need your help."

CHAPTER TWENTY-NINE

FRANKLIN DELUCA STILLED AT THE SOUND OF THE FRONT DOOR unlocking. Stuffed inside the hall closet, he tightened his hand on the knife while raising it chest high, ready for action when the door opened. He was patient, methodical – he had to be in his line of work. He never made mistakes or had errors in judgment when dealing with an assignment ... until this one. That's what he got for making a swift decision in the parking garage. He never intended to kill Scott Henson there, but the situation presented itself. His rash decision caused a domino effect of poor executions. The fire. Then the car accident. Now he was playing catch up and adding more players to the game.

He hushed all movement when footsteps outside the door walked by. Finding Julia Anderson was top priority. After a day of coming up empty, desperate times produced desperate measures. He really didn't want to hurt anyone else, but he needed information.

The only way he knew how to get her whereabouts was from the woman on the other side of the door, Lucy Williams. Knees slightly bent, he placed his hand on the knob, ready to emerge, but paused when her phone rang.

Grunting mixed with a thud. "Hey, Ava." A pause. "Sure, I got a sec. Can I put you on speaker? I'm running behind and need to pack up my paints and a few pieces to take into the gallery."

"No problem," the woman, Ava, said.

"How's your weekend going?"

"Great. Matt and I finished up the rest of unpacking today. It's a good feeling to be all done."

"I'm sure. Are you two going to make it to the folks for dinner tomorrow?"

"I think so, but that's sort of what I'm calling about. I just got a call from Derek." Frank's ears perked up. Derek was the cop Julia dated.

"Everything okay?" Lucy asked.

"I'm not sure. Derek called, asking me to come to his parents' cabin where they're staying."

"Tonight?"

"Yes."

"The cabin is in Galena, right? That's a couple hours away. You're going alone?"

Frank leaned his ear against the door. Julia's whereabouts had just dropped into his lap. He might not have to hurt Lucy after all for the information. As long as she didn't come into the closet.

"No. Matt is going with me. He doesn't want me to drive so far this late at night."

"Good plan."

"The thing is, we are dog sitting for Derek's dog, Max. Is there any way you can swing by the house in the morning to let him out and feed him? Josh can cover the afternoon. We should be back in time for dinner."

"Sure. Not a problem."

"Thanks."

"Text me when you get there so I know you made it safely."

"Okay, I will. Love you."

"Love you, too. Bye."

A smile slithered across Frank's lips. He'd wait until tomorrow night to head to this cabin in Galena. It'd give him a day to figure out the destination and to come up with a new plan on how to get rid of Julia.

Footsteps passed by again while he held his breath. The front door opened and closed, leaving him alone once again in the house. He waited twenty minutes and then snuck out of the house and ran down the road to his car.

CHAPTER THIRTY

JULES LAID IN BED THE NEXT MORNING WITH THE SHEETS TUCKED up to her chin, a tissue box at her side and her heart ripped in half. She still couldn't believe she had broken up with Derek. Never would she have thought walking into his parents' house last night that she would be walking out the way she did. His reaction, his determination to fight for her, didn't come as a surprise. But the emptiness and regret that followed did.

It was for the best – at least that's what she had been saying to herself over and over – despite the pain and the urge to run to him and beg for him to take her back. She wanted him. Every fiber in her being desired to make it work. But it was pointless to wish for something that would never be. She was doing the best thing for him. Someday he would see it. Maybe if she could fully allow him to love her, they might have had a chance. But she couldn't. And she didn't know why. Derek deserved to be in a relationship that didn't always tip the scales one way. He gave everything while she gave only what felt safe.

Last night she came back, took her pain pills with a sleep aid and cried herself to sleep. She wanted to be asleep before Derek returned to ensure she didn't have to talk to him. New tears drenched her face. Rolling on her side, she drew her knees up to her chest. How could she go out the door and face him? They could be here for days yet. The clock announced nine o'clock in the morning. She grunted. Soon she would have to leave this room and see him – form words and act as if everything was fine.

And she wasn't just grieving over Derek, but also the buried pain that had been dug up about her parents and their history. When she was a child, a teenager, and even to this day, she had dreamt of what it would be like to have a family dinner together. To have the chance to sit around sharing about a person's day, laughing together, everyone caring for each other.

She got a good glimpse of that with Derek's family last night. She yearned for it herself. No, his family wasn't perfect, but at least they were not perfect … together. Funny, in not a humorous way, how different their fathers were. David Brown was overbearing and cared too much about Derek's future. While Barry Anderson couldn't care less about his daughter and what happened to her. She understood Derek's frustration toward his dad, but if she had a choice, she'd rather have a dad that cared too much than one that didn't care at all. Maybe she should tell him her little revelation. She drew the covers up over her head, or maybe she'd just stay in bed all day and ignore any confrontation.

Knock. Knock. Knock.

Groaning escaped her lips. Ready or not, she had to face him. What if she kept quiet, would he give up and leave her alone for a little longer? Because she was not ready to look into those baby blue eyes and keep her conviction of not being together.

"Jules?"

Jules flung the covers back and sat straight up. That voice was like milk and honey to her ears. "Ava?"

"Yeah, can I come in?"

"Yes, of course!" Scrambling out of bed, she slipped on

her robe and slippers and met Ava halfway, gathering her into the tightest hug. "You're here! I can't believe it!" She finally released her, soaking in the dark haired beauty. "I'm so glad you're here," she tilted her head to the side, "but why are you here?"

"Derek called me last night." Ava rubbed a hand up and down her arm. "He thought you could use a friend."

God bless that man. Even though she had hurt him horribly last night, he still had her best interests at heart. "Did you just get here?"

"No, Matt and I came last night. You were asleep when we arrived and I didn't want to wake you."

As much as she would have liked to see Ava last night, it was probably good that she waited. The sleeping aid she took last night would have made their reunion quite groggy. A lump formed in her throat. Had Derek told her about last night and that she had made herself throw up? She didn't think he'd betray her confidence and share her secret. But what if he did?

"Did Derek tell you what happened?" Her pulse thudded against her chest, wrists and neck, waiting for the answer.

"No, not really. Just that you had a rough night." Ava's eyes softened. "Care to tell me what's going on?"

Of course he respected her wishes. Shame washed over her. Even if they weren't together, she knew him better than that. Now she needed to tell Ava what happened. She deserved to know everything – even about the eating disorder. As hard as it would be to tell her, it had to be done. It should have been done months ago if she hadn't feared her struggles coming to light.

"There is a lot going on and many things I need to tell you," a defeated breath huffed out, "first of all being that I broke up with Derek last night."

Shock and confusion flashed across Ava's face. If she only knew the worst was yet to come.

"Why? What happened? When you left two days ago you were both so happy together."

"Reality happened."

"What does that mean?"

Her insides constricted. Her stomach churned. Her breaths shortened. She wasn't ready for this conversation. Telling Ava would happen, just not at this exact moment.

"I'll tell you everything, just let me get some clothes on and brush my teeth first."

"Sure. How about I get us some breakfast?"

Jules smiled. "You're going to make breakfast?"

Her frame straightened. Known over the years for her lack of skills in the kitchen, Ava became the source of many jokes over it. "I'll have you know my cooking skills have improved immensely over the last couple months." With hands on her hips, Ava's eyes sparkled with a joy in them Jules had only seen over the last week. Married life looked good on her.

"I'll take Greek yogurt with granola."

"Sounds good. If I screw that up, there really is no hope for me."

Ava turned to leave. "Wait!" Jules' voice came out much louder and panicked than she expected. "I don't think I can go out there. I just can't see Derek yet."

"Okay, don't worry. Matt and Derek just left for a run. They should be gone for about an hour."

Relief unknotted her muscles. "All right. I'll be out in a couple minutes."

Dressed, Jules stood in front of the mirror, running a comb through her hair. Puffy eyes reflected back at her from the hours of crying. And the crying would continue the rest of the day. She opted to just put on a layer of foundation and skip the eye make-up. What would be the point in about ten minutes when she would confide in Ava. *Lord, I really messed up not talking to Ava about this sooner. Please give me the words as I share what's been going on over the last couple of months. Give me strength to overcome my urges to throw up, and when I get those urges to keep my thoughts on you. Guide me in my decisions, especially concerning Derek. Help me to do what's right in your eyes.*

Five minutes later, Jules sat next to Ava at the kitchen table, which was tucked into the bay windows. Outside appeared beautiful with the sun shining in a cloudless sky, deceiving of the cold temperature. Head down, she said a blessing over their food. They ate their first couple bites in silence before Jules worked up enough courage. Time came to rip off the Band-Aid.

"Ava, you know you're my very best friend, and I love you, right?"

Her lips tipped upwards. "Yes. Right back at you."

"The thing is, I've been keeping something from you, from everyone, and it's time I told you."

Ava set her spoon down and adjusted in her seat. A look of trust drove a stake right through Jules' heart. "Okay, I'm listening."

"I, um … I've been struggling with an eating disorder since this summer."

Jules didn't hold back. She started at the beginning with Scott breaking up with her, to not eating and overly exercising, to finally gaining control – or more so, letting God have control over her life – to the couple times she made herself throw up over the last couple weeks, but leaving out last night. She'd cover that next.

Ava sat uncharacteristically quiet, never interrupting, with tears pooling in her eyes. Unable to read her reaction, Jules finished with, "I'm so sorry I didn't tell you. I totally understand if you're mad at me."

Blotting her eyes with a napkin, Ava shook her head. "I'm not mad at you. I'm just sorry that you've been dealing with this alone for so long. And I feel guilty that I missed it. I should have seen the signs or noticed things. Over the last few months I've been so wrapped up in what was going on in my life, I missed what was going on with yours."

Of course Ava blamed herself. Jules should have seen it coming. "Ava, this is not your fault. This is my struggle, and I chose to keep it hidden."

Ava's gut-wrenching tears pushed her over the top. She joined in. Simultaneously, they blew their noses. Oh, it felt so good to get this off her chest. Derek had been right. Satan wanted you to keep things hidden so you could fester in your darkness alone. To have Ava hear the truth and cry alongside her brought such freedom.

"So you're doing better?" Ava asked.

"I'm doing better. Not healed yet, but better."

"Does Derek know?"

"Yes. I told him the night we started dating. He encouraged me to tell you."

"Smart man."

"Yeah." Just one of his many attributes she loved. Loved. Yes, she still loved Derek. But like she told him in the bathroom last night, sometimes love just isn't enough.

"What happened last night, Jules?"

She took a bite of her yogurt, mulling around where to even start. "I told Derek I loved him."

A firecracker sparked in Ava's eyes. "What? That's great, and yet so confusing at the same time. You also broke up with Derek yesterday, right?"

"You have no idea the emotional roller coaster of yesterday."

With her coffee mug in hand, Ava crossed her legs and leaned back in her chair. "Tell me everything."

So she did. About arriving at the cabin, their walk through the woods when he proclaimed his love, the dream she had and how Derek stayed the night in her room. She covered the spontaneous shooting range he'd created for her, to her finally telling him that she was in love with him, to the kiss that made her feel weak and powerful all in the same moment.

Ava listened, only interjecting a few times with questions. It hurt to walk down memory lane and the happiness she had felt not even twenty-four hours ago.

"So your last few days sound amazing," Ava agreed. "What happened?"

"Derek's family dinner happened."

"I didn't think his family was supposed to be here."

"Neither did we, but when his dad heard we were coming, they flew up from Lexington right away to see him."

"And that's where the family dinner came in?" Ava asked.

"Yes. His sisters came, too. And that's where the drama started. Get this," she leaned forward, elbows on the tables, "Derek's dad asked him to take over running the estate here since they are officially moving to Kentucky."

"What!" Ava's eyes grew big. "But Derek loves being a cop. What is he going to do?"

"I don't think he has decided yet. But that is just the beginning. His dad knew that Derek and I were together and without even meeting me, decided I wasn't good enough for his son, so he had Derek's sister bring Chelsea to dinner last night to remind Derek how perfect they are for each other."

Just talking about it brought back the harboring sadness of being rejected and unwanted. Ava sat with her mouth open. It wasn't often that someone could make Ava speechless.

Finally she replied, "Wow. What did Derek say about all of that?"

"He apologized for his dad and said he doesn't want to be with Chelsea."

"Well, anyone that has seen the two of you together knows he loves only you."

Jules gave her a blank stare. "That isn't helping."

"So let me get this right. You broke up with a man who is deeply in love with you because his dad wants him to return to the family business and get back together with his ex?" Ava lifted her brows and bit her lip.

It did seem silly when put that way. But it went so much deeper. "We're just too different. There is a good chance he's going to return here. I don't belong in this world." She threw her arms up, waving around the grand cabin. Admitting this next part didn't come easy. "Last night when I overheard him and his dad talking, I went into the bathroom and made myself throw up again. He deserves someone better than me, Ava."

She stood and deposited her half-eaten yogurt in the trash. Ava followed, tight on her heels. "Don't you think that decision should be left up to him?"

"He's too wrapped up in his feelings to see the big picture. It's never going to work out. Sooner or later he is going to see that. It's better to just end it now."

Ava didn't say anything in return, just wrapped her arms around her and pulled her into a hug.

See, even Ava saw that it would never work.

CHAPTER THIRTY–ONE

D EREK'S LUNGS BURNED FROM THE COLD AIR AND THE LONGER than usual run. He had to get the tension out somehow. Exercise seemed like the best avenue at this point. Entering a boxing ring with his dad didn't seem appropriate. Matt stopped beside him, bending over with hands on his knees, sucking in air. "Since when do you keep that fast of pace for that many miles?" he asked between breaths.

"Sorry, you should have said something. I would have slowed down for you."

"Never."

Derek smiled. Matt was just as stubborn as he. Pulling off his hat, he extended his arms above his head to get more oxygen into his lungs. "I needed to burn off steam."

"Mission accomplished?"

"Not really."

"Care to expand?"

He placed his hands on a nearby tree and stretched out his calves and thighs. "Jules broke up with me last night."

"Sorry, man."

This morning he woke up with a resolve to fight for Jules without pushing. As to how that was going to happen, he wasn't sure yet.

"Yeah, it's a big mess, which is why I asked Ava to come up – Jules needed a friend." He stepped forward and laid a hand on Matt's shoulder. "I'm glad you came along. I could use a friend and some advice myself."

Matt intersected his fingers and pushed out his hands, palms out. "You've come to the right guy. I have a way with women."

"I don't need love advice."

"Right, cuz it's going so well for you now."

"Touché." He rubbed a hand down his face. "But right now I could use your opinion on something else." Matt nodded, so he continued. "My dad came here for the weekend. We had a talk two nights ago, and he made me an unexpected proposition. He and my mom are moving down to Lexington year round, and he wants me to run the Brown Estate here in Galena."

He decided to leave out what happened last night with his dad inviting Chelsea and their ensuing argument. He wanted Matt's honest insight without mucking up his opinion with his dad's poor choices in actions and words.

Matt swung an arm across his chest and used his other to push it back in a stretch. "That is quite the offer. I didn't know you were interested in returning to the horse business."

"I'm not sure I am, but this is about my family's history and the inheritance I am supposed to uphold. You know my dad has never liked the idea of me leaving to pursue law enforcement. In his offer, he asked that I commit to two years running the ranch and if after that time I still want to be a cop, I'll have his blessing to return."

Scratching the scruff on his face, Matt gave him a look that seemed to be dissecting his inner thoughts. "Hmmm, tough dilemma. I can see both ways, as I'm sure you can also. I followed in my dad's footsteps, so I can understand how your dad desires for you to do the same, and I'm sure that is creating a pull for you, too. On the other hand, you have to be true to what God has called you to do." Matt blew into his hands and rubbed them together. "Either way, I'll support your decision."

"Thanks." For nothing. He felt back at square one.

"Ready to head back to the cabin?"

"Sure. Why don't we walk the rest of the way back, and I'll tell you everything that happened with Jules last night. I guess I could use some advice."

Matt smiled. "I thought you'd never ask."

Over the next fifteen minutes he filled Matt in on all the events, minus Jules throwing up in the bathroom. That wasn't his story to tell. They entered the cabin to find the girls hugging in the kitchen. His heart ached to see Jules and not be able to walk over and draw her into his embrace. He longed to touch her, hold her in his arms, thread his fingers through her soft curls, and feel her skin beneath his lips. Instead he settled with a smile. "Good morning, Jules." He kept a safe distance.

"Hi."

He didn't intend to stare, but he couldn't help it. Puffy and red from crying, her eyes didn't look right; however, she seemed relaxed in her skinny jeans and college sweatshirt standing next to Ava. Hopefully having her friend here would help lift the sadness that clung to her features, dampening the sparkle that usually radiated from her.

Ava didn't leave Jules' side but made sure to make eye contact with Matt. "How did the run go?"

"Besides Derek trying to kill me with a hard run in twenty degree weather? Fine."

Jules kept her eyes on the ground, clearly avoiding him. He hated the tension between them. Directing his question to Ava, he asked, "Have you two decided what you're going to do with your day before you and Matt leave?"

Jules jerked her head up and looked at Ava. "You're leaving today?"

Ava nodded. "Tomorrow's Monday. I have to get back to

school and teach, and Matt is on the schedule. We'll leave late this afternoon."

"Take me with you," Jules begged. "I'm ready to go back." A fist in the face wouldn't have hurt worse than Jules wanting to get away from him. Derek's resolve to patiently fight for her began to dwindle with each breath.

"Jules, staying here is for your safety," Ava reminded her calmly.

"We don't know if this shooter is even after me. Plus, we could be stuck here for days, maybe weeks yet." It hurt that she would rather gamble her safety by returning to Rockford than to spend a couple more days here with him.

At that moment, Derek remembered he hadn't had a chance to tell her about his conversation with Trevor. "My talk with Trevor last night was very encouraging. They have a name – Franklin DeLuca. Trevor is in Las Vegas today doing some interviews. It's just a matter of time, Jules. Until we find the shooter, it's just safer for you to stay out of the city."

She turned to Matt, like a child trying to pit the parents against each other. "Please, take me with you. I could stay at your place. I'd be just as safe there as I would here."

Stick a fork in him, he was done. Derek didn't even care what Matt's answer would be. At this point, he was tempted to go pack her bags and send her on her way. Matt flashed a look at him. He put his hands up in surrender. The decision wouldn't be up to him.

Massaging the back of his neck, Matt rolled his head to the sides. He looked between the girls and then crossed his arms over his chest. "Jules, we need to stick to the plan. You're the safest here, and I think you need to stay here unless that changes. Plus, having you at our house might put Ava's life in danger, and I'm not willing to do that."

Jules nodded. "You're right." She spoke slowly, articulating each word. "It's best if I stay here. I would never want to put anyone else in danger." She finally made eye contact with him. "Derek, are you still okay if I stay here?"

"Yep." He couldn't stop the terse snip with the word.

"Okay, so it's settled," Ava said, putting her arm around Jules' shoulder. "Let's make the most of our time here together."

Time together would not involve him being around Jules right now. "I'm going to head up to the main house for the day. I'll be back later." He moved to the door.

"I'll go with you," Matt called after him.

"All right, I'll meet you outside," he said over his shoulder, ending his sentence with the slam of the front door.

CHAPTER THIRTY—TWO

TREVOR PUSHED THE ELEVATOR BUTTON THAT TOOK THEM TO THE top level – the Penthouse. His stomach rumbled from the movement and because he hadn't had anything to eat yet today. Nerves knotted his stomach, and all he could get down was a horrible cup of coffee from the hotel lobby. He turned to Detective Hank O'Brien from the Las Vegas Police Department. He had called before arriving in Las Vegas to team up with one of their detectives. He wanted to be in good favor with them in case he needed their help in bringing the DeLuca family to justice. Plus, it helped to have someone that knew the area. The police department was more than willing to help and promised to dispense anyone to his service that he might need. For now, he asked for a detective to help with the interviews so that after he returned to Rockford, someone from the LVPD was already in the loop if he needed anything further.

They already had one interview under their belts – Scott's old college roommate, Randall McGuire. Randall gave a lot of back story to Scott's downfall of gambling, coinciding with Emma's statements as well. The one thing that brought this case together and finally made sense of it all was the verification that Scott did use Vince DeLuca for a loan. That much they figured, but to hear Randall support that theory gave their interview process with DeLuca a stronger foundation and more leverage.

Randall also revealed that Scott had turned the tables on
Vince DeLuca. For weeks, as Scott was trying to gather the
money he owed, DeLuca began to threaten him, saying if he
didn't get his money by a certain time, his family would be
in danger. He even went so far as to blackmail him by threat-
ening to expose him at the hospital with his addiction and
substantial debt.

The weekend before his death, Scott went to Las Vegas
to ask for an extension. DeLuca refused, so Scott told him
he would go straight to the authorities if Vince continued to
threaten him and his family. It explained his edgy demeanor
that Jules noticed. Scott had been trying to turn his life around,
pay off his debt and start fresh. Instead, he went up against the
devil and lost.

The downside that stacked the chips against them – Randall
McGuire refused to testify. All the information they had been
given was great, except they had no proof and now, no witness. He didn't blame Randall. You don't go up against a loan
shark without painting a target on your back.

This interview with Vince DeLuca had to go well or they
would be stuck in a frustrating situation with a guilty man
they couldn't press charges on. "You got a plan?" Detective
O'Brien asked as they passed the eighth floor. "He won't
crack easily. We've been trying for years to stick him to a
crime and have come up empty."

"I know he's not going to just come out and say he ordered
the hit on Scott Henson. The plan is to catch him in a lie and
get him flustered so he makes a mistake."

The elevator doors opened right into the Penthouse. A
woman dressed in a maid's outfit welcomed them. "Good
morning, detectives. Mr. DeLuca is on a conference call. He
said to have you wait in the sitting room until he can join
you."

"Thank you," Trevor said as he got in step behind her, with Hank bringing up the rear. They passed the grand entrance and took a right through the kitchen and into the sitting room. Marble flooring magnified their steps marching in rhythm. The maid excused herself, leaving them alone. Trevor headed over to the wall of glass windows overlooking the strip. How many times had Vince DeLuca stood here as a king on his throne?

Ten minutes later Vince DeLuca walked in, every bit the way Trevor imagined he would look. He was in his early fifties and had dark hair with a splash of gray on his temples. Short but stocky, his shoulders were back and his head up as he controlled the room with his mere presence.

"Good morning, gentleman. I apologize for keeping you waiting. Business never rests on a Sunday, does it?" Vince said.

"Thank you for meeting with us on such short notice, Mr. DeLuca." Trevor spun around. "Your place is great." He pointed out the window. "And your view is astounding." Trevor had learned earlier on in his career that it was easier to catch flies with honey than vinegar. Trevor closed the distance between them, extending his hand. "I'm Detective Trevor Hudson with the Rockford Police Department." He turned to Hank. "And this is Detective Hank O'Brien with the Las Vegas Police Department."

"Mr. DeLuca," Hank said as they shook hands.

"Please call me Vince." Vince turned his attention back on Trevor, rubbing his chin. "Rockford. Where is that?"

Okay then. Let the games begin. "Northern Illinois."

"Why would a detective from Rockford, Illinois want to speak with me?" He didn't look confused. In fact, he had a smug grin that tipped up the corners of his mouth.

"We have a case we are investigating. One we think you can help us with."

"Is that so?" He strutted over to the couches. "Please, have a seat," he said as he sat down in the plush chair. "Can I get you a drink?"

Trevor didn't need a drink, but breakfast sounded appealing. It probably wouldn't be professional to ask for eggs over medium, toast and a couple slices of bacon. "No, thank you," he replied, taking a seat next to Hank.

They sat eyeing each other for a brief moment, the only noise coming from dishes clanging in the kitchen. Trevor collected his thoughts and plan of action. "On Friday, January 9th, a doctor by the name of Scott Henson was shot in the parking garage of Rockford Memorial Hospital."

Trevor looked for any signs up distress, but Vince only held a blank stare in reply. "Sorry to hear that, but what does that have to do with me?"

"We believe that your cousin, Franklin DeLuca, is the man that shot him."

Vince leaned back in the chair and laid his arms on each of the arm rests. "Frank? Why would he do something like that?"

So Vince's strategy was to play dumb. Got it. "You are a loan shark, correct?"

"I'd like to call it an upscale loan officer. People need money, I help them out."

"With outrageous interest that causes people to struggle financially," Hank inserted.

"We all have to make money somehow. It's not my fault people get in over their heads. I'm giving them money when no one else will," Vince noted.

"We have reason to believe that Scott Henson borrowed money from you," Trevor tightened his rein on the direction of questioning.

Using his fingers, Vince played with his bottom lip. "The name doesn't sound familiar. I would have to go back through my records to be sure."

"Does Franklin work for you?"

"He's my cousin. I like to keep things in the family. He's one of my middle men and collects the payments for me."

"When was the last time you spoke with him?" Trevor asked, pulling out a pad of paper to take any worthy notes.

"A couple of weeks ago. Business has been slow." Slow, as in dead.

Another lie. They were starting to stack up to his chin. "Franklin's phone records show that he has contacted you more recently. In fact, he called you a couple times on January 9th and also a few days ago. Tell me what you talked about."

Vince shifted in his chair. A nervous trait? "It obviously wasn't important if I don't even remember the calls."

"Do you know where he is?"

"I'm not my brother's keeper." He shifted again. "So tell me, why do you think Frank is guilty of shooting this Henson guy?"

"We have camera feed of him leaving the parking garage around the time of the murder. He also came into town under an alias."

Vince laughed. "What proof do you have? Does the bullet match his gun? Do you have an eye witness that put him at the scene? Or a motive? I'm sorry, detectives, but you seem to be grasping at straws."

"At this time, we don't have proof, but it will come, especially when we find him. As for a motive, we believe your business is our motive."

"My business?" He shifted again in the chair. "Detectives, in case you don't understand how my business works, if a client dies, I don't get paid. Why would I have someone killed who owes me money?"

"We have reason to believe that Scott turned the tables and threatened to turn you in to the authorities for blackmailing him. That seems like a good enough motive to have him eliminated."

"And you have proof of this or someone to testify for your accusations against me?" Trevor and Hank sat still, neither able to defend their case. "I didn't think so."

Vince stood up and they followed suit. "Gentlemen, so far you have come here and accused me of many things that you cannot back up with proof. You have accused my cousin of a terrible crime just because he was in the same vicinity as the victim. We all know you have nothing that will hold up in court. You've done nothing but waste my time here. Our meeting is over. Layla!" His eyes darted to the kitchen. The maid returned. "Please show our guests out."

Dread filled Trevor's stomach like lead, slowing his steps as they walked back to the elevator. Vince was right. They had nothing. Without Randall, they had no witness to vouch for the motive. Without Jules, physically seeing Franklin shoot Scott, it all rode on assumptions. Without Franklin, they couldn't connect him to the crime at all. And even if they did find him, what if he'd already pitched the gun? Looking for it would be like searching for a needle in a haystack. Without the gun, they would never be able to connect him to the shooting to verify that the bullet found in Scott came from Franklin's gun. First step, they had to find Franklin. And then hope everything else fell into place.

CHAPTER THIRTY-THREE

JULES FOUND A SPOT NEXT TO AVA ON THE COUCH AND SPREAD out a blanket between them. Today had been just what she needed to get out under her cloud of doom. This morning after breakfast, they watched a movie and took a short walk in the woods. After lunch, they looked through Matt and Ava's wedding photos picking out which ones to print.

Derek and Matt had yet to return. But she didn't expect them to. She had upset Derek with her request to go home. The pain etched in his drawn eyebrows and tight lips explained enough. The slam of the door was the icing on the cake. She had seen him mad before, but never at her. She didn't like it. Not one bit.

"What are you thinking about?" Ava asked, pulling her from the thoughts.

"That Derek is really upset with me."

"I'd have to agree with that assessment." She paused. "Do you blame him?"

"No."

Elbow on the back of the couch, Ava leaned her head to the side against her fist. "Can I ask you a question?"

"Sure."

"I think I already know the answer, but I'd like to hear it from you." She waited a beat. "Are you still in love with Derek?"

It would be pointless to lie. "Yes." She wondered when Ava would finally cave and start asking her more questions. It wasn't like her to get that much intense information and then say nothing about it.

"Can I just be honest with you about something?"

And here it was, four hours later. That had to be a record. "Yep, bring it. I've been ready for it." She smirked. Being defensive in this situation wouldn't help. Ava would only want the best for her and she respected any advice given, even if it came unsolicited.

"Being on the outside looking in, I've noticed a couple things. I'm not here to change your mind about being with Derek. It's your life, your decision. I think he's a great guy, truly loves you and would do anything for you – but you already know all those things. What I want you to hear is that Derek is not like your father."

Whoa. She didn't see that coming. "I know that." But did she?

"Just hear me out. I have been your best friend since, well, since forever. I know you've been hurt by the rejection of your dad." She took hold of her hand. "And I am so proud of you for taking the initiative to work through those issues. I've seen a lot of healing in you over the last few months, and yet I still notice you have your guard up. Hearing your reason for breaking up with Derek makes me wonder if it's more about you struggle with allowing him to love you and less to do with your differences. If you ended things with Derek because he's not the right guy for you, that's one thing, but if you did it because of fear, that's another, and one you need to do some soul searching on."

Ava went on, "Sometimes I think it all goes back to you keeping God's love at arm's length. Until you fully allow God to love you and understand that love – you will never be able to accept Derek's, or anyone else's, for that matter. You've never really had a father's love before, or at least an earthly example of it. That can mess with your mind and heart. Just know God loves you unconditionally, Jules, no matter what you say or do. He will never love you more or less than he does right now." Ava took a big breath and continued, "And Jules, just because you struggle with an eating disorder doesn't mean you don't deserve God's love … or Derek's."

That was a lot to process. Everything Ava said rang true and began to clear the fog of uncertainty that had been building since she arrived at the cabin, but she needed some time alone to do that soul searching she talked about. Jules leaned forward and gave her a hug. "Thank you. You've given me a lot to think about."

Ava patted her leg. "Can I get you a Diet Coke? I could use one before the drive home."

"Sure. And maybe some caramel rice cakes? I feel like living on the edge today."

"Got it." Ava laughed and jumped up, retrieving their mid-afternoon snack. Plopping down next to her again, she handed over the beverage and bag of rice cakes. "How can I help you walk through this eating disorder?"

In life, God gave her so many blessings. She had a great job, a roof over her head – well, currently she was homeless, but that was beside the point – good health and freedom. The one blessing that hadn't changed since she was five years old – Ava. Never, throughout all the ups and downs in life, had she ever felt alone during the constant years of people walking out of her life, because she always had Ava by her side. And she would never have to walk through this struggle alone.

"I could use someone to keep me accountable."

"Like someone to ask you the hard questions and give opinions whether asked for or not?"

"Something like that. Know of anyone?"

"That is totally out of my comfort zone, but I'd be willing

to give it a try for you."

Laughter erupted between them.

§ § § §

AFTER AVA AND MATT LEFT TO RETURN HOME, JULES FOUND herself alone in her bedroom, sulking. She hadn't seen Derek since he left that morning. Stormed out was a better description.

She missed him. Consecutive days in a row of being around him had become addicting. The walls began to close in, suffocating her. She could only read a book and stare out the window for so long. She needed to get out of this room. Maybe she could go out for a drink of water and just run into him for a couple minutes. Just a glance, a moment in his presence, to calm the withdrawal.

Feet padding out into the kitchen, disappointment sagged her shoulders down. Empty. She slowly added ice to her glass and filled it with water by a slow drip from the faucet.

Returning to her room that had become her personal dungeon since Ava left, she took the long route through the living room as a way to stall. Music came from outside on the deck, pausing her beside the fireplace. She quickened her steps, hoping not to be noticed, and then hunched down against the stone work, peering out the window. Squinting her eyes through the darkness, she caught Derek's shadowy figure perched on the front edge of the wooden Adirondack chair, playing guitar.

With the back of her head against the stone, she closed her eyes and drank in the chords he played – simple, calming, and just loud enough to soothe her conflicted heart. Then, he started to sing. His deep tenor voice filled in the cracks of her hardened resolve. She let the words of the worship song wash over her:

"On and on and on and on it goes
It overwhelms and satisfies my soul
And I never, ever, have to be afraid
One thing remains...
Your love never fails, it never gives up
It never runs out on me"

Chin on top of her knees, tears began to spill onto her cheeks – the beauty of the words, the sincerity of Derek's voice when it cracked through his emotions, the realization that God's perfect love casts out all fear and gives hope. All of these experiences were more than she could bear. With blurred vision, she rushed back to the sanctuary of her room.

For years she had categorized God's love in with human love. Today, she finally comprehended that concept needed to change. Her talks with Derek and Ava about God's love consumed her thoughts, swirling around without a pattern. Her heartbeat thumped wildly against her chest. Like the clouds parting after a storm, her eyes opened to the revelation of God's love. "You really do love me, God," she said out loud, "but why?"

Because you're mine.

She smiled through the tears, for the first time in her life feeling truly loved. She remembered lying in bed as a nine year old, crying in her mom's arms about not understanding why her dad left. Why he didn't love her enough to stay? How she felt if maybe she'd been good enough maybe he would have.

At this moment, in her weaknesses, her struggles, her poor decisions – she was wanted and loved by the Creator. Even if she threw up every single day, He would still love her. However, this love didn't give her a free pass to do whatever she wanted. If she truly accepted it, it needed to change her from the inside out. This love made her strive to be a better person and to fight against her sins and shortcomings. To understand that love finally completed a hole in her heart she had been trying to fill through others. She had expected Derek to fill that role, a burden no one should ever be given. Now that she had been made whole, did that give her and Derek a chance to be together or had her revelation come too late?

CHAPTER THIRTY-FOUR

JULES FILLED TWO MUGS WITH COFFEE AND SET OFF IN SEARCH OF Derek. Checking his room earlier, she noticed he was already up for the day. The main level empty, she bounded down the stairs to the bottom level. The workout and game rooms stood deserted. The only options left were the mud-room and office. She headed to the office. Outside the door, she peeked through the crack to find him sitting at the desk chair, his head resting in his palm. Taking a deep breath, she pushed the door open with her foot. "Good morning."

Derek jerked his head up and swiveled the chair around. He didn't look pleased to see her. "Hey. Did you need something?"

You.

She stretched out her hand to give him the mug. "A peace offering."

He accepted. "Thanks." He took a sip.

"Any news from Trevor?" she asked, deciding to break the ice with business first.

Derek nodded. Taking a paper from the top of his desk, she noticed his Bible open. Whoops. Maybe she had interrupted his reading time.

"I spoke with Trevor early this morning. The interviews went as expected. Vince DeLuca weaseled his way around the questions, but Scott's friend had some good information.

Looks like Scott had turned the tables on DeLuca and had threatened to turn him into the authorities if he didn't stop blackmailing him over the money he still owed."

Scott really was trying to turn his life around. Jules took a few seconds to process that new information. "So what does that mean for me?"

"It means we sit tight and let Trevor handle this. He's heading back to Rockford and closing in on Franklin. We just have to be patient."

If he was irritated by having to stay here longer with her, he didn't show it. She'd take that as a good sign. "Listen Derek, I'm really sorry for asking to leave yesterday morning. You're going out of your way to keep me safe, and I didn't mean to sound disrespectful or ungrateful by asking to leave with Matt and Ava." She stepped closer into his personal space. "Thank you for protecting me."

He stood up, edging away from her. Dressed as if he just finished a hard workout, his cutoff shirt clung to his chest, showing off his biceps etched in muscle. The basketball shorts revealed trim legs. Her eyes trailed back up his body. A body she wished to lean into and wrap her arms around.

"No problem. It's my job." She caught the distance in his eyes. Getting back in his graces wouldn't be easy. He shifted toward the door, lifting his mug. "Thanks for coffee. I'll see ya later."

"Wait!" she blurted out, panic shooting through her veins. So much for surface talk. She had to say something, dig deep and help him understand. "Can we talk?"

He waited a few seconds before responding. "Sure."

Hands clammy, she shifted back and forth, deciding where to begin. She couldn't think straight with him towering over her. "Would you sit down?" She motioned to the chair.

"Why?"

"Because I need to talk to you, and I'll lose my nerve with

you all tall, broad, and gorgeous while standing over me." Again, she motioned to the chair. "Please."

With the briefest grin that he didn't contest, he just sat without saying a word. Arms crossed over his chest, he waited for her to begin.

"Last night I had an awakening with God, and I finally understand how much He loves me. I did some soul searching and my eyes were opened to the fact that He loves me just the way I am, and it's a love that will never go away."

Derek held a faint smile. "That's great, Jules."

"And my eyes were opened to you. Us." She stepped closer. "I'm sorry I broke things off with you. I was scared and allowed my feelings of inadequacy to misguide my judgment. I want to make things work between us."

He shook his head.

"Derek, I love you." She put all her emotions into those four words. His eyes changed, turning into a puzzle she couldn't figure out. "You don't believe me?"

Lips pursed, he leaned forward in the chair. "It's not that I don't believe you, Jules. I'm just not sure you believe it. I think you're just saying you love me because you're afraid to lose me."

Tears poked the corner of her eyes. "So you're going to give up on us," she snapped her fingers, "just like that?"

He scrubbed his hands over his face, letting out a growl. "You mean like you did Saturday night? Talk about calling the kettle black, Jules." He straightened and walked across the room with his hands resting on his hips.

"You're right, and I'm sorry. I shouldn't have given up so easily. I was wrong, but I really know we can make this work." She reached out and touched his arm. "We're good for each other, and I know if you just give me another chance I'll—"

"Stop." He pulled away from her touch. "I'm done. I can't

keep going back and forth like this. I gave you everything of me and only got half of you in return. I feel like that's all I've been doing lately – working hard to get the approval of my family, hoping for them to love me just for me, and then giving everything, trying to get you to do the same. I'm tired, Jules. I'm here to protect you, and I will do the best job I can, but that's all I can give right now." And with that, he walked out of the room.

Frozen, Jules stood staring at the empty doorway. His words had hurt, but they were true. The only one willing to fight for their relationship lately had been him. And alone, he had been fighting for his family's approval. In an instant she saw the big picture. No one had ever fought for Derek.

Well, that was about to change.

CHAPTER THIRTY—FIVE

D EREK FOUND HIMSELF IN THE ONE PLACE THAT BROUGHT HIM solitude and peace – the horse barn. He approached Captain's stall, needing a good ride to work out his frustrations and clear his thoughts. His talk earlier this morning with Jules had not only been unexpected, but full of lies on his part. Acid ate at his words, eating away the truth word by word. He rejected Jules' attempt to repair their relationship when all along he wanted to agree and wrap her in his arms, shielding her from the world around. Instead he lied and said he was done.

From the outside looking in, it would appear he was playing hard to get with her. Not the case. Even though he wanted to make things work between them, he had to make sure she was for real this time. *Fool me once, shame on you. Fool me twice, shame on me.* There was no way he would get back together with her until she could somehow prove to him that she was sincere on trying.

Captain snuffed as he approached, nodding his head up and down in excitement. "Hey buddy, I feel the same." He stroked Captain's nose and kissed the tip.

Derek grabbed a brush from the top of a nearby crate and unlatched the lock to let himself into the stall. He rubbed his hand along Captain's side. The strong smell of hay teased his senses and brought back the many memories of his time with this beautiful and strong animal. In slow strokes, he brushed, remembering the competitions, the unending rides through the countryside, the day he brought Jules here to ride. What if her riding experience had been different? Would she have looked differently at the lifestyle here or feel more compatible with him? He didn't care that she wasn't interested in horses and didn't want to ride. It would be great if she did love horses, but it wasn't a deal breaker. He knew pilots whose wives hated to fly and musicians whose girlfriends couldn't sing or play. Lots of relationships had that dynamic.

"There you are."

Jules stood on the other side of the stall. Luscious red curls framed her face with a matching green beanie hat and scarf that brought out her eyes. Her face glistened in white porcelain except for her rosy cheeks and nose. After their earlier encounter, he expected her to be upset and keep her distance.

"Did you walk all the way here?" he asked, perching his arms on the top of the gate. The horse barn was at least a half mile from the cabin.

"Yeah, I needed some fresh air." She started toward Captain, but stepped back, startled, when he leaned in her direction.

Fear of the animal kept her at bay. "Do you want to touch him?" Derek asked gently. She nodded. "Lift up your hand, palm facing him. Let him sniff your scent and get familiar with you."

Taking baby steps, she shuffled closer, leading with her palm. "Like this?"

"Yep." Captain nudged her hand. He had always been a flirt with the ladies. "Now stroke his nose slowly from the top down."

At first her hand flattened stiff against the nose, but after a few strokes she began to ease up and relax, even stepping closer. "Can we go for a ride?"

248

His eyes widened. "Are you sure?"

"Yes." But doubt clouded her features.

He could feel his defenses breaking down by wanting to reach out to her when her eyes glassed over. Wisely, he stayed on the opposite side of the gate. "You don't have to do this, Jules."

"I do." Her resolve straightened her frame. "Did you know I was close to my grandpa, my dad's dad, before he passed away my sophomore year of high school?"

She hadn't shared much about her extended family. "I didn't."

"He lived in southern Illinois, so I wasn't able to see him much, but he was a great grandpa. When I was about twelve years old, he let me ride his moped around his property during a weekend while visiting. I took a curve too tight, spun out, tipped and slid sideways along the gravel."

"Did you hurt yourself?"

"Not too badly, just a few cuts and bruises."

"And you've never ridden on a moped or motorcycle since?" She cocked her head to the side and smiled. Why did she have to look so adorable when he needed to keep his distance?

"I walked the moped back to my grandpa's house and told him what had happened. Instead of consoling me, he made me get back on and ride again so I wouldn't fear it." She stretched her hand out, rubbing Captain's nose again. "I have to do this."

There was that spirit, that flare that matched her hair. "All right then, let's ride." He exited the stall. "Would you like to ride Gracie again or try a different horse?"

"I'm a firm believer in second chances. I'll ride Gracie." Her rueful smile made her point and punctuated the double meaning of her statement.

He led Gracie out of her stall and brought her to Jules. Panic flashed across her face. Her chest rose from ragged breaths. Her hands trembled at her sides. Maybe she wasn't up for this. "You don't have to do this, Jules."

She nodded, catching her bottom lip in her teeth, staving off the tears with her thumbs. "I hate being weak."

Derek caught her elbow and tugged her to his side. "You're the strongest woman I know." Desire clogged all reasoning. Eyes closed, he backed away, afraid of her touch. He had to think clearly and couldn't do that with her so near.

"Let's start off small and work up," he suggested. "Ride with me on Captain until you are comfortable, and then you can switch over to Gracie."

She looked between him and the horse. "All right, but no taking off in a sprint or rounding barrels."

He laughed and held up two fingers. "Scout's honor."

§ § § § §

FRANKLIN DELUCA SAT PERCHED IN A HUNTING STAND FIFTEEN feet up off the ground. Binoculars pressed against his eyes, he scanned the cabin and surrounding woods in search for Jules. Once he had her in his sights and knew for sure he had the right place, he would come up with a plan.

His cell phone started to vibrate. Pulling it from his pocket, he answered quickly so as not to alert anyone of his position. "Yeah."

"Frank! I thought you said you had everything under control?" Vince barked through the ear piece.

A call from Vince was the last thing he needed. "I do."

"Then tell me why I just had two detectives at my place asking me questions about you because they are investigating the murder of Scott Henson and are linking his death to my business. I said keep it clean!"

Two squirrels hopped along the branches above him. Did they understand how easy and simple their lives were?

"Vince, I'm in Galena now tracking her down. I'll take care of Julia Anderson by tomorrow, and then I'll disappear. They can't convict either of us if they can't find me."

Hoof steps approached . He hunched lower into the stand. "I have to go. I'll call you when it's done."

A horse with two riders came into view as he slipped his phone back into his pocket. Auburn hair bounced in the short distance. Julia Anderson. She leaned back into her boyfriend's chest as he held the reins, leading them along the trail. Derek appeared on edge but she looked happy, content even. Poor girl had to be at the wrong place at the wrong time. This could have all been avoided had she not walked down to the parking garage with Scott.

He'd let them go past for now. Let her have one more day of bliss. This Derek guy seemed to be at ease with her protection, not keeping her under lock and key. No clue that the enemy lurked so close…or right above him. Frank would head back to his hotel, grab his rifle and return tomorrow.

CHAPTER THIRTY-SIX

DEREK OPENED THE CONTAINERS AND TOOK A WHIFF OF THE food. The steam settled around his face. Annabelle had outdone herself. He took two plates and filled them with the food.

"What is that delicious smell?" Jules asked as she walked into the kitchen, looking relaxed in wet hair from her shower. How this woman could pull off jeans and a long sleeve t-shirt to look like she could be a runway model, he'd never understand.

"Dinner."

"You made this?"

"Annabelle. I wish I could claim this feast was my doing." He gathered their plates and placed them in front of the bar stools.

"Annabelle made grilled salmon on a bed of rice with steamed asparagus just for us?" she asked while they leaned against opposite sides of the island, facing each other.

His parents had asked him to come up to the house for dinner tonight. He refused, not in the mood for round three with his father. Annabelle graciously made extra and sent it their way.

"No. She made this for my parents also."

Her eyes slanted. "Did your parents invite you to the main house for dinner tonight?"

"Yes."

She frowned. "I hope your decision didn't rest on me. I would have understood if you wanted to spend the evening with them."

Filling up two glasses with water, he explained. "Hanging out with my dad tonight didn't rank very highly on my priority list." Staying here seemed like the lesser of two evils. Tolerate his father and the endless ragging of disappointment or spend the evening with his ex whom he stilled loved but couldn't have.

They took their seats and he blessed the food. Thank goodness he had the food to keep him occupied, because he caught himself glancing in her direction too many times – the scent of her coconut shampoo, her full lips sliding across her fork with each bite, her elbow that sat a mere inch away from his. Maybe he made the wrong choice. Plan B: He needed to eat and then excuse himself as quickly as possible. A man could only stay strong for so long. He had kept his distance and his emotions in check during their horseback riding although he probably didn't need to hold his arm around her waist the entire time, but he wanted her to feel extra safe.

And she did great. He'd been so proud of her for tackling her fear. After a half-hour of riding with him, she switched over to Gracie. This time he didn't let her out of his sight. Further into the ride, he could see a natural stance emerge. She might have even been enjoying herself.

"Have you had a chance to talk to your dad since Saturday night?"

"No." Derek had pretty much avoided all contact with his father.

Out of his peripheral vision, he could tell she had stopped eating and had her eyes on him. "Have you decided what you're going to do about his proposition?"

He wasn't even close to a decision, and time was running

out. His dad gave him until the weekend to make his choice. The brief encounter he had with his dad yesterday proved to be the norm for them: disappointment in his dad's eyes and words and frustration building between the two of them, ready to explode. At this point he was ready to just draw straws.

"Not really. I have a good list of pros and cons, but nothing that makes me lean one way more than the other." He crunched on his ice, relieving aggravation.

"Sometimes it helps me to talk it through." She bit her lower lip, exposing her vulnerability. "I can make a pretty good sounding board."

What would it hurt? Friends could talk about deep, important things, right? Friend? What a joke. Pretty sure friends didn't think this way about each other. She wanted him to share his thoughts and feelings about his future. Well, the future he wanted crashed and burned forty-eight hours ago.

He must have waited too long because she waved her hand in the air. "It's okay. You don't have to talk to me about it. I understand."

No. The problem was, she *didn't* understand. "It's fine, Jules. We can talk about it." He moved his rice around on his plate with his fork, stalling.

"Okay. Give me the cons to taking the job."

Suck it up, Brown. He could do this. "I love being a cop. It's all I've wanted to do for the last decade. I want to stay in Rockford. My dad and I already don't get along. Throw in business and it could be a disaster. I walked away from this lifestyle for a reason. I'm not sure I want to come back."

She listened intently. Leaning forward, she rested her chin on her fist. "And the pros?"

"I do miss the horses. It's my obligation to uphold the Brown legacy. Just once," he stuck up his pointer finger, "I'd love to hear my dad tell me he's proud of me. Plus, the Bible tells me to honor my father and mother. Am I sinning if I go against their wishes?"

Her eyes softened, and she rubbed a hand down his arm. He had to get some space. Taking their empty dishes to the sink, he turned and leaned back against the counter. She hadn't taken her eyes off him.

"What would you do?" he asked her, wishing for some sound advice.

"I'm not sure. I don't think anyone can tell you what to do, Derek. This has to be your choice. But I can tell you, honoring your parents doesn't mean that you have to do what they want you to do. You're an adult. It's your choice. Biblically, honoring our parents means to respect them, with our actions and words. Forgiving them, even if they don't deserve it."

Ouch. She had a point. He had not been honoring his dad the last few years. Holding a grudge and harboring bitterness, yes. Respectful, not even close.

"Sometimes I just want to say 'yes' to my dad because that seems like the easy way out." He ran a hand through his hair. "Honestly, I just want him to love me with no strings attached, and I'm not sure that will ever happen unless I go along with his plan." Had he really just admitted that? But it was true. Standing against his father for so long became tiring, and he just didn't know how much fight he had left.

Jules slipped from the stool and leaned her hip against the sink, while he stood with his hands in his pockets, his attention steadily centered on her. "There are so many things I love about you, Derek, and baring your heart right now is one of them." She inched closer to him. "Sometimes the path of least resistance isn't always the right one. You just have to be true to yourself and allow peace to direct your steps."

Just by her words he could see the changes she'd made. Maybe grasping the depth of God's love for her would trickle out into other areas of her life. "I just wish my dad would have offered the position to Claire," he admitted. "She's the one who deserves it."

"And I think she really wants it, too." Jules noted.

His lips parted and then closed. Did Jules know something he didn't? "Why do you think that?"

She shrugged. "I don't know for sure, but when your dad announced at the table that he offered you the position, she seemed disappointed, upset even. Like she had been hoping he would offer it to her."

Interesting piece of information. "Really? She never mentioned anything like that to me."

"From the two hours that I've known Claire, I don't see her pushing anyone down to get what she wants."

It always made the most sense to have Claire put in charge of the Galena estate. She knew those horses better than anyone. Did she really want the position, or had Jules read her wrong? He had a lot to think about tonight. And thinking had nothing to do with his next reaction. He reached over and picked Jules up, spinning her around in a circle. "Thank you."

She giggled as he set her down. "For what?"

"For giving me an idea." He pushed away a strand of hair that caught in her eyelashes. Her soft, silky skin rubbed against his fingertips. His eyes dropped to her lips. She must have sensed what he was thinking because she stepped into him gently. He had to get out of here before he wouldn't be strong enough to leave. "I have to go." He stepped back like she had pushed him.

"Where are you going?" Her sheepish grin told him she knew exactly why he was making a quick exit.

Anywhere but here. To take a cold shower. Maybe a brisk run in the dark. "I need to check the grounds, make sure everything looks good for the night," he mumbled over his shoulder, grabbing his hat and coat from the hook by the door. "Call me if you need anything. I'll be back later." He walked out into the night, needing the fresh breath of air.

CHAPTER THIRTY—SEVEN

"I LOOK LIKE THE ABOMINABLE SNOWMAN." JULES WADDLED TO-ward Derek decked out in snow pants, a puffy coat, gloves, scarf and boots — all over two layers of clothes and three pairs of socks. She'd die from a heat stroke before hypothermia.

"It's necessary. Trust me, once you get going fast on the snowmobile, you'll thank me."

It was Tuesday morning, and they decided at breakfast to get out of the cabin for a couple of hours. She suggested going snowmobiling, one of his favorite pastimes. Not only did it sound fun and adventurous, but she wanted to show him that his interests were important to her.

Derek seemed more relaxed today. He continued to keep his distance, except for that glorious moment after dinner last night when his façade broke slightly, and he almost kissed her. Unfortunately, he did an impeccable job of reining in his desires. She understood it would take awhile to prove she had changed and truly wanted to be with him, but it gave her hope that maybe, just maybe, she had a chance to repair what her foolishness had broken.

"Don't forget this." He handed her a bulky helmet. As if she didn't look ridiculous enough.

"Thanks," she replied dryly.

"Are you sure this is a good idea?"

"The helmet? No. You'll understand when you see my hair after I take it off."

He laughed. "I meant snowmobiling. The helmet isn't up for debate."

On Sunday, she would have said "no", but since yesterday her aches and pains had subsided, and she almost felt normal again. She hadn't needed any pain pills since yesterday morning. "I'll be sure to keep my reckless tendencies to a minimum."

He shook his head, flashing a smirk that elevated her temperature. They exited the cabin through the walk-out basement doors to find two snowmobiles ready for them. Derek ripped their cords, bringing them to life. "Follow me!" he yelled over the noise. "We'll stay along the trails in the woods and throughout the grounds." He grabbed the right handle on her snowmobile. "This is the gas," he pointed, "and here is the emergency brake."

Okay. She would be learning by the hands-on approach. "Got it."

Derek took off in a smooth, even acceleration. Jules pinched the gas lever. Nothing happened. When she pressed harder the snowmobile jerked, throwing her body back from the burst of power. She let go of the lever, coming to a gradual stop, laughing at herself.

Second try went much better. Not as graceful as Derek's, but at least it was minus the whiplash.

They started through the woods and moved to the open spaces of the fields. Some of the horses came up along the fence, running beside them, as if taunting them to race. Derek was right about the amount of clothes. They had been out for a long time, and she hadn't gotten cold yet. Plus, the helmet wasn't only just good for safety, but also to block the spray of snow in her face.

Jules kept a good distance behind Derek. If he turned,

she turned. If he picked up speed, she picked up speed. If he slowed down, she tried to slow without hitting him. A couple times were a little too close for comfort. Maybe it was the brisk air or the adrenaline pumping through her veins, but a revelation came to her while trailing him. She realized if he chose her, she'd follow him anywhere for the rest of her life.

Derek made a swoop of his arm in a circular motion. They must be heading back to the cabin. Taking the left path that rounded to the south of the cabin, they hit a patch of trail that had tiny hills – almost mini jumps. The first couple she took with ease. The last, biggest one, she squeezed the gas and burst over the jump. Her squeal turned into a scream as the snowmobile tilted too far to the left. A thud sent her twisting, unable to straighten out. On target with a tree, she let go of the handles, sailed through the air and smashed head first into the ground.

§ § § § §

"JULIA!" Derek turned around just in time to see the snowmobile soar through the air and crash into a tree. Pushing the emergency brake, he came to a sudden stop, jumped off and ran to her side. Jules lay on her side, chest shaking. Taking in the sight of her collapsed body on her side pulled at his heartstrings. He'd never forgive himself if she got hurt, or if he didn't make things right with her before he lost his chance.

"Jules?" Afraid to ask, but did anyway. "Are you hurt?" He dropped to his knees beside her. Turning her slowly, he adjusted her to lay flat on her back, careful not to jar her much in case of neck or spinal injury. He slid her visor up to find her laughing. The crazy woman was laughing. Derek sat back into the bed of snow and slipped off his helmet. "I thought you were crying, but you're laughing."

Rolling to her side, she rested her weight on her elbow, joy dancing her in eyes. "I took the jump too fast and had to bail." Her laughing stopped, and her smile turned into a frown when she looked over his shoulder. "Oh no, did I wreck the snowmobile?"

He followed her gaze to the snowmobile lying on its side, smashed up against the tree. Tree, one. Snowmobile, zero. "It's definitely seen better days…and better riders," he spoke under his breath. She slapped his chest. He scanned a quick glance over her. She didn't appear to be in shock. No bones were sticking out. Not that he'd probably see any under all the layers.

"Well, Evel Knievel, let's get you back to the cabin." He stood, extended his gloved hand, and pulled her up. "You can ride with me."

"What about the snowmobile?"

"I'll have Henry come and get it."

"I'm sorry I broke it."

The snowmobile wasn't the only thing she broke while here. His heart still had to heal from her rash decision to break up and throw his love back in his face. He saw the changes since Saturday night, but enough for him to give them another chance, he didn't know.

"It's fine. Henry is a magician, he can fix about anything."

Back at the cabin they got out of their snow gear and confirmed that she had nothing broken. Up on the main level, Jules started a pot of coffee. Opening the cupboard, he grabbed two mugs. He turned to find her standing right next to him, in his space, smelling like lavender and a hint of cinnamon from her gum with green eyes that drew him in. He set the mugs on the counter beside the coffee maker and tried to shuffle around her. She stepped in the way. "I had a great time this morning," she confessed with a smile that stretched from ear to ear.

She reached up on her tip-toes and hugged him. Unwrapping her arms, he stepped back. "Jules," her name came out strangled with emotion.

"I love you."

He closed his eyes, wishing he could believe those three little words that packed a punch in his gut. "Smiling at me and telling me you love me isn't going to fix this."

She nodded, and he hated himself for the tears he caused to form in the corner of her eyes. "I know." After filling her mug, she began to walk away but stopped after she rounded the island. "But just so we are clear, I'm going to keep fighting for you."

And with that, she retreated back to her bedroom. He followed suit, filled his mug and headed to his room, needing some space and time to think. He sat on his bed and opened his Bible that sat on the night stand. He didn't take the decisions he needed to make lightly, and the only way he would find the peace he desired would be keeping his eyes on Jesus.

Knock. Knock. Knock.

Derek opened his door to find Jules' blue journal and a note lying on the ground. With both in hand, he shut the door and sat on the edge of the bed. He opened the handwritten note first and began to read:

Derek,

I know I've hurt you, and for that I am truly sorry. I wish I could go back and change things, but I can't. I want you to read my journal entries so you can truly see how much I love you. It wasn't on a whim. I didn't say it because you said it. I simply allowed my fears to reject the best thing that ever happened to me. I hope you give us another chance someday. I understand if you don't, but until you tell me to stop, I'm going to keep fighting for you.

Love Always,

Julia

❧ A Rescued Love

At the bottom of the note she told him he could read whatever he wanted, but to please read the dates she suggested. He ran a hand over the leather cover, not sure what to expect. He opened up to the first entry she'd asked him to read. He remembered her reading off the first part at Lucy's house about Scott, but the second half she hadn't mentioned.

December 14th, 2013

"Oh God, tonight I realized that I am in love with Derek. And more than that, I think he might be the one you've created for me. It's the most exciting and yet terrifying emotion ever. Help me to not let my fears ruin this. But I know I have to mend the relationships with my parents first before I can accept this gift you have given me or be the woman Derek deserves."

She had been in love with him that far back? His hands quickly turned the pages to the next entry she suggested.

January 14th, 2014

Today was Scott's funeral. My heart grieves for the loss of his friendship and because I'm not sure where he is spending eternity. Lord, I hope and pray it's with you and that someday I'll see him again. The one thing that made this day bearable was Derek. He is such a good and decent man. Besides Ava, I've never had anyone else that I can completely be myself around. I think about him all the time, and it goes deeper than just admiring him...it's respect, utter trust and most importantly, love. Derek has a way of putting others before himself. He is ambitious and never stops fighting for what is important to him. He stays true to himself, a follower of Christ, and doesn't change his morals, values or who he is for others. Thank you for putting him in my life.

He could barely wrap his mind around the words that

flowed onto the page. How had he not realized the depth of her feelings or how she viewed him? It made him want to be a better man. He turned a couple pages to the last entry she asked him to read. His heart squeezed.

January 17th, 2014

"Jesus, help me. I broke up with Derek tonight. Is it possible for a heart to literally break, because I feel as though mine did? Even through my pain, I want the best for him. And the best for him might not be me. Plus, sooner or later he's probably going to leave me. It's better to end it now, right? But I can't help but wonder if I made a mistake..."

Derek sat stunned by her revelation. Why would she assume that he would leave her? Separating the confusion, understanding began to make itself clear. Her dad had left her. Her mom had left her. Scott cheated on her and then left her. When times got hard, the people in her life turned away from her. And he did exactly what she expected him to do. He walked away.

With a new confidence, he left Jules a note in the kitchen telling her he was heading up to the main house and would be back soon. Time had come to make some decisions.

CHAPTER THIRTY-EIGHT

ONCE DEREK HAD HIS FAMILY SETTLED IN THE LIVING ROOM, HE took a seat across from his dad in a chair. His mom and Claire sat together on the couch. Lauren had already returned to Chicago for work. He wished he could have seen her longer, but when she left, so did Chelsea…and that was more than okay with him. Hanging out with Chelsea didn't make it high up on his priority list. In fact, he dodged her every chance he got until she left. He texted Lauren his reasoning for being absent, and she replied back with understanding. They made tentative plans to meet up in Chicago early next month.

"What's this about, Derek?" his mom questioned.

He strummed his fingers along the white, cloth arm rests. *Help me, Lord.* "I've made a decision about dad's proposition."

David clapped his hands together. "Excellent."

He took a deep breath. "First, I just want to apologize. I'm sorry that I've turned my back on the family for so long. Starting a new life didn't mean I had to dismiss the old." He looked between his parents. "And I'm sorry, Mom and Dad, for the years I have disrespected you with my words and attitude. I appreciate all you have done to give us kids a great and comfortable life with a strong legacy."

Kathleen reached over and patted his hand, her rings

knocking against his dry skin. "Thank you, dear."

He looked straight at his dad. "Dad, I'm sorry for being so angry with you and allowing that anger to cause a barrier between us. You have raised me to be proud of the Brown name and to live it out with excellence, and I want to do that, but in my own way."

The hope that shined in his dad's eyes quickly darkened as they slanted and his lips thinned. "What does that mean?"

"It means I appreciate the offer, but I have to decline. I'm honored to be a Brown, but I am a follower of Christ first, and He has called me to be a police officer."

His mom gasped. Claire gave a knowing smile. He had pulled her aside before he called the meeting and questioned her about her desire of position in the family business. Together they came up with a plan of attack.

David's face turned red, but he stayed mute.

"Thank you for believing in me and entrusting me with this position, but there is someone else that is better qualified and deserves it more." He turned to his sister and smiled, "Claire."

"Claire doesn't know the first thing about running this estate," his dad objected quickly to his suggestion.

As if Derek knew how to run it? "Dad, just let us tell you our plan."

"This is absurd. I'm handing you a life of prestige on a golden platter, and you refuse me?" He jabbed his pointer finger at him. "I'm still in control of your stocks. Don't bite the hand that feeds you." Derek didn't so much as flinch. When would his dad see life wasn't about money?

"David." His mom cut in with a voice that he hadn't heard since he was a kid. "Hear them out. Please."

He crossed his arms over his chest, his features turning to stone. "Fine."

Derek began, a calmness melting over him. "Dad, you built this estate to continue the Brown legacy. Why can't it be run by a combined family effort? Claire knows these horses better than anyone. Lauren is already working with the finances. Henry is practically family and can run this estate like a well-oiled machine. I'm not sure yet in what area I can contribute, but I want to return as much as I can to help out where needed." It was true. He wanted to be a part of his family again. Being a cop didn't mean he had to give up helping out around here. "Let us do this together, Dad."

He couldn't read his dad's reaction to his proposition, but his mom looked pleased and that was already half the battle.

"David, it seems like a fair offer." His mom wrapped an arm around Claire's shoulders and gave him a smile. "How wonderful to have all three of the kids working together." She leaned her head against Claire's. "I remember the days when you'd all be outside riding the horses together and calling yourselves the 'Three Musketeers.'" The memory warmed the air.

"Derek was probably in his sweat pants," Claire teased.

"Hey, they were comfortable."

"And a fashion nightmare at my events," Kathleen chimed in.

Before his dad could answer, Henry rushed into the room. "I'm so sorry to interrupt. Derek, I need to speak with you."

Henry never interrupted anything unless it was important. "Sure." He left his family and met Henry out in the hallway to secure the privacy of their conversation. The man's rigid shoulders had the hairs on the back of his neck standing at attention. "What is it, Henry?"

"I just got the snowmobile back to the shop to work on it." The aged man raked his fingers through his gray hair. "I found something I thought you'd want to know."

"What is it?"

"I found a bullet hole in the seat."

Derek stepped back. *No.* He already had his phone out,

placing a call while he asked, "And we don't allow hunting on the grounds, right?"

"No, sir."

"And it wasn't there before we left?" He already knew that answer.

"No, sir."

Why had he left Jules alone in the cabin? Stupid. He'd gotten too comfortable here and it might have cost her life.

Trevor picked up. "Derek, I was just getting ready to call you." He didn't wait for a greeting. "We have a hit on Franklin's vehicle. The local police in Galena found it deserted, tucked in the woods a couple miles from your family's estate."

Already running to the door, he called over this shoulder. "Henry, get my family and the rest of the staff off the property now!" In a full-out sprint to his truck, he answered Trevor. "I need back-up as soon as possible."

"I already sent Matt your way. He should be there within the hour. The local law enforcement is sending officers to do a sweep of the property. Just keep Jules with you and stay inside until we figure things out on our end. I'll be there when I can, but I'm overseeing the extraction of his car, hoping to find some evidence to nail this guy to the wall."

Skidding into the driveway of the cabin, he was out the door before he got it totally in park. "I'm on my way to find Jules now. I'll call you later."

He ended the call and unlocked the front door. Barreling into the cabin, his breath hitched when he didn't find her immediately. "Julia!" He ran around the kitchen, through the living, panic setting in. "Julia!" Nothing but an echo of his voice in return.

She had been a sitting duck here for the last hour. If Franklin had been watching, he would have seen him leave, prime time to come and finish off the job. Vomit stuck in his throat.

Running down the hallway, he was ready to bust down her door, when she swung it open, dressed in workout clothes and her hair up in a high ponytail. The most beautiful sight he'd ever seen.

"Derek, what's wrong?"

He couldn't find his voice to answer. Instead, he just wrapped her into his arms and held on tight.

CHAPTER THIRTY—NINE

PERMANENTLY IMPRINTED IN HER SENSES WAS HIS WOODSY CO-
logne. She took in a deep whiff of him. Jules didn't
mind being enveloped in Derek's arms, but something was
wrong. She repeated her question, chest tight from his hold.
"Derek, what's wrong?"

He released her. "Stand in the hallway." She obeyed while
he entered her room and began closing the blinds. She instinc-
tively balled her fists to her sides when he released his gun
from his side and inspected the bedroom and bathroom. His
intense movement brought a chill down her spine. She had
never seen him in cop mode like this before. And the "why"
made her throat close.

"Derek?"

He met her in the hallway, his eyes softening as his fin-
gertips traced the length of her shoulder. "I got a call from
Trevor. They found Franklin DeLuca's car not far from here.
We are in lockdown until he's found."

Her insides rolled. Fear and peace mixed in a strange com-
bination. Franklin was here and after her, and yet Derek was
here protecting her. She'd put her money on Derek any day.
Everything would be fine.

"Stay here. I need to check the rest of the cabin. If you hear
or see anything out of the ordinary, scream." He checked each
of the other bedrooms and bathrooms and then ducked around

the corner to search the remaining rooms and lower level.

She stood on edge the entire time he left her side. After returning, he leaned against the opposite wall. His whole body slumped in defeat. Her hope dimmed. He wasn't telling her something. Their breath shared the same rhythm as she waited him out. His shirt stretched across his shoulders, tightening from the muscles as he crossed his arms. "Henry found a bullet hole in the seat of your snowmobile. I think Franklin already tried to take a shot at you."

That was new information she could have done without. Her chin trembled, even with her best efforts to try and make it stop. Her breath hitched when she caught the underlining of his defeated stance. He blamed himself.

"Hey, but I'm fine." He became blurry from her tears.

"Not because of me. You're only alive because this guy has a horrible shot." He put his head down, unwilling to look her in the eyes. "I never should have left you alone in the cabin."

"No one had any idea that Franklin had found us. We had no reason to be overly cautious."

"I let my emotions get in the way, Jules. That's unacceptable."

She couldn't stand for him to think badly of himself. Courage filling her movements, she stepped forward and took his hands, bending slightly at the knees to force him to look her in the eyes.

"Derek Brown, I love you. There is no one else in this world I would want to be my protector. I believe in you." She'd spill her guts a hundred times over if she had to. At this moment, giving him confidence outweighed winning over his heart. She expected him to push her away, needing space from her like he had been doing over the last couple of days. Instead, he shifted, pulling her closer.

"I read your journal."

She swallowed past the knot in her throat. "And?"

"Did you mean it?"

"Every word."

His thumb trailed a line down her cheek, drifting down her neck. His soft touch sent her pulse into overdrive. "I love you, Jules. And if you're willing to give this stubborn, hot-headed guy another chance, I want –"

She didn't let him finish. Throwing her arms around his neck, she pressed her lips to his. Her fingers threaded in the hair at his nape, causing an explosion of passion between them. Derek deepened the kiss, a moaning coming from the back of his throat. Hoisting her body up and against him with an arm around her lower back, her skin turned to fire. He ran his free hand down her thigh and then hooked it around her knee, pulling it up to his side. A warning alarm went off in her head. She slipped her hands down his shoulders, gripping his arms, knowing she needed to push away before they couldn't stop. He must have sensed the same thing, because his lips slowed and the intensity began to diminish. He let her leg down but cupped her face instead. His gesture was as endearing as his baby blue eyes soft with an agreeing smile. She closed her eyes and leaned into him as he placed a kiss on each eye lid, each cheek. The front door creaked open. Derek had her behind him and gun drawn before she could blink. Down on the balls of his feet, he moved quietly down the hallway.

"Derek?" Matt's voice rang out.

Derek stood up tall and walked around the corner. "Hey Matt, perfect timing as always."

CHAPTER FORTY

SHEETS AND BLANKETS RUSTLED WHILE JULES SETTLED INTO BED. Derek kept his gun close to his side but hidden to keep her at ease. All afternoon and evening she kept an upbeat attitude, but as nighttime fell and the sky darkened, her anxious traits picked up – playing with her fingernails, curling her hair around her finger. Distraction – she had zoned out most of dinner.

Leave it to Matt to come up with the stellar idea of bringing Derek's dog Max with him. Not only would he be good company for Jules, he could help them with protection.

"Why don't I have Max sleep in here with you tonight?"

Her eyes brightened from his suggestion. "You wouldn't mind?"

"Nope, but I'll warn you. He's a bed sleeper and hogs most of the space."

"I don't care, I could use the company."

He whistled. Nails scratched along the hardwood floors, closing in on them. The golden fur ball burst into the room and sprang up onto the bed, snuggling in beside Jules. "See what I have to live with?"

She giggled and began stroking his head. "You better be careful. After this trip, I might become his favorite."

"He has no alliances. Whoever treats him the best has his undying love. Don't let it go to your head." Derek walked over to the bed and sat down on the edge. "A couple weeks ago the mail lady left a treat in the mailbox. Since then he stands at the front window and wags his tail, completely smitten."

Jules rubbed her cheek into Max's fur. "You just know a good thing when you see it."

"He must get that from me." He leaned in and gave her a brief kiss on the lips. Sitting in her bed, he refused to let it be any more than that.

She reached out and took hold of his hand. Hers trembled slightly in his grasp. "Can you go over everything with me again?"

"Sure." She leaned back against the headboard, her hair spilling over her shoulders. With her make-up removed, he noticed the black circles under her eyes. From lack of sleep or stress, he couldn't wait for this nightmare to be over so she could rest peacefully again. "For tonight, the local authorities are keeping watch on the grounds and are in charge of the wide perimeter of the cabin. Matt and I will stay here with you, taking shifts monitoring the inside and just outside the cabin. First thing tomorrow morning we will transport you to a safe house until Franklin is captured."

"It just all seems so surreal."

"I know, Babe, but it will all be over soon."

"I'm afraid I won't be able to sleep."

"I wish I could give you sleeping pills, but I need you to be able to wake up quickly if need be."

Nodding, she shimmied further down in bed. "I've gotten really good at counting sheep."

He fingered her hair that splayed over the pillow. She tried to play it off, but he could tell she didn't want to be left alone. He couldn't blame her. He didn't want to leave her either, but he had to keep on high alert. But maybe a few minutes wouldn't hurt. "I can sit in the chair until you fall asleep."

She bit her lower lip. "Are you sure?"

"Yep. I have some e-mails I need to catch up on." He bent over, their noses a mere inch away.

Her fingers curled into the front of his shirt. "I love you."

"I love you, too."

Laugh lines pinched the corner of her eyes as she smiled. "I don't think I'll ever tire of hearing you say that."

He kissed her cheek. "I don't plan on ever stopping."

Derek pushed to his feet, drawing himself tall. He shut off the lights, turned the chair around to face the bed and got comfortable. Within ten minutes her breathing changed, deepened, spaced out. He let himself out and shut the door behind him. He found Matt at the island with a phone pressed to his ear. "Sounds good, Trevor. We'll see you in the morning."

Derek made his way into the kitchen and poured himself and Matt a couple cups of coffee. He handed one to Matt. "What's up with Trevor?"

"He found a safe house for Jules. An old friend from his last precinct has a house in Tennessee they use on occasion."

Rounding the island, he took a seat next to Matt. Somehow he'd have to finagle his way to go with her to the safe house. Having Jules that far away didn't sit well with him. Best option would be to find Franklin tonight. "She is packed and ready to go when necessary." He took a sip of the scalding coffee, which burned the tip of his tongue. "You want me to take the first shift canvassing outside the cabin?"

Matt shrugged. "I can go first in case Jules isn't fully asleep. If she wakes up, she'll want you," he pointed out. "For the shifts outside, I think we should check at random times. That way if Franklin is keeping a watch on us, we don't give him a regular pattern to follow."

"Good plan. We'll start rotation in twenty minutes."

§ § § § §

FRANKLIN HUNCHED DOWN IN THE THICKET OF BRUSH WAITING for his moment. The cold seeped through his coat and into this skin, but he refused to move an inch. Over the last two hours, he had made his way toward the cabin from the south side of the estate. Local authorities kept circling the grounds, but they did in a rhythm he caught onto after watching long enough. He prided himself on patience. This morning he had taken a foolish shot at her on the snowmobile. After missing, he could have shot again but decided to wait for the prime time. He had been trying too long to make it look like an accident as if hunters had missed or misjudged their target.

Tonight he wouldn't miss.

All night as he drew closer to the cabin, he began to question his decision to continue his hit on Julia Anderson. Vince claimed the cops didn't have a witness that put him at the scene. Julia might not have seen him, but one thing kept him moving forward. In his profession, one could never show weakness. If he walked away from this hit, he would never be respected again in his circle.

Lights began to shut off throughout the cabin behind the blinds. He couldn't make out the person but was able to watch the shadows shift throughout the rooms. The boyfriend and the other cop took shifts patrolling the outside of the cabin, mixing up their pattern of time and direction. They were skilled. He'd give them credit where credit was due. Knowing he was up against trained men gave his adrenaline a spike and would give him enjoyment to watch them fail. The front door opened and the dark haired man emerged. Franklin smiled.

CHAPTER FORTY-ONE

JULES WOKE WITH A START. CONFUSED BY HER SURROUNDINGS, she laid still, allowing her eyes to adjust to the darkness and shadows. Max sat at the foot of the bed, growling. She slipped out of bed, fumbling in the dark for her robe and slippers. The red light from the alarm on the side table screamed 2:37 in the morning. What had Max so agitated? Maybe he needed to be let out to go to the bathroom. Changing her mind, she switched to a hooded sweatshirt. Going back to sleep would be difficult. At least one of the guys would be awake. She'd rather go out and join them than lie in bed and panic over the unknown. Reaching for the doorknob, the door swung open. She yelped and jumped backwards. A man's silhouette stood in the doorway. "Derek?"

"Yeah, it's me. I didn't expect to find you awake. Are you alright?"

"I'm fine, but Max seems worked up about something."

Derek bent down to one knee and ruffled Max's fur through his fingers. "What's up, boy?"

Max growled again. "That's what he's been doing," Jules pointed out.

Derek straightened his frame and took the few steps to turn on the lamp, giving the room a soft glow. The light betrayed the stress that knit his brows together. "I don't have a lot of time to explain. Matt didn't respond at check-in time. The airway has been silent for far too long. Help is still at least a ten-minute walk away. I have to go out and check on him."

Her breath caught in her chest. "Of course." Thoughts immediately tormented her about everything negative that could have happened. What if Matt was hurt ... or worse? She would never forgive herself if Ava's husband died while trying to protect her.

Derek withdrew a gun from his side and placed it in her hands. "This is the gun you practiced with. When I leave, barricade yourself in the room and turn off the lights."

She tried to give the gun back to him. "Derek, I can't use this."

He refused her attempt. "You shouldn't have to. It's just a precaution. I'll be back soon."

Turning to leave, she grabbed his arm, delaying the inevitable for only a moment. "Be careful."

He nodded and shut the door behind him. An ill feeling slithered throughout her stomach. Jules set the gun on the floor, too uncomfortable to hold it.

Scanning the room, she chose the chair Derek had used and dragged it over and propped it against the door, obeying his request. She shut off the lamp and curled up into the chair, with her chin resting on her knees. Watching the red numbers like a hawk, she waited.

§ § § § §

AFTER GRABBING HIS SPARE GLOCK, DEREK RAN THROUGH THE cabin shutting off the rest of the lights. Making his way down to the lower level, he exited out the mudroom door, locking it behind him. Moonlight lit the way as he skirted around the trees. He didn't even know where to start looking for Matt. In their attempt to be cautious, they had no pattern for their walkabout. Derek knew the perimeter they covered, but Matt could be anywhere within it.

Starting south of the cabin, he headed west, working his way around clockwise. Down on the balls of his feet, gun in hand, he swiftly stepped, staying light on his feet so as not to bring attention to himself. Not being able to call out for Matt, he had to rely on sight. Canvassing the ground, he continued to zig-zag through the trees. Following a set of footprints, he observed a second pair that mingled together. Looking forward, Derek's heart squeezed at the body laying ten feet away. He dropped to his knees beside the figure. A chill ran down his spine. Matt.

He checked his breathing and pulse with his fingertips. Thankfully, both seemed strong. Shaking him slightly, Matt groaned. "Matt."

His eyes fluttered open. Head flinching back slightly, he brought his hand up and palmed the back of his head. With a blank look, he gave a slack expression. "What happened?"

"That's what I was hoping you could tell me."

Jaw clenched, Matt looked skyward. "I remember walking the perimeter." He spoke slowly, working hard for each word. "I got hit over the head with something. At least that's what it feels like."

Beads of sweat formed on his forehead. Someone had gotten close enough to the cabin to attack Matt, and that could only mean one person: Franklin. "I have to get back to Jules." He gripped Matt's hand and pulled him up to a sitting position.

Matt's squinted eyes lacked focus, but he waved his hand to dismiss him. "Go. I'll be right behind you."

Derek took off in a run. Gaining speed, a shot exploded the quiet night. A buzz whipped by his ear, splintering the bark from a nearby tree. He dove into the snow and army crawled behind a tree. Hopefully Matt was coherent enough to seek cover. He'd shoot back, but he had no idea the position of the shooter. Giving it a few minutes, he tried again. Crawling again, he padded straight for the closest tree. Another shot. He sprawled on the ground. Until the shooter moved on, he was stuck. He'd be worthless to Jules with a bullet in him. As long as he was the one being shot at, that meant Jules was safe. He pulled out his cell phone, praying help would be on the way soon.

CHAPTER FORTY-TWO

JULES JUMPED AT THE GUNSHOT. THE FIRST SHOT MADE HER NER-vous. The second one, sounding closer, freaked her out. Eyes zoned in on the gun lying on the floor, she blew out a series of short breaths to gain control over the panic attack setting in. Should she stay here or go see if Derek needed her help? He'd given her his gun. She just couldn't let him stay out there unarmed. What if he or Matt was lying somewhere wounded and each second she sat here debating, their condition deteriorated? She was a skilled nurse, their best option in the middle of nowhere.

Without giving herself time to change her mind, she pushed to her feet. Her hands shook as she tied her tennis shoes.

Max whimpered beside her, in tune with her emotions. She couldn't have him draw attention to her. Grabbing hold of his collar, she ushered him into the bathroom and shut the door. Pushing the chair aside, she eyed the gun again. Her clammy hand wrapped around the handle, drawing it to her side. She unlocked the door, opening it a crack to get a view of the hallway. Empty.

She slipped out of the bedroom. Keeping her back along the wall, she took short baby steps. Her palm grazed the textured drywall. Her legs wobbled, nearly buckling beneath her. At the corner, she stuck her head around to get a limited view of the living room and kitchen.

Empty.

Where should she go? Head down to the lower level? Go outside through the front door?

Leaving the shelter of the hallway, she disrobed all sense of security. Shuffling her feet in the open entryway she made a decision. For no reason other than it was closer, she headed for the front door.

A creak in the floorboard behind her gave her time to turn to see a figure approaching, but not enough time to do anything about it. Strong hands gripped her arms and threw her onto the ground. Tumbling along the floor, she lost her grip on the gun. The metal scraped against the wood as it slid a couple feet away from her. Up on her knees, she crawled, knees knocking against the floor. A hand grabbed a fist full of her hair and pulled her back. She let out a scream, slicing the soft tissue in her throat from the strain. She swung her leg around, cutting the man off at the calves, throwing him off balance. Hair tore from her scalp as he pulled away from her. Scrambling on her elbows, she gained distance to the gun. Extending her arm almost out of socket, she gripped the weapon. Rolling to her back, she aimed the gun at the shadow looming over her.

Beady eyes edged in hatred glared back. Jules' finger skimmed along the trigger. She had to shoot him, but couldn't, frozen in place. Despite the darkness, Franklin's white teeth illuminated his smile. With a hand reaching behind his back, he produced a gun.

A shot rang out. All noise dissipated except for the intense ringing in her ears. She dropped the gun and covered her ears, rolling on her side. Franklin crashed to the ground beside her.

Derek jumped on top of Franklin, yanking his arms behind his back. A moment later, Matt picked her up and rushed her out the front door. Her head throbbed as she yelled Derek's name, but Matt never stopped momentum.

Pushing her with support down the steps, he guided her behind Derek's truck. He shoved her frame down into a squat. "Stay here!" He turned, retreating back into the cabin.

Leaning against the back tire, she let out a huge breath. The cold air turned her warm breath into a cloud of white around her. Minutes ticked by as she waited. Finally footsteps approached. Derek rounded the front of the truck. She rose, and with an unsteady walk, reached out to him. Tripping over her feet, she caught herself before she collapsed into his arms. She burrowed her face into the crook of his neck and let his strength hold her up. Her shoulders shook as the tears escaped. He pulled her in tighter against him. Sirens drew closer, symbolizing the finale of this horrible night.

CHAPTER FORTY—THREE

FRANKLIN DELUCA SAT IN THE CHAIR, HIS FRAME JUST AS BROAD as the desk he leaned his elbow upon. Hands clasped together in handcuffs, he bowed his head, the light from the overhead florescent lights shining off his bald scalp. His chest and shoulder, wrapped in gauze, had begun to bleed through again. Derek's shot had gone right where he wanted it to, puncturing Franklin's upper right side of his chest as a through and through. He knew they needed him alive to bring down Vince and his inexcusable business, and yet injured enough he could take him down with ease. They had an EMT check him out, assuring them he wouldn't bleed to death and gave him some pain medication. After interviews, they'd get him checked out at the local hospital before transporting him back to Rockford.

The small, quaint town of Galena had just been rocked tonight. Tucked in alongside the Galena River, its 19th Century architecture and family feel gave them an easy place in the Top Ten best small towns in America. With a population that barely topped three thousand, they weren't in need of a large police department, hence, the mere nine officers that surrounded the edges of the cramped room. The majority of the officers had never experienced the type of action they had over the last twelve hours or spent a long cold night canvassing the woods for a dangerous person of interest.

Trevor emerged from the police chief's office. "Bring him

in." Derek grabbed his left arm and dragged him to the room Trevor had prepared for the interrogation, sitting him in the seat opposite of Trevor.

"Mr. DeLuca," Trevor began, "We are charging you with the murder of Scott Henson and the attempted murder of Julia Anderson. Now that we have your gun and car, we have plenty of evidence that is going to put you away for life." He leaned forward. The sheer determination for justice laced his eyes. "Unless we make a deal."

Franklin leaned back against his chair. "What kind of deal?"

"We know that you alone didn't place the hits on Scott and Julia. Give us Vince, and I'll have the DA lighten your sentence."

Laughing, Franklin adjusted his large frame in the scrawny metal chair that looked ready to fold from his weight. "You don't get how this works. I give you Vince, and I'll be dead by morning. Family or no family, my world doesn't tolerate betrayal."

For the next ten minutes, Trevor tried to convince him otherwise, pointing out all the options from a high security prison to protective custody.

Derek's skin itched, watching the scene before him, unable to keep a still stance. Wringing his hands together, he realized his impatience had nothing to do with the conversation, but the fact that he hadn't seen Jules since he held her in his arms by his truck. Now mid-morning, the exhaustion of a sleepless night and the ache to have Jules near him shifted his priorities. Trevor could handle this. The only reason he tagged along for the interview was to watch Franklin squirm.

Trevor took a break to answer a phone call. Derek seized this as a good opportunity to leave. He leaned over to Matt. "I'm going to go get Jules and take her back to the cabin." He had called Claire once Franklin had been escorted off the property, asking for her to take Jules up to the main house until he could return.

"Sounds good. I'll keep you updated," Matt ensured.

Derek squeezed his shoulder as he passed by. "Thanks."

Driving up to the main house, he parked in the front next to his parents' car. Stalling, he gripped the steering wheel and lowered his forehead to press against it. Every muscle ached and his eyes burned from lack of sleep. He didn't have it in him to walk into the house and endure another round with his father. Maybe he could get in and out under his radar. Walking in the door, he realized that wouldn't happen. His dad met him in the entry. "Derek, good to see you're alright, son." Derek didn't expect the hug, but accepted it.

"Thanks." He scanned the area. "I'm here to pick up Jules."

"She's not here. Your mother decided to treat the girls to a spa day. She mentioned something about massages and getting their nails done. I just spoke with her. They are out for brunch now and should be back shortly." He cocked his head in the direction of the hallway. "Walk with me?"

Derek gave a curt nod and followed his dad down the hall and into his office. At the doorframe, he stopped short. "Listen, Dad, I'm tired and not in the mood to argue."

David didn't answer, just pulled bottled water out of his mini-fridge and handed one to him. "The whole town is talking about what happened last night. Seems you made quite the impression on the chief of police and fellow officers."

It didn't surprise him that word would spread quickly through the small town. "I couldn't have done my job without their help."

His dad stroked his jaw. "It's seems I've underestimated you and your love for your job." Derek blinked a few times, not sure he heard correctly through the fog of exhaustion. "I'm proud of you, Derek. You stand for what you believe in. I can't fault you for that. Do I wish you'd come back here full-time?

Yes, and I probably always will, but I promise to back off and let you live your life."

A tentative smile grew as Derek let his father's words sink in. His dad had actually uttered the words that he was proud of him. Miracles did happen. "What changed your mind?"

"Besides your mother reaming me out?"

They shared a laugh. "Yes, besides that."

"You made me realize our legacy didn't ride on you taking it over. Our legacy is our family. The girls deserve to be a part of what your grandfathers and I have built just as much as you do." He unscrewed the cap of his bottle and took a swig. "You gave me an offer I couldn't refuse."

They tapped their bottles together. What a moment to celebrate. He and his father, in the same room, without tearing at each other's throats. He couldn't wait to tell Jules. The thought of her brought up one more subject. "And what about Jules? I love her, Dad, and I need you to respect that."

David put a hand on his hip and used the other to straighten out his glasses. "I've already apologized to Julia for my behavior on Saturday."

"Mom again?"

"That woman can put me in my place faster than Hugo can win a race."

Woman's voices floated down the hallway. "Sounds like the girls are back. I'm going to grab Jules and return to the cabin."

With a hand on his shoulder, his dad walked with him to find Jules. "Don't be a stranger anymore. And I hope you make an effort to come see us in Kentucky."

"I promise to visit more often."

David hung back as the group went through their hugs and goodbyes. It would take time to get the relationship Derek had always wanted with his dad, but at least there was an effort on both sides.

Derek and Jules returned to the cabin. He slipped his hand into hers as they ascended the steps. She didn't seem to hesitate, but this place would stir up many emotions and memories of last night. "Are you okay going inside?"

She squeezed his hand. "I am."

Max greeted them with his tail swishing to each side. Derek helped Jules take her coat off, hanging it on the rack. Arm around her lower back, he drew her into his chest. "Do you know what I want to do right now more than anything?"

She tilted her head, eyeing him suspiciously. "No."

He ran a hand up her neck and traced his fingers along her jawline. Lips hovering in front of her mouth, he admitted, "A nap."

She giggled. "That's the best thing you've ever said to me."

"Even more than, 'I love you'?"

She laid her head on his chest. "It might be a close second."

Guiding her over to the couch, he flopped back first and tucked an arm behind his head. She found a spot at the other end. "Nope." He smirked, wiggling his finger for her to join him.

"You're crazy. We both won't fit."

He scooted to the inside and patted the open space in front of him. "I just need to feel you next to me." After what they had just been through, he didn't want her out of his sight, but also not away from his touch.

"Alright, but no funny business." She crossed her arms. "I'm serious about wanting a nap."

He laughed at her attempt to look unyielding. As if one kiss behind her ear wouldn't change her mind. "Me, too." He reached up and pulled her down onto the couch next to him.

She grabbed the blanket off the ottoman and covered them, situating herself into the grooves of his body. Placing a kiss on her temple, his body finally relaxed. He closed his eyes, anticipating his first restful sleep in over a week.

CHAPTER FORTY–FOUR

J ULES AWOKE TO FIND HERSELF ALONE ON THE COUCH. SHE MUST have been sleeping deeply if Derek could slip out from behind her without waking her up. Who was she kidding? She was dating a ninja. Last night he barreled into the room, gun blazing, saving her life, and she had yet to really thank him. Up on her feet, she went looking for him. Coming up empty on the lower level and bedrooms, she heard the strumming of a guitar just outside the front door. Pulling on her coat, hat and gloves, she made her way outside. Derek sat on the porch swing with his guitar, humming along with the chords. He stopped when she stepped out.

"Don't stop for me. I love hearing you play." She took a seat beside him.

He nodded and began playing again. "It's what I do to un-wind."

They hadn't talked about what happened last night. Or Franklin. A lump formed in her throat from the memories rushing back. Thank God it was over, but she still had a lot of emotions to process. She wasn't naive enough to think she could walk away from the last two weeks without any reper-cussions. She turned her head away and bit her lip, sucking in air through her nose, but couldn't stave off the tears.

"Jules?" With a shake of her head and a weak smile, she tried to downplay the tears. But he couldn't be fooled. "Oh

Honey, come here." He sat down the guitar and wrapped her into his arms, pulling her into his chest. He didn't say anything, just let her cry.

Through time and deep breaths, she began to gain control. Maybe even be able to utter a word or two. She palmed her cheeks, pushing off the tears. "Thanks for saving me last night."

"You seemed to be holding your own pretty well."

"I couldn't shoot him, I just froze. If you hadn't come when you did..."

"Hey, it's over. You're safe now. Franklin's going to jail for a very long time."

"How did the interrogation go? Did he come clean and confess?"

"Not at first. Trevor had to really work to get him to say anything." He stroked the outside of her arm with his hand. "To put you more at ease, Matt called while you were sleeping to let us know that Franklin gave up Vince. I guess Vince got an anonymous call that Franklin had been captured and was talking. Franklin found out about the call and decided to talk to ensure protective custody."

"Hmmm, anonymous?"

Derek gave her a silent, knowing grin. She leaned her head against his shoulder and threaded their fingers together. "Speaking of last night, I have to ask. Why were you out of the bedroom?"

She figured he wouldn't be too happy about that. She scrunched her face. "I heard the shots, and I couldn't stand sitting in the room wondering if you were hurt and needed me." Straightening, she left a mark on his cheek. "In case you haven't noticed, I'm kind of fond of you. The thought of losing you outweighed the fear of Franklin finding me."

His eyes shifted from a playful adoration to an affectionate burn that warmed her all the way down to her toes. They sat nestled together, their legs in a matching rhythm as they pushed the swing back and forth. His mind seemed to be racing while he stayed uncommonly quiet – a perfect time to pick his brain. "So when I showed up at the main house, you were talking with your dad. Have you made a decision?

Keeping his focus on the woods, he didn't answer right away. She didn't push. "I have. I had a good talk with Claire. You were right. Together we proposed our own offer to my parents to let the three of us and Henry run the estate. We haven't worked out the logistics or exactly what my part will be yet. I'll continue being an officer and live in Rockford, but after being back and finally working things out with my dad, I want to be as involved as I can be."

His decision didn't surprise her, but he held reluctance in enthusiasm – almost a hesitation in telling her. Did it come from an uncertainty in his decision or concern for how she would react? She had continually expressed her discomfort in being here and not feeling like she belonged; however, in the last couple days, she began to see things differently. No, she might not belong here with this lifestyle, but she belonged with Derek. And that's all that should really matter.

"I think that's great." She squeezed his hand. "This morning your dad apologized to me about all that happened on Saturday."

He smiled. "He told me. I actually think his ice cold heart is melting some."

"I hope you'll bring me back with you when you come. This place is growing on me."

"Really?"

"If I don't, Gracie will miss me. And we're like this." She crossed her fingers.

He threw his head back and laughed. She jabbed his side with her elbow. Once again they swung in silence, appreciating the silent comfort between them. With the sun shining on them, tucked out of the wind, she could sit here the rest of the day.

"I had a good talk with Ava while she was here. I told her everything."

He kissed the top of her head. "That's good. One more step in your healing process."

"I finally began to see that my eating disorder doesn't have to define me. And you're right. It's a process. Today I might be fine, but tomorrow I may struggle, but I don't have to fight this battle alone. Christ died to ensure that the victory is mine."

They both had done a lot of healing while staying here implanted in their own personal bubble of the world. Sometimes she wished they could hide out here forever.

As if reading her mind, he asked. "Are you ready to go home?"

They planned to head back to Rockford later this afternoon. "Yes and no. It will be good to get back into a normal routine, but sad that I don't have a home to go back to."

Being here made it easy to forget all the things she had left behind and her long to-do list. Work out finances with the insurance company. Start construction on the house. Find a new vehicle since hers was totaled. Go back to work and get used to the norm of Scott's absence.

Derek stopped the swing and let go of her hand. He rubbed his hands along the top of his thighs. In a smooth repositioning, he dropped to his knees in front of her and braced his hands on the swing on either side of her. His cheeks flushed and his eyes turned a tender yearning. "Let me be your home."

"What do you mean?"

"Marry me. Let me be your home."

Her skin tingled as her shaking hands covered her open mouth. She leaned back against the swing, needing more support. Joy mingled with shock made her blink with a hopeful grin. "You're crazy."

"I'm crazy in love with you." He pulled her hands away from her face and leaned his chest against her knees. "I don't have a ring. Yet. I don't have a plan or any eloquent words prepared. But sitting here beside you I realized that next to you is where I want to be for the rest of my life. I want to walk with you through the good and the bad. I want to wake up next to your beautiful face every morning and kiss you goodnight each night. I want to be your home, Jules." He leaned in with a soft smile. "Marry me."

His baby blue eyes turned into a liquid pool. She traced his face, savoring each detail. She loved this man. They had only been dating a short time, but she'd known for a while her heart would always be his. This was the life she had always dreamed of. Now, finally, a reality.

"Yes," she said, barely audible.

"Yes?"

She nodded, her vision blurring from a fresh batch of tears. "Yes," she repeated with conviction, full of passion.

He let out a whoop and pulled her off the swing, twirling her around. Their laughter blended together. He set her down gently but kept her tight against him. With an arm around her waist, he took a hand and cupped the back of her neck, rubbing her cheek with the pad of his thumb. "I love you."

Her throat squeezed. She didn't take or give those words lightly. "I love you."

And then he kissed her. Pouring every ounce of him into it, she felt the joy of the moment, the hope of their future and the anticipation of the many tomorrows yet to come.

A PERSONAL NOTE
FROM THE AUTHOR

Dear readers,

This book holds something extra special for me because I am able to share a bit of my testimony in it. When my son, Brayden, was two-years-old, he had Kawasaki Disease. The storyline of Brandon Spencer is very near and dear to my heart, because that is mostly our story — minus a few details and the husband shooting the doctor, of course! Greg was so supportive and a rock through our whole experience!

At the end of May 2009, Brayden came down with a high fever for a few days. We took him to the pediatric doctor that we had just switched to and were told he just had a virus. After a few days Brayden woke up from a nap with a golf ball sized lymph node. We took him back to the doctor and were sent home again because they said it was a virus. A few days after that, his eyes became bloodshot. We called the doctor, only to be told once again it was just a virus.

Still struggling with high fevers throughout all of this that lasted over two weeks, we began to notice he became more fatigued and his hands and feet would at times become swollen. On a Thursday morning, I went to my great uncle's funeral, and when I got Brayden out of the high chair, he started crying, refusing to walk. The next day I called the doctor to inform him of this, and they said that sometimes viruses can work into the joints and cause him not to walk. They said if he wasn't walking by Monday, to give them a call back.

On Sunday night Brayden was still not walking, but he could get around by crawling. In the middle of the night he came crawling into my room, asking for food. I took him into the kitchen and got him something to eat. Looking at his bloodshot eyes, weakness and his small body anguished with fevers and pain was truly heartbreaking.

I don't really know if I can describe the next moment other than to say I felt like God spoke to me through a burning bush, almost as if I could literally hear his voice. The words I heard in my soul shook me to my core, "Natalie, your son is dying and he needs help." I stood there in my kitchen and cried, terrified, wondering how long he had left.

The next morning Mama Bear emerged, and I called the doctor's office, informing them that I was bringing my child in, and I was not leaving until they did something or found out what was wrong with him. At the doctor's office they agreed something was wrong and did some blood work. That afternoon the office called to inform us that his inflammation levels were extremely high, and they scheduled an echo for him the following morning.

We still stand in awe of how God worked out the details such as the fact that the technician used to work at Riley Children's Hospital in Indianapolis and had seen many Kawasaki cases and upon doing the echo was able to identify right away that Brayden had the disease. The children's cardiologist was out of town, and it would have taken some time to get the results back, but since the technician saw it, she was able to let our doctor know immediately so action could be taken.

By the time we got to the doctor's office from the echo appointment, he already had the results back and informed us that Brayden had Kawasaki Disease. At first, we sat there in shock. Then we felt very upset about the time frame it took to figure it out, terrified of what this could mean for our sweet blond-haired, blue-eyed little boy. Right away we returned to the hospital for our four-day stay as Brayden started on the immune gamma globin.

That first night his fever spiked from nothing to extremely high in a matter of minutes. His body started to convulse, and the fear that he was dying strangled me. As a believer, I know when I pray it needs to line up with the Lord's will... and that terrified me. I cried for my husband to help, I cried for the nurses to help, but I was terrified to ask God, because I didn't know if it was in His will to heal Brayden.

Once again, the Lord spoke to me and said, "Natalie, do you believe that I love Brayden and want what is best for him?"

"Yes, Lord."

"Natalie, will you still serve me if I don't heal Brayden here on earth?"

"Yes, Lord."

"Then ask me."

So I did. From that moment on Brayden began to improve. I

truly believe that God spared my child. And not only spared him, but also showed off by completely healing his heart. By the next year, Brayden's heart was completely back to normal with no signs of the disease that tormented his body despite the extremely low percentage for recovery he was given because of how long he had the disease!

To God be the glory!

Thank you for reading this book. I pray that as you read these words, your spirit stirred. Maybe you related to one of the characters and their struggles, and through watching God rescue them from their situations and circumstances you realized that you, too, need rescuing. Maybe you struggle with forgiveness, an eating disorder, decisions, or understanding how you can be loved — and that weight continues to hold you down. Let God help you release that and find freedom! Or maybe this was just an enjoyable read as you escaped from everyday life for a few hours. Whether this book is read by one or thousands, my heart's desire is to serve the Lord and that HE will be glorified in all I do!

— Natalie Replogle

Natalie Replogle is a busy stay-at-home mom of three young kids and a wife to her heartthrob, Greg. She enjoys escaping the glamorous life of after-school homework, meal preparation, dirty dishes and laundry by losing herself in writing novels drenched in romance and suspense. She is the author of two other novels in the Come to My Rescue series, *A Rescued Heart* and *A Rescued Hope*. She and her family reside in Northern Indiana. You can connect with Natalie online at www.nataliereplogle.blogspot.com.

Coming soon
Trevor and Lucy's story in:

A RESCUED LIFE

Chef and rising artist, Lucy Williams, has found herself in uncharted circumstances. Lifestyle choices and being at the wrong place at the wrong time has landed her as a suspect in a murder investigation. Her family rallies around her, determined to clear her name, and against her plea, they ask the one person she can't stand to help her.

Detective Trevor Hudson would do anything for the Williams family that he has grown to love as his own – except spend time with the flighty-spitfire youngest sister. He will need to dig deep, keep a professional front and bypass his dislike for Lucy when he agrees to take on her case.

As Trevor and Lucy work together, the case takes many twists and turns and becomes more dangerous than either of them imagined – for their safety and their hearts. Secrets are uncovered and feelings begin to change and deepen as they search for the truth that will hopefully set them both free.

48257277R00186

Made in the USA
Charleston, SC
30 October 2015